After the fire

patti diener

This is for those who risk it all, those who put in on the line every day. The emergency response teams of Lake County, California, you are all like angels.

And to those who suffered loss in the Valley Fire, of Lake County, this is a love letter to you.

CHAPTER ONE

ARRIVAL

"*WHERE DO YOU go, when there is nowhere to go?*"
Gabriel read the words from the crisp pages of his complimentary newspaper left outside his hotel room door. That was all he read before tossing it onto the unmade bed and rushing to work that morning. Returning now to the quiet room, he surveyed the mess he'd left, and considered the paper once more, the headlines still talking of the tragic fire from a few months ago. A heavy sigh, he squinted his eyes, folded it in half, then tossed it unread onto the cheap hotel desk. Too much to think about.

Gabriel was in a foul mood. The excavating company he worked for brought him to this rural community in northern California, to clean up after the Valley Fire swept through and destroyed over one thousand homes. It wasn't the work that was upsetting. It was the fact that it was the holidays, and that particular time of year always tore at his heart. He thought being in a strange place would distract him. The truth was it made him feel more alone than ever.

The company was putting them up in the only large hotel chain in the area. The Best Western was the tallest building in the small town of Clearlake, reaching four stories high. Being the foreman, he didn't have to share a room with other guys. He was alone and able to sulk all he wanted.

Three years earlier, it had been raining that Christmas Eve, and it was all over before Gabe even knew what hit them. The papers said the multi-car pileup on the freeway was caused by poor weather conditions, limited visibility, and high speeds. Gabe suffered his share of injuries, a fractured arm, clavicle, ribs, and punctured lung, but Shelly's side of the car was what took most of the hit. The doctors said she died instantly.

Once the casts were off, Gabe went to work. It was the only reason he had to get out of bed.

Coming to Lake County, to help rebuild the lives of so many that lost everything in the Valley Fire, he thought would lift his spirits. Being lonely around the holidays was just something he couldn't shake. This particular Friday the thought of driving hours back to his apartment just didn't sound like it would help so he stayed at the hotel while the rest of the guys went home. Maybe if he had a dog or something, he would have a reason to go, but alone here or there was still alone.

After showering and shaving, Gabe decided to head downstairs to grab a burger and a few beers. Maybe watch some football on the TV, if it was on. To his surprise, the small town bar was slammed and lively. There were loads of people shooting pool, watching the game, and talking loudly over the jukebox.

There was one lone seat at the far left of the bar, furthest away from the television, but closest to the kitchen entry. He could smell the aroma of cooking onions, and sizzling beef. Suddenly he was famished.

"What's your pleasure my man?" The gentleman taking Gabe's order had deep dimples that accompanied a kind smile.

"Oh, a Coors Light please, and can I order food?"

"Of course. Do you need a menu or can I make a suggestion?" the bartender asked.

"Um…well, sure. What do you recommend?"

"Well, the chicken fried steak is always good, but my personal Friday Night fav is a thick, juicy burger with sautéed onions. We have shoestring fries that go great with it too."

Gabriel thought the guy read his mind and quickly agreed to the burger and fries. The cheery bartender winked at him and said he'd place the order right away. The long-neck bottle of Coors Light was placed in front of Gabe as the bartender disappeared into the kitchen.

The Stanford game was on the TV but the sound of Bruno Mars was blaring out from the jukebox. Gabe swiveled his barstool around to survey the room while taking a long swig off his beer. The group was mostly his age or younger.

At thirty-three, Gabe was an old soul. He never was a big partier and preferred more intimate gatherings. But somehow, being swallowed up in a crowd right now was comforting. It was easier than being back in the city, with Shelly's and his friends feeling sorry for him. Nobody knew him here, or his story, and that's the way he liked it.

The woman bartender appeared in front of Gabe, placing his plated burger in front of him along with a bottle of ketchup. She gave him a brief smile and quickly walked away to grab a chilled wine glass and a bottle of chardonnay to pour for another customer.

Just as the dimpled bartender promised, the burger was exactly what Gabe needed. The crisp, salty fries were cooked to perfection and he washed it all down with the beer. Before he could even ask for another, the guy just appeared in front of Gabe with a knowing look.

"Ready for another cold one?" The bartender leaned over to grab Gabe's empty bottle.

"Yeah, you have great timing," Gabe said.

As the bartender reached into a refrigerator under the counter, Gabe took a better look at him. The guy seemed a little older than he was with slightly weathered good looks. His light brown hair was a little long, and they were about the same height. His deep-set, dark eyes smiled just like his dimples. Although he was tanned, somehow, Gabe knew it wasn't from being on the lake a lot. This guy seemed more like the outdoorsy, working kind of guy, like himself. That and his hands looked rough like his own. This guy didn't spend all his time inside bartending that was for sure.

"So, what do you do?" Gabe asked as he took a swig of beer.

"Well right now, I'm your friendly neighborhood bartender. But I dabble in many fields. How about you?" the bartender asked.

"I'm here with the contractors for the fire clean up. I'm staying at the hotel."

"I'm surprised you didn't head out this evening like the others then. Don't feel like going home for the weekend?" he asked.

"Let's just say, I can be just as occupied here as there." Gabe replied, having another pull on his bottle.

"Well, it's a pleasure having you here. I know there are a lot of folks really grateful for any help speeding up the recovery process. That fire really kicked this community's ass. Folks need hope, ya know?" The bartender got distracted by something and Gabriel turned on his barstool to see what was going on.

Three women were heading into the bar. The first was a lovely blonde with typically over-highlighted hair, jeans and heels. The next was a brunette in a long-sleeved dress and high-heeled boots. Finally, somewhat behind and entering more slowly, was a thin, honey haired girl with her head down. She wore simple jeans, tennis shoes, and a flannel shirt with a tank-top under it. When she looked up in the direction of her friends, her light green eyes were piercing, and something caught in Gabe's chest. He couldn't take his eyes off her.

"You, uh...Ok there my friend?" the bartender was asking.

Gabriel realized he hadn't heard a word the guy had said. His focus was on the green-eyed girl.

"Sorry, man. No, I'm just fine, thanks," Gabe smiled somewhat embarrassed.

"It's understandable. I'm guilty of the same distractions," the bartender said while staring in the girl's direction himself. A dark shadow fell over the face of his otherwise cheerful bartender. "If you will excuse me, I need to grab some stuff, but I will be back," and he disappeared down the hallway.

When Gabe returned his attention back to the girls, he saw a waitress over taking their orders. He didn't want to seem too obvious with his intrigue, so he turned his barstool sideways to watch the TV screen and pretend to be interested in the game.

Gabe hadn't dated or even thought of dating anyone since Shelly. He just didn't have the heart to let go of the past yet, despite all their friends trying to set him up. He insisted it was too soon and he wasn't ready to even think about it.

He snuck another glance in her direction. She looked like he felt, when HE was with his friends. Distracted, and uncomfortable, but trying to go along with the facade of the evening, she sipped her wine and looked around the room.

Suddenly, the girl locked eyes with Gabe and he felt a rush of heat flush his chest and face. She'd caught him looking. Gabe tried to slowly, casually turn his barstool back towards the TV.

"Be careful with that one," the bartender said pulling Gabriel from his fog.

"What are you talking about?" Gabe pretended. He wasn't ready to admit to *himself* that he felt interested in a woman, much less admit it to anyone else.

"She's fragile. Don't give it another thought unless you can respect that about her."

Gabriel looked into the bartender's eyes. He was dead serious.

"Not that I'm interested, but I take it you know her."

"Everyone does," he said. "She's as local as it gets. But she's had her fair share of hard knocks so, that's why the warning."

"Broken heart or…" Gabe's question was left hanging in the air as the bartender stared at her pondering a response.

"More like shattered. She's not recovered. Oh, she puts on a brave face, but… Anyway, it will take a very special guy for her to ever trust again," and the bartender turned and started washing dishes.

Gabe drank more of his beer and turned his stool back to look towards the girl's table. The green-eyed girl was shyly glancing towards Gabe periodically but then turned her chair to face her friends more directly. Gabe got the hint.

"Must have been some stupid guy to hurt a girl like that," Gabe said in the bartender's direction. "I have never been the player some guys are. I know something real when I have it. And anyway, who's got the time for that?" and he finished off the last of his fries.

The friendly bartender turned and gave a small smile to Gabe, as he took the empty plate away and wiped the counter. "It's too bad not more people have the same outlook as you. Truth is my friend, that most folks are always looking for the next best thing. Nobody is ever quite satisfied with what they have. Especially if things get rough, that's when the weak give up."

"So that's what happened? Some guy left her in hard times?" Gabe asked.

The face of the bartender seemed pained at the question and soon Gabriel was sorry he asked. It was beginning to look like there was more to this story than the bartender had first let on and Gabe immediately felt like he should retract any further questioning.

"Hey, I don't mean to pry, you don't need to answer that. It's really none of my business," Gabe offered.

The bartender gave a forced laugh, "No, no. It's quite alright. We all move on and so will she, but everyone here kind of watches out for her. Just so you know," and he winked at Gabe then walked back into the kitchen with the plate.

He knew he shouldn't be, but Gabe was now more intrigued than ever about this green-eyed beauty. It seemed so unfair that something as gentle as she could have gone through such trauma.

And even though he was always missing Shelly, Gabriel had a yearning to get to know this girl. Approaching her in a bar was NOT the thing to do though, and Gabe knew it. She'd only think he was some slime ball trying to get her into bed. Some, out-of-towner looking for a one night stand. That couldn't be further from the truth, so he dismissed the idea entirely.

Defeated, he decided to ask for the bill.

"Hey man, I think I'm ready to settle up," Gabe said.

"Sure thing," he said and pulled the bill from his apron. "I suppose we will be running into each other periodically since you are here for awhile."

"Yeah, I suppose so. I'm Gabe, by the way," and he extended his hand to the bartender.

Wiping his hand off on his apron, he reached to shake Gabe's hand, "Max, and it's great you guys are here to clean up so folks can rebuild."

As he stood to go, Gabe leaned in to ask one last question of Max, even though he wasn't sure what he'd do with the information.

"Hey, Max? I don't know why I'm asking, but…what's her name?"

Max eyes sparkled as he smiled at Gabe, letting him know it was ok he asked.

"Sarah. Her name is Sarah," and he winked, then disappeared back into the kitchen.

∽

Sarah McKinney put on a brave face during the day, but each night, with the setting of the sun, her heart sunk with it. Her body was on constant autopilot, going through the motions of life just to get by.

Then the Valley Fire struck, leaving her best friend Michelle, homeless along with so many others. Diving into opportunities to serve, Sarah found she was able to put her own issues aside for a bit. That's the only reason she was here tonight. Michelle's husband took the kids to a movie so she could have a girl's night out.

"Wow! I almost forgot what going to a bar was like," Michelle said.

"A few years back and this would have been normal for a Friday night," Stacy said.

Sarah scanned the room, trying to remember what all the hype was when they partied years ago. Nearly thirty now, she felt much older.

"Holy Cow," Stacy said quietly. "Would you get a load of that guy at the end of the bar?"

They all looked up at the man sitting at the far left of the bar nursing a beer and trying to act as if he wasn't looking at them.

The dark hair, athletic build, and strong jaw line were very appealing, but when the others looked away giggling, Sarah looked back and his cerulean blue eyes nearly stopped her heart. He was definitely not a local.

"Sarah is the only one that could act on this opportunity," Michelle stated.

Sarah snapped her attention back to the girls. "What are you talking about?"

"You should go over and talk to him. My, my he's a hunk of burnin' love," growled Stacy.

Her friends laughed but Sarah couldn't imagine doing that.

"Geez, yes. Let us live vicariously through you Sarah. If it weren't for Caleb I'd be jumping at or on that," Michelle said drinking from her glass.

"No way. You guys are crazy," Sarah said casually turning to get a second look at the G.I. Joe stud at the bar.

He was watching television but turned just in time to lock eyes with Sarah, leaving her stunned, momentarily paralyzed. His stare bore right into her like he could see and know every part of her. Suddenly, Sarah felt very vulnerable so she turned her chair to face her friends more squarely.

"This would be a great way for Sarah to get back in the saddle. And by saddle, I mean *ride 'em cowboy!*" Stacy snorted a laugh.

Smacking both her friends on their shoulders and struggling to not laugh out loud and make a scene, Sarah protested.

"Oh, I totally agree," Michelle chimed in. "God knows it would be one helluva release. Hmmm."

"STOP IT. Are you guys insane? You know there's no way in hell I'm gonna go talk to him. Oh my God. Quit."

"Well you might miss your chance. Looks like he's paying his bill," Michelle said.

They all watched the muscular guy in tight blue jeans turn to leave and the three women followed him out with their eyes. But there was something in Sarah's stomach and throat that fluttered. Something that pulled as she watched him open the glass door to the bar and walk out, that felt vaguely familiar. Sipping her wine she realized what it was. Yearning.

CHAPTER TWO

COINCIDENCE

THE WEEKEND FLEW by and all Gabe managed to do was drive around the county to survey the destruction of the Valley Fire. Since he'd decided to stay, he was curious to see what kind of damage wildfires did in California. Coming from Oklahoma, he'd seen how tornados could rip apart a house on one street, leaving the homes next to it completely untouched. It would seem that wildfire could do the same.

Monday morning the crew was all back and they were working with the Valley Fire Ops Chief and Cal Recycling for assignments. The debris at each site had to be surveyed before removing any of it. The Department of Toxic Substance Control and the Environmental Protection Agency were coordinating with everyone, as well as the Office of Emergency Services. It was by far the largest collaborative job Gabriel had ever worked on.

Once Gabe's crew was given addresses for their assignments that week, they drove up the winding roads through the thickly forested hills. When they came upon the Valley Fire's burn scar, everything opened up due to the lack of foliage. Enormous black sticks that used to be trees felt eerie, like a skeleton forest graveyard. The ashy landscape with its thick smell of soot seemed as foreign as being on the moon. It felt dead.

This was their third week working on clean up, and Gabriel still couldn't get over what devastation he saw. They were told they'd be staying on the sites on Cobb Mountain for the remainder of their time in Lake County. They began in Middletown, a small country town at the base of Cobb Mountain, and that town was hit pretty hard. But seeing the rolling hills and valleys of Cobb left bare, save for the blackened stick trees, was far more unsettling. Everywhere was black or gray, everything was bare, and you could see there were few routes the residents would have had to get out.

Even though he didn't experience the fire himself, Gabe could feel the ominous sorrow of the place. It was as if the land itself was mournful. Driving the roads now, he imagined the panic of hundreds of people, trying to flee on these narrow, two-lane roads, with smoke and fire baring down on them like a dragon from Hell.

Once they arrived on Evergreen Lane, there were no homes, only foundations, fireplaces, and paved driveways as far as he could see. Crudely painted signs posted at each site by Cal Recycle and other state partner teams provided the addresses they needed.

Gabe parked and got out to look around. The pungent smell of charred wood filled his nose. On a normal Monday morning this area would have been full of busy people headed to school or work, but now it was deathly quiet.

Double checking all of the home site's information on his clipboard before they began, Gabe pointed to where the boys were to pull in the equipment, and they all suited up in Tyvek. Before long, they'd begun hauling off the remaining debris of 14650 Evergreen Lane.

Throughout the morning they never saw another civilian car come by. Only PG&E trucks, AT&T trucks, and even the Army Corp of Engineers, but just before lunch break, a minivan drove past and parked at the top of a long driveway, just a few sites away. His quick glimpse of the girls looked familiar. He heard the soft voices of women talking as they got out of the van.

"Hey Gabe. Where ya going, man?" Barry hollered. Barry was their water truck driver and the oldest guy working on the crew.

"Be right back. Just gonna check something out," Gabriel waved him off and kept walking, carrying his large bottle of water.

As he approached, Gabe could hear the women talking.

"I'm not sure if you think I'm crazy for even trying, but I'm glad you agreed to come look with me one last time."

He didn't want to intrude and realized that it was a little too late for that. Both women looked up and stared right at him.

And there she was, the woman with the incredible green eyes. Suddenly, Gabriel found himself speechless and had to shake his head to find words to explain his being there.

"Um…Hello. I uh…We are working down the street and I heard voices and thought I'd come see…well if you needed anything.

The other woman stepped forward, elbowed Sarah and extended her hand. "I'm Michelle. This is…well, *was* my home. My friend, Sarah here, is being nice enough to help me try to find anything left of this place that's even remotely salvageable."

Gabe shook her hand and said, "I'm truly sorry for your loss. My boss's company was subbed out to help in the cleanup process for the fire and we were assigned right down the street."

He locked eyes with Sarah then and she slowly approached Gabe, putting her hands in her pockets as she walked over.

Gabe nodded to her, "Sarah, you said? Hello, I'm Gabriel Hart."

"Yeah, I'm Sarah McKinney. Hello," she offered back, very apprehensive but continued to keep eye contact with Gabe nonetheless.

"I know it has to be done," Michelle started, "but I just know I'm going to lose it when they have to haul off this ash pile. My husband is at work and we must have been here half a dozen times together already. I just wanted to try one more time. Believe it or not, I've found my mother's wedding ring. My friend, Charlotte, she lived a couple of blocks from here, she also found jewelry at her place. Strange huh?"

Michelle started pacing a little, wringing her hands as she looked around her gray and blackened property.

"I guess we are just lucky to be alive. I keep telling myself that whenever I get emotional. We almost didn't make it out. I had just come home from the store and was unpacking groceries and didn't want to answer the phone. I let it go to the machine but the damn thing kept ringing! I heard sirens but they were off in the distance and I didn't pay it any mind. Caleb, that's my husband, was out working in the garage. Our kids were at his brother's house, *thank God*. By the time I had three phone calls in a row I decided I'd better answer it. It was my sister-in-law and she was rambling so fast I thought something had happened to one of the kids. She said for us to *get out now! We had to leave. We had to go because fire was coming our way!* I had no idea what she was talking about. My husband's brother is a fireman and they'd heard about it over his radio. Well I slammed the phone down and ran outside. I smelled smoke but that was it. I thought…they must have been mistaken. It HAD to be far from us."

Sarah wrapped an arm around her friend and rubbed her back. Michelle had lost so much. She couldn't spare a moment to worry about what Gabriel might be thinking of all this, instead she stood close to her friend and let her talk. Tears were building in Michelle's eyes, her hands shook, while a flush of pink crept up her neck to her face as she relived her story.

"I ran to tell Caleb and he came outside and looked too. He said we should pack some stuff and go, just in case. But what the hell do you take? I grabbed a photo album off the coffee table that had our vacation pictures from last year in it, a change of clothes for each of us…*just a change*. I mean, we were coming right back, right? I grabbed our dog, Sadie, and threw her into the car and got her kibble. I even fed the fish. Why, I don't know. They didn't have a chance. Thank God Caleb remembered to grab our flash drives.

"By the time we were loading stuff up a man was running up and down the street screaming for everyone to get out. GO NOW, he was shouting, and there was such thick smoke then, I was really getting scared. When we got to the bottom of the hill and had to decide which way to go, we panicked. What if we made the wrong choice and got stuck! The fire was baring down on us and cars were flying down but seeing was difficult and it was hard to tell which direction the fire was going. Caleb chose to go towards Lower Lake and it worked out for us, obviously. But yes, this is what we returned to after waiting for a week to come see if we had a house or not."

Michelle wiped her tears and nervously laughed at herself. "I must seem like a crazy person to you. Here I am telling a perfect stranger my tragic little story."

Simultaneously, Gabriel and Sarah said, "No, you are not."

They three laughed, breaking the tension of the moment.

"Listen," Gabe said reaching into his shirt pocket to pull out a few business cards, "I'm in town until our contract runs out. I really don't know how long that will be because the powers that be have been unsure themselves. However, I would like to help. If you find you need extra hands over the weekend, I'm staying at the Best Western with some of the crew. They usually go home on the weekend but I've been staying so, if you find you could use a hand with…I don't know, anything, just call."

Sarah took his card and felt a tingle as their fingers touched. "The Best Western? We saw you there last Friday night at the bar, didn't we?"

Again, Michelle's elbow, and she was jumping in. "You know we did. He was the interesting guy at the end of the bar. Sarah noticed you and…"

Sarah reached up and gave Michelle a sharp squeeze on the back of her arm.

"Anyway, we just knew you were there," Michelle finished.

Gabriel blushed, smiling at them with his incredible dimples and perfect teeth. He was too adorable, she thought. Dangerous.

"I won't take up more of your time but I hope to hear from you. The guys are probably wondering what happened to me though. I should get back to work."

Sarah just nodded but Michelle spoke up, "We certainly will call Gabriel. Have a great day and thanks for coming over."

As he turned to leave, he gave Sarah one last flash of those amazing eyes and she watched him walk away. Oh Lord.

When she looked back at her friend, Michelle was grinning from ear to ear, mocking her knowingly.

"WHAT?" Sarah hissed quietly.

"Oh…you are in so much trouble my friend," Michelle giggled. "It's all over your face."

◆

That night at the hotel, Gabe sat in a chair near the fourth floor window of his room. Three years cloaked beneath the suffocating, dark shroud of loss left Gabe unaware of the suffering of others. Being in this place, listening to Michelle's story, he'd felt *something* for the first time in a long while. It was strange to admit to himself but this was the most *alive* he'd felt since Shelly's death. Gabe wanted to help these people. Somehow, sharing in their pain and wanting to do something to better their situation made him feel like he found something to live for.

And there was something else. It was the undeniable feeling he got in his chest when he thought of her. Emotions Gabe thought were dead forever inside of him, welled up more powerful than he could fathom. The soft sweetness of a girl, somewhat demure, had a hold on him in only two times that he'd ever seen her. He was either going to be saved by this woman or she'd surely be the end of him. But for the first time in a long time, Gabe felt like taking a chance. When he closed his eyes that night to sleep, the last thing he remembered was the touch of her hand, and the look in her eyes.

❧

For the next few days it was business as usual with more home sites needing clean up and Gabe was starting to feel like maybe he'd not handled the chance meeting with Sarah very well. Neither she nor Michelle had called him. By Thursday, Gabe was feeling somewhat down about it, foul mood returning.

After work he wandered into the bar looking for Max but the only bartender was the lone woman and the only customers were a couple of elderly gentlemen talking loudly about who caught the bigger fish. Gabe decided on calling for pizza and pouting alone in his room.

Jeopardy was on TV and Gabe was working on his second piece of pizza when his cell phone rang. He turned down the sound and picked up his phone.

"This is Hart," Gabriel said after swallowing.

"Hello, I don't know if you remember me from Monday, but this is Michelle Hollings. I met you with my friend Sarah McKinney, at my house site, sifting through our stuff. Do you remember?"

Gabriel's heart jumped and he quickly shut off the TV and started pacing. "Of course I remember you. I remember you *both*. How are you doing Michelle?"

"Well, my husband Caleb and I are renting this little place in Hidden Valley and were wondering if you'd like to come over tomorrow night for dinner. Sarah will be here too. We are getting some furniture from my parents and, well, I was hoping I could bribe you with a home cooked meal in exchange for your help."

His smile spread so big across his face that Gabe was sure

Michelle would know it right through the phone. He tried to sound nonchalant as possible but his enthusiasm was very apparent. "You bet. What is the address and what time? Can I bring anything?"

Michelle laughed, "It's 2425 Big Sky Court, and just bring yourself. I know *Sarah* likes wine though, if you were so inclined."

"What kind? She was drinking white when I saw her at the… bar," he realized he'd given away too much to Michelle about how fascinated with Sarah he was, but it was too late now.

"Good eye. She loves all wines but lately she's been on a Sauvignon Blanc kick. We'll see you around seven? Sound good?"

"Excellent! And thank you Michelle. It will be my pleasure to help out. Have a good evening."

They hung up and Gabe just stood there stunned. He felt like a teenager going on his first date. He quickly looked through the small hotel closet for a clean button down shirt but he only had t-shirts and heavy flannels. Dating hadn't been on his agenda when he left the Bay Area. Gabe leaned in to smell them then laughed at himself and sat down on the bed.

Suddenly he felt guilty. Would Shelly approve? She had been the love of his life and all he'd ever expected to come home to. When she was taken from him, he felt a strong sense of loyalty that he had to live for the both of them. He felt he was supposed to stay true to her. It should have been him that died, not Shelly. Gabriel took out his wallet and stared down at Shelly's picture. Her beautiful soft smile, light brown hair, and dark brown eyes made him ache. But this new woman, he was sure Shelly would have liked her. It had been three years. He was only thirty-three and all their friends had been trying so hard to get him to move on. Maybe now, in this new place, he could try.

The next day, Gabe and the boys had their last assignment for the week at 12585 Spruce Street. The day went quickly with nothing too unusual about it. On Spruce Street, not many homes were lost. The bizarre pattern of burned homes was erratic, proving that some building materials, some fire clearances, and pine filled gutters or over hanging tree limbs, could make a difference in which burned and which didn't. But he'd heard this fire had a mind of it's own regardless.

The big boss, Tommy, called Gabriel mid day. "Hey, looks like local contractors will be handling the rest of the clean up. Lots of folks are turning to their private insurance companies and not going through FEMA right now. Our contract is coming to an end so looks like Tuesday, Wednesday at the latest you guys will be back down here. Bet you're ready to come home huh?"

He wasn't sure of that at all, but Gabriel still said, "Yeah. Sure. So I guess I will wait to hear more. I'll tell the guys. They will be pretty happy." The crew did their job, loaded up the equipment, hauled it back down the mountain, and left for the weekend. They were told there may only be enough work for a few days the following week and Gabe could see the guys were happy about the prospect of working close to home again. They all had girlfriends, and Barry had a wife and kids, so the weekly drive and hotel living was taking its toll.

Keeping his mind off the following week and just looking to the evening ahead, Gabe headed to the hotel after work. He showered quickly, shaved, and used a little cologne he always carried. Dressing in his nicest blue t-shirt and flannel, he gave himself one last look in the mirror.

"You are ok, man," he said to himself as he ran a shaking hand through his hair.

On the way, he stopped off for a bottle of wine for Sarah, and flowers for Michelle. He knew it was sort of old fashioned, but his mother taught him to always bring the lady of the house flowers. No matter if it was a friend, girlfriend, or grandmother. Regardless of his confident good manners, his palms sweat and hands continued to shake.

The GPS on his phone brought him right to Michelle and

Caleb's driveway. It was a modest tract home, a light tan color with white trim and the garage door was open. It was also the only house on the street without Christmas lights. A large, white, Ford F250 was backed into the driveway with the tailgate facing the garage and a few large pieces of furniture were in it, with a tarp draped over.

Gabe parked along the street just beyond the driveway and killed the engine. With one last look in the visor mirror, he took a deep breath and silently hoped that he was doing the right thing. He turned the light off by the visor and grabbed the flowers and wine in the dark. His heart began to race and there were pterodactyls flopping around in his chest. *Get a grip man.* This was ridiculous, it was just dinner. Just dinner and nothing more.

With a calmer attitude, Gabe opened the truck door and stepped down onto the street. As he approached the door, the smell of something familiar and wonderful wafted through the air. Suddenly he realized he was hungry and not just an apprehensive mess. He rang the doorbell. There was no going back now. Someone was headed to the door and his heart rate felt like a rabbit's again.

"You must be Gabriel. I'm Caleb Hollings," A large, blonde, fair-skinned man with a beer in his hand opened the door. He wasn't taller than Gabe, but much bulkier with a thick neck, and had a smile that spread across his entire face.

The guy extended his huge hand and shook Gabe's enthusiastically. "Come on in."

At least the guy seemed sociable and at ease. It helped Gabe to relax a bit.

"Hey Michelle! I think I have competition here. Gabriel brought flowers and I'm betting they aren't for me," he laughed.

The short entryway opened into the living room where the TV was on a music channel, playing Jason Aldean's, *She's Country.* A Christmas tree was in the corner, but the house was otherwise not decorated. Gabe quietly acknowledged to himself how hard it must be for them losing everything, especially this time of year.

The women were in the kitchen around the corner to the right and Michelle came around wearing an apron and blue jeans with a white blouse under it. Her dark brown hair was swept up in a loose bun and her fair skin and light freckles were endearing when she smiled a truly delighted smile at Gabe.

"Oh, Gabriel. For me? They are beautiful but you really didn't need to do that. How sweet. Oh. And wine too? Sarah, Gabriel brought wine."

Sarah slowly came around the corner just as Gabriel was headed towards the kitchen. They nearly bumped into each other and Gabe was mesmerized again by her jade green eyes. They pulled Gabe in like a hypnotized juvenile. He found it difficult to speak.

"I love Sauvignon Blanc. Did Michelle tell you?" Sarah spoke first breaking the spell Gabe was momentarily under.

Caleb chimed, "I have some beer outside, Gabriel, if you like Coors Light or Sam Adams."

"You can call me Gabe. Coors Light is great, thanks. Michelle, it smells wonderful, whatever you are cooking."

"It's pot roast and potatoes. Hope you are a meat eater, Gabriel," she said handing Sarah a bottle opener.

"Oh, I grew up on a ranch in Oklahoma. We all eat meat," Gabe said opening his beer. He was suddenly very warm.

"Oklahoma? What the hell brings you all the way out here to California?" Caleb asked.

"Friends. I just thought Cali would be an adventure I guess," Gabe wasn't going to get into his Shelly story tonight. That's all he needed. He hoped the subject could be changed quickly to something else.

"Well, we are glad you found us here in Lake County, Gabriel. Where is it you said you live?" Michelle asked pouring her and Sarah a glass of wine.

Sarah was standing at the counter looking straight into Gabe's eyes, waiting for the answer and it was killing him because he found it hard to concentrate.

"Uh, Danville. I live in Danville over in the east bay," he took another pull from the bottle and made a mental note to pace himself and not drink too fast just because he was nervous.

"So how much longer will you be working in Lake County?" Sarah asked taking a sip of her wine.

"I'm really not sure," he lied. "I will find out soon though." Gabe didn't want to get into the fact that he was leaving either. It might scare Sarah off and he wouldn't be able to even get anything started between them.

"You sure I can't help? I know my way around a kitchen," Gabe said feeling guilty for sitting.

"Oh now don't let them hear you say that, Gabe. I can't boil water and you will make me look bad in front of my lady." Caleb winked at him then motioned to the kitchen table and took a seat.

"It's true," Michelle said. "But he is so great in other ways that I keep him around. Besides, we are nearly finished in here. You can earn your dinner helping that burly guy move in the dresser and night stands my folks gave us. Everything you see here was either given to us, bought at goodwill, or picked up from town donations. That's why it's all mismatched and hodgepodge. We don't have a stereo, but the cable company offers music channels so that's a two for one."

It hadn't occurred to Gabriel about the furniture or other household items. He kept forgetting that anything and everything they had was lost along with their home. They had to start all over again.

"I think it looks great, Michelle. So where are your kids tonight?" Gabe asked.

"OUT." Caleb said, "We traded them for magic beans."

"Don't listen to him. My parents kept them *and our dog* when we went to pick up the furniture. They are getting their grandparent fix and we get a grown up night alone," Michelle said.

"Well, that's nice, I guess," Gabe was running out of small talk and wished Sarah would say something.

He looked up at her working with Michelle in the kitchen and she seemed to float about, very natural. Despite his anxious feelings, Gabriel was thoroughly glad he agreed to come.

❧

She brought the salad to the table and tried to steady her shaky hands. The wine would help. Sarah took her seat across from Gabriel and smiled at him, thrilled he was there but terrified just the same. He held her gaze a little too long so she spoke.

"The dinner looks amazing, Michelle."

"Well, pot roast is one of Caleb's favorites and it's really quite easy so I hope it tastes yummy. Dig in everyone," Michelle commanded.

Sarah was in a wet knot before driving over to Michelle and Caleb's house. She didn't know what to wear, how to feel and, as much as she loved her friends, she was feeling nearly thrown at this guy. Strangely though, Sarah *really did* want to see him again, which only made her feel guilty.

At any rate, here they were. Together. The four of them. She pushed her food around nervously with her fork, appetite waning, and catching glimpses of him looking right into her again while her heart raced.

Caleb and Michelle did all the talking. They all laughed at the stories of how Caleb and Michelle met in high school and how she and Sarah were inseparable. They also talked about their kids and how much trouble the son was going to be if he was anything like Caleb was, and how their daughter would be in charge of anything she wanted if she was like Michelle.

His smile was genuine, and his laugh was full and warm. This stranger, who came to help clean up a community he didn't even live in, and now he was helping her friends, too. *Who was this guy?*

"When do you want to tackle the furniture?" Gabriel asked as they finished eating.

"How about now? We can knock it out and then won't have to worry about it the rest of the evening."

The guys headed out as the girls moved to the couch. Michelle poured both of them more wine and they shared a school girl's giggle.

"Oh my gosh, Michelle. Can you tell how nervous I am? Am I hiding it ok or do I look like a fool?"

"No, no, you are doing great. So he has looks *and* he seems really sweet too. Bonus!"

Sarah sipped more wine and shook her head in protest. "I know, I know. He's the whole package but I'm not sure I'm what he's looking for, you know? What if I'm not ready for this? What if he sees right through me?"

"And sees what? That you are not only a natural beauty but a wonderful person as well? Geez that would be terrible, wouldn't it? Come on, Sarah. He's not proposing marriage. He is just here getting to know you…and *don't you wanna get to know some more of THAT?*"

They laughed. Sarah guessed Michelle was right. What harm would there be in spending time with an insanely good looking man that was kind to boot? They clinked glasses together and drank.

◈

When they were safely outside, Gabriel asked Caleb some questions as he hopped up into the bed of the truck.

"So, Sarah was ok with Michelle asking me over? I mean, I'm sure you could have gotten any number of friends to help you guys. Not that I mind *at all.* It's just sort of obvious Michelle has set us up. I mean, I'm good with that…but is she? Or is she just humoring the situation?" Gabe realized he was rambling and grabbed a corner of one bed side table.

Caleb laughed a huge belly laugh. "Man, Michelle jumped on

the idea of having you two meet up again, because Sarah doesn't *ever* show interest in any guy. She got all shy and blushed talking to you up at our place on Cobb so much that after you left, Michelle teased Sarah mercilessly. Sarah is shy, but she's into you man. We can tell. We've known her since we were kids. So to answer your question, no, she don't mind."

That was all Gabe needed to hear.

When they got back to the living room, Caleb brought them each in one more beer. The women were on the sofa, so Caleb walked to the recliner. This made it clear Gabriel was to sit next to Sarah, who was in the middle of the sofa.

"My wonderful sister-in-law gave us this coffee table or we wouldn't have anything to set our drinks on tonight." Michelle said. "And the sofa and recliner came from Griffins' Furniture in town. They were offering discounts to people in our situation."

"It's really nice, Michelle. Things will start to look up," Gabriel offered nodding to Caleb as well then taking a drink of his beer.

"Well, I don't want to talk about this sort of stuff anymore tonight," she said shaking her head. "How about you tell us when you will be back around here? Do you go home tomorrow for the weekend?" Michelle asked.

Sarah looked up into Gabriel's eyes then for the answer.

"I guess that all depends. I was planning to. I mean, I need to check on my apartment and get some clothes for next week. I haven't been there in awhile. But, maybe…I mean I could go and come back. I guess I haven't decided," he stammered.

"He doesn't need a plan, Michelle. Guys like us like to wing it. Right Gabe?" Caleb came in to the rescue.

"Oh, yeah, I mean, of course. I was just being nosey as I always am," Michelle laughed.

"What were your plans for the weekend, Sarah?" Gabe asked feeling awkward now.

Sarah started to wring her hands in her lap but smiled while looking at the floor. "I haven't decided."

Both Caleb and Michelle looked at one another and nodded towards the kitchen.

Caleb stood, "Hey Babe? How about I help you with the dishes and let these two talk awhile?"

Both Gabe and Sarah laughed nervously while the other two departed. Although he was grateful for a moment alone, he couldn't think of a single thing to say. He reached for his beer then realized it was empty, and set it back down.

"Look," Gabriel started, "I don't want you to feel pressured into seeing me or anything like that. It was just so great to hear from you guys and I was very happy to see you again tonight. You look wonderful, by the way."

Sarah smiled and looked up at him, again with apprehension. Her hair fell into her eyes and without thinking, Gabriel reached up and swept it away from her face. She didn't pull away.

"I'd like to see you. It's just been a really long time since I've done this. Sorry if I'm a little awkward. I feel like a baby deer trying to stand for the first time," she laughed.

"Well, no more awkward than me. I haven't seen anybody in a really long time either. Three years to be exact," then he wished he hadn't said that. Either way, he was being honest.

"But remind me to thank Michelle later. I was wondering how I was ever going to see you again."

"So when DO you think you are going back?" she asked.

"Well, I really should drive down to Danville tomorrow to check on my place, pay some bills, and grab new clothes. How do you feel about taking a drive? I mean, it would be a long day, but if you don't have any plans, I'd love the company. And we could stop in the Napa Valley on the way back for dinner. A real date."

From the look on her face, Gabe knew that was the wrong thing to say. He was going too fast and she was about to tell him so. Then after a few seconds that seemed like minutes, she laughed and shook her head. He tried to keep a brave face up while his heart dropped in his lap. *Good job buddy. Scare her off in the first ten minutes you are alone with her.*

"No, I'm sorry, it's not that I don't like the idea. I was just thinking of moving around some of my plans so I could go. I was going to breakfast with my father tomorrow, but I will tell him I have a date with a friend. He will understand. So, I'd love to come. Sure," she said.

Gabe blew out a breath he didn't know he was holding. His chest filled with nervous, divine, feelings of anticipation that happen when you know something extraordinary is ahead. He felt his goofy grin but didn't care how he looked. She'd said yes and tomorrow they'd spend the day getting to know one another.

"I'd better get going so I can be ready for tomorrow. What time do you want to leave?" Sarah asked.

"Oh, um probably pretty early so we can get down there and back in the same day. It's 3 hours. Is that ok with you?"

"Sure. Like 7:00, OK? You can pick me up at the coffee house in Lower Lake on Main Street if that's ok?"

"I know the place. Sure 7:00 works for me. Maybe we should go talk with Michelle and Caleb and I will walk you out," he said, standing up and reaching for her hand.

As he pulled Sarah to her feet, they stood smiling at one another. Her small frame was so near to his, it made his heart start to race again. The warmth of her radiated so that he could feel the connection between them without even touching her. She was maybe five foot four and looked up at him with those amazing eyes of hers that pulled at Gabriel's heart strings.

Sarah broke the tension by laughing and pulled at Gabe's shirt, "Let's go say our good-byes."

After thanking both Caleb and Michelle for a lovely evening,

Sarah grabbed her purse and they walked out into the cold December night.

Sarah had on a light jacket that Gabe knew couldn't possibly keep her warm enough. He followed her to her red car and they stood facing each other a moment. He knew he should keep the conversation brief so she didn't freeze, but saying good night was so hard. Still, the night ended up being so much better than he ever expected. She gave him something to look forward to.

✍

"Well, I guess I will see you tomorrow then," Sarah began.

"Yes, tomorrow. I'm really looking forward to it. You sure you are up for that much traveling?" Gabe asked her wincing.

"Of course! I could use the change of scenery," Sarah said.

Dealing with her own grief and then all the recovery efforts from the Valley Fire had become all consuming for Sarah. For months, depression had grabbed a hold of her like a dark demon in rough seas. Then the guilt from surviving the fires without a scratch made her dive head first into countless hours of volunteer work. It had been a very long time since she'd taken any time for herself.

"I didn't mean that the way it came out," Sarah retracted immediately. "I love helping Michelle and Caleb. I mean, I feel terribly guilty I even said that. My best friends just lost *everything* and I still have my place and all my things."

He stepped closer. "Well, Michelle didn't lose quite *everything*. She has her family and you. I can see very clearly that means the world to her."

Gabriel grabbed both her hands and they stood dangerously close together. He leaned as if he would kiss her and she froze in anticipation, but he brought her hands up to his mouth and kissed them both gently. Sarah let out a small gasp and smiled broadly.

"I can't wait to see you tomorrow. Thank you for agreeing to come. You get in now and warm up. I'll drive behind you. Be safe," he said and opened her car door.

What a gentleman. She tried not to question it, but the thoughts were still there. *What was he doing here with her? This wonderful, great looking guy that could be with anyone he wanted to. Why was he here with her?*

It took her a few moments to shake her thoughts from her head and start the engine. Gabe followed her to the intersection of highways 29 and 53. She turned right into her town of Lower Lake, and he continued onto Clearlake, to his hotel. Sarah couldn't help but to roll her window down and wave at him. Gabriel honked as he flew by and she wished the night hadn't ended.

CHAPTER THREE

THE DATE

THE ALARM WENT off at 6:00 am but Gabriel had been awake since 5:30 thinking about what to say when he cancelled his date with Sarah. What in the world was he thinking asking a beautiful woman to spend the day with him. His own crew didn't particularly like working with him for eight hours a day, and most of the time they were in separate vehicles. He had been in pain after Shelly died, and over time that pain evolved into anger. He wasn't angry any more, not really, but he sort of held on to being grouchy all the time because he didn't really know what else to be.

Something about Sarah was more captivating than Gabriel had ever experienced. Shelly was attractive and forward. He adored her and they had been good together. But Sarah was different. She was shy, but there way this gentle kindness about her too. It was as if she was the light at the end of his long, lonely tunnel. He couldn't stop smiling. He couldn't cancel.

He was early to meet Sarah at the coffee shop so he sat in his truck to wait and see if she wanted to go inside and grab a cup of coffee for the road. Time inched by at a snail's pace while he waited, but when her red Honda pulled up next to him, Gabe's heart raced again.

Gabriel was beaming with excitement as he jetted from his truck to help Sarah out of her car. The sun shined on her long, honey-colored hair like spun gold. The light green pashmina scarf she wore made her eyes glimmer like emeralds.

"Good morning. Wow, you look amazing," Gabriel said taking her hand.

"Thanks, you too. I have to grab my coat out of the back seat. Can we grab a coffee? I didn't get a chance to have any."

"Of course, I was thinking the same thing. If you are hungry we could grab something to eat too." Gabriel grabbed her coat from her so she could lock her car up.

"They do have amazing muffins here. Do you like blueberry? Or they have these really great apple cinnamon ones too," she said with a mischievous smile.

"Anything you wish, my lady."

The day was clear and the morning was pretty chilly, but the weather promised to be more mild than the previous few days. Gabriel was dressed in his usual t-shirt and flannel. He made a mental note to grab some nicer clothes for his return trip, just in case.

They ordered coffees and muffins to go and before long, they were driving south on Hwy 29, headed out of town.

For awhile they just talked about how great the morning was. With the little amount of rain that had already fallen, the coun-tryside was already turning green with sprouts of grass and the contrast between the blackened tree sticks and the green ground was astonishing.

"Do you want to listen to the radio? I usually have it on for background noise, or just company because I drive alone a lot, but we don't have to have it on if you don't want," Gabe was getting nervous and too chatty, he thought.

"Oh, I love listening to music. My car has the radio on always.

I have to remind myself to actually listen to the engine once in awhile," Sarah admitted. "What do you like?"

"I listen to a lot of country, but I love classic rock and some R&B too. Anything you like. You choose," Gabe said.

Sarah picked a modern country station and kept the volume low, so they could talk. Once they established the food was yummy and the weather was nice, there was awkward silence.

Gabe didn't want Sarah to feel uncomfortable so he decided the direct approach was best. "So I'm totally out of practice on what to say on a first date. I was just thinking, I hope you are still glad you came today. I was so nervous this morning I woke half an hour before my alarm just thinking of seeing you."

She smiled a shy smile and looked out her window at the passing landscape. A little embarrassed laugh escaped her throat, then she turned to look towards Gabe. He could briefly see in those eyes of hers that she had so much to share, so much to say. He just had to be patient.

⌁

"I was nervous too. I changed three times. I haven't dated at all since…" Sarah stopped herself before she just blurted it out. *Great Sarah. Now you have to tell him. Smooth,* she thought.

"Since…" Gabriel prompted her to finish.

Here goes nothing, she thought.

"My husband died in a car accident little over a year ago and I just haven't been interested in dating. I haven't thought of it actually. I didn't even think until you asked me to come today, that you and I would date. But here I am. On a date."

Not exactly the conversation she was hoping to have so early in their date. She couldn't decide what would have been worse. If she had told the truth how her friends wanted her to jump his bones that first night, or the fact that she just talked about her dead husband in the first fifteen minutes of their date. She picked up her coffee again, hiding behind the cup and staring out her window.

"I'm really, truly sorry you've had to go through that. I hope that doesn't mean you felt pressured into being here, because that's the last thing I'd want to do."

That snapped her attention back. Sarah put her hand on his shoulder and rubbed it reassuringly, a small curve of a smile forming on her lips.

"No Gabriel. I'm not feeling pressured. That's the strangest part. It's all been…very unexpected."

After that their conversation went a little easier. She told him of her job working for the Wildhurst Winery, in Kelseyville. They also talked about how she and her father, brother and sister were all very close since the death of her mother. Her dad had retired a few years back after being a butcher at Safeway for thirty years. How he fished a lot and was thinking of going into business with a friend of his, buying and selling antique fishing tackle and other paraphernalia. She talked about her older sister that lived in Sacramento with her husband and kids, and about her little brother that was in college at Chico State.

Then Gabriel shared a little about his own life. He told Sarah he was an only child. His parents were Jack and Beth Hart, and they'd tried to have more kids but it just never happened.

Sarah winced at that statement. Gabriel must have seen her because he quickly continued.

"I wasn't lonely growing up though, because I had cousins around all the time. Both my parents have brothers with families who lived only a few miles away. We all went to the same schools and every holiday was like a family reunion. Everyone was always in everyone's business," he laughed. "It was a good childhood."

Big family, she thought. Another conversation she wasn't so sure she was ready for.

"What made you come out to California? Don't you miss them?"

Sarah asked changing topics. She fidgeted in her seat and wadded up her napkin in her hand, tightly balling it in her fist.

Just breathe Sarah. You are doing fine.

❦

Gabe had to decide to tell the whole story or just part of it. Shelly had been the love of his life, and he'd lost her. But Sarah's story was out in the open, as far as Gabe could tell. He didn't want to get too heavy so early in their day, but he also didn't want to hold back from her and seem untrusting.

"Well…I was on a vacation and I met someone while I was here. She and I became involved and I moved here to be with her," Gabe began slowly.

"So I gather it didn't work out," Sarah inquired while drinking more of her coffee.

Gabriel sipped slowly on his own cup while pondering his response.

"No, it didn't work out. But not for reasons that you might think. Three years ago I was in a car accident on Christmas Eve. I survived, but Shelly didn't."

And there it was, his life's drama out in the open in his truck's cab, in the first hour of their morning together. What a great first date.

"I am so sorry Gabriel. I had no idea. That must have been a terrible loss. I don't even know what to say," Sarah said touching his arm.

"Well, looks like you and I are both the survivors of lost loves. But hey. We are dealing with it right? I mean, look at us today. We are out meeting new people, greeting this glorious day, and getting through it one day at a time. I think we should be proud of ourselves," Gabriel said to lighten the mood.

"I suppose you're right," Sarah said and shared a small smile with him.

❧

Eventually, they pulled off the highway and into Gabe's apartment complex, he pulled into the parking garage and killed the engine. Walking out of the truck, the air was crisp and fresh feeling. They turned left on the walkway, through shrubbery, ivy, and pergolas with dormant wisteria and bougainvillea. Gabriel's apartment was on the top floor of Building C, number twenty-two.

Gabe dropped his suitcase in the entry and helped Sarah out of her coat, laying it across the back of the sofa. He motioned with his arms, "Well, this is the palace. Your standard, bachelor's one bed, one bath, apartment. It's not a castle but I call it home...for now."

She smiled and looked around thoughtfully. She said nothing at first but nodded a lot as if approving of the space. Gabe tried to see it through her eyes and realized how stark it was with white walls and nothing on them except a big screen TV. Sarah walked over to the entertainment console and looked at his CD collection and DVD's he had.

"*Lonesome Dove? Open Range?* I'm sensing a Robert Duvall obsession," she said smirking.

"Um...yeah, I guess you caught me. I think there is a *True Grit* in there too," Gabriel smiled.

"He's one of my favorites," she said. "Agustus McCrae, was my favorite character ever. But...what's with the music here? You have Tammy Wynette mixed in with Lynyrd Skynyrd over here. What's with that?" she laughed.

Gabe stuck out his chest, "Yes. Yes, I do. And George Jones. Somewhere there might even be a Conway Twitty with Loretta Lynn, but I like modern country too. Brad Paisley's not bad."

"The Coalminer's Daughter. Now *she* is perfectly acceptable, and Patsy Cline. I love those women. My dad listens to them, I'm more modern." Sarah smiled up at Gabe.

"Just not Tammy Wynette, right?"

"Well, the whole, 'Stand By Your Man,' thing is a bit sexist. No offense. I just couldn't get past it so…" Sarah looked away suddenly.

Gabriel wasn't sure if he'd hit a nerve or what. He decided to not over think it and keep things moving. "Well, how about a tour of the rest of the place? It's quite a castle."

He showed her the bathroom, then the master bedroom, barren accept for his bed and dresser. He asked if she wanted to help him pack up some new clothes or listen to his terrible collection of old country music while he packed for the upcoming week. She opted to listen to music.

Choosing a more modern country channel on his stereo, Dierks Bentley came out of the speakers, then she ventured out onto his small balcony outside the sliding glass door off the living room.

Gabriel felt flustered and unable to concentrate but he managed to assemble a week's worth of work clothes and a couple of dress shirts this time, in case he was fortunate enough to get Sarah to meet him for dinner. In the hallway there was a pocket door that he slid open to expose a stacked washer and drier. He quickly threw in his dirty work clothes from the previous week and started the machine, then closed the door.

Back in the living room, Gabriel found Sarah had taken off her scarf and boots and put them near her coat on the sofa. Having her in his place made him both nervous and happy all at once. He was glad she'd made herself at home.

He found her sitting on the balcony in one of the two small chairs, with the door slid open to hear the music. He only had two chairs and a small round table out there because he never invested in plants or even a BBQ. But it was a lovely view of the lawn and garden courtyard below, even though it was all in the dormant stage.

Just as he stepped out to join her, his cell phone rang. He looked and it was Tommy Dermont, his boss and best friend.

"I'm sorry, I should take this. It's my boss," Gabe said apologetically.

She nodded at him so Gabe stepped back inside the apartment, pacing around.

"Hey Tommy."

"Gabriel Hart! How the hell are ya?"

"Pretty good. No complaints. What's going on?"

"I was just checking in on you, my friend. It was great for the company to get the Lake County gig, but I'm really glad you guys are coming back later next week. We have lots of jobs I've been bidding and I think this will be our busiest year yet. It's all because of you, man. You've worked like a dog these past few years and helped so much to build this place up that now I can't do it without you. Seriously, your desk is overflowing with shit you're gonna have to weed through when you get back in here. Anyway, I bet you are ready to come back and stop living out of a suitcase huh?" Tommy asked.

Tommy had been there for Gabe from the day he moved to California. When he needed a job, Tommy believed in Gabe. But after he lost Shelly and everyone else was hovering around him and saying stuff like, "you will feel better in time," Tommy said when he was ready to work there would be work for him. That had been the lifeline he needed to get out of bed in the morning, and he had practically buried himself in work ever since. Now Tommy needed him to help continue with the growth of Dermont Excavating. Guilt washed over him as he thought of how much he wanted to be closer to Sarah.

"Yeah, I'm ready to stop living out of a suitcase," he said running his hand through his hair and staring out the glass door.

"Well rest up this weekend and probably by mid-week, you guys will be packing it up to return permanently. I'll be in touch. Call if anything comes up."

"Sure thing, Tommy. See you soon."

He ended the call and took a deep breath feeling awful. It was a distraction he would rather not have had. Instead, he watched Sarah for a moment as she pulled her hair over one shoulder and tucked her feet up underneath her legs. Instantly, he refocused on just them being together. He didn't want a work call to ruin the progress they were making. He'd worry about the future another time.

⌁

It was strange how comfortable Sarah felt sitting on Gabriel's balcony, waiting for him to pack and finish up a work call. She was uncharacteristically at ease and found being with him almost natural. But when he returned onto the balcony, she could see he was distracted now.

"Hey you want something to drink?" he asked. "Soda, water, hot tea maybe? It's only the boring old Lipton tea I make sweet tea from. Nothing fancy, but it's warm."

"Actually I'd love some tea. I can help."

"Oh, you really don't have to. I can bring it. Just sit back and relax."

He disappeared into the apartment and she turned her attention back to look below at the lawns and the random people walking by.

Once he returned, they sat and sipped in silence a moment, just breathing. Soon the silence grew awkward and they both smiled at one another. Sarah's chest fluttered with excitement at his stare. He didn't look away and she immediately felt him draw her in.

"The tea is good, thank you," she said breaking the intensity.

"You're welcome," he said finally looking away.

"Need any help packing?" she asked.

"Hmmm? Oh, I think I did fine but I'm washing clothes so I hope you're not in a hurry. We could go grab a small bite if you're hungry. There are dozens of places we could go."

"I'm fine right here. Actually, I'm not hungry just yet. This is nice," she said sipping her tea and locking eyes with him over the rim of her mug. She suddenly wished he'd touch her.

Gabriel continued gazing right through her, sending waves

of electricity into her body that made her weak. She smirked and looked away, breaking his spell.

"Gave up on Conway Twitty huh?" he teased.

"Oh, no…I will not venture to listen to that twangy old stuff. He was my *grandmother's* favorite. That should be telling you something." she laughed.

"Your grandmother must have been adventurous." he laughed back.

After the laughs died down, Gabriel turned to Sarah and said, "I'm really glad you are here. I've, um, not brought a woman to my apartment before. I thought you should know that. It may sound strange to you, but just having you here makes me feel like I need to put a feminine touch around this place. It must seem pretty drab to you. I tried looking at it through your eyes and I guess it could use some homey touches, huh?"

Sarah laughed and was touched by his sentiment. He continued to impress her with his charm, and the easy way about him. He wasn't pretentious, wasn't arrogant, and had such sex appeal without trying that it left her off balance around him.

"I don't think it needs a thing," she said. "I like its simplicity. It's clean. You probably have everything you need."

"Not everything," he said smiling, and he grabbed her hand.

Holding her hand, Gabriel realized being with Sarah just felt right. Sitting together, watching the birds, people coming and going, and the faint sound of traffic off in the distance, Gabe knew he wasn't living the life he was meant to live. City living wasn't what he knew. It was simply what he accepted. He had loved Shelly so much and she was the one that loved the city because it's all *she knew*. But with her gone, the only thing keeping him there was Tommy.

Gabe gently squeezed Sarah's hand, then dropped it, and slowly crushed his coke can. He set it down on the small table and ran both his hands threw his hair, exhaling loudly.

"I don't even know what I'm doing here," he said out loud. He hadn't meant to, but there is was.

"Don't you like it here?" she asked furrowing her brow.

"Danville is ok as far as cities go. It's a bit upscale and has everything right at your finger tips. But I mean really, who needs country clubs, seven days a week dry cleaning, and Indian food? I don't even know what that is. I've never eaten Indian food and probably won't. I don't golf. I mean, I was raised with acreage, grew hay, and ate beef. I rode horses and drove tractors in Oklahoma. I was willing to give that all up because Shelly made me so happy. Then I landed this excavating job, which made me feel the most at home I'd felt since I left Oklahoma, and I stayed. Then Shelly died and…well, here I am."

Sarah pursed her lips and looked a bit confused. "Why do you stay? Why didn't you go back to Oklahoma?"

"It's complicated," he said shaking his head.

He wondered just how much he should share, this being their first date. Sarah was so easy to talk to, things just came out of him.

"Truth? Guilt. I have a tremendous amount of guilt, I guess. Before, leaving felt like abandoning Shelly. I thought I was supposed to feel terrible and stay where we promised to live our lives together. I know that sounds strange. But now… I think it's about Tommy, my boss. He really needs me and just now, on the phone, he told me he, 'couldn't do it without me.' I don't know what to do about that. I guess nothing right now."

He looked up to see Sarah's reaction then. She raised her eyebrows, wide-eyed, then kind of stared across the apartment complex to the buildings opposite them. She took her time before speaking and he guessed she didn't really know how to respond to all that. Maybe he shouldn't have shared quite so much.

"I'm not trying to be a kill joy here," he said grabbing for her hand again.

She didn't pull away, but squeezed his hand and looked back at him with her killer eyes. She gave him a weak smile, but it was warm and understanding nonetheless.

"I don't pretend to have the answers, but don't you think Tommy would want you to do whatever it is that makes you happy? If he's your friend, maybe you should be honest with him. I mean, if you decide to make any changes that is."

God, she was lovely. Her gentle, non-judgmental approach to him made him feel like he could really fall for her. She wasn't just beautiful to look at. Sarah was an amazing person and friend too.

"You know, I haven't really thought about what would make me happy. Not in a long time. I guess I always thought I'd be on a large piece of land somewhere, doing something meaningful. I love working outdoors, but here I mostly tear down old buildings so new ones can replace them. Or we work rich people's land to reconfigure it for expensive homes with cliff top views, or golf courses, or build vineyards. It's great and all, I just feel something is missing. I don't feel at home here. The city isn't where I belong. I'm a fish out of water. I'd like to live out in the country where I know all my neighbors and they know me."

Sarah leaned in closer, laughing a bit and said, "Aw, you really are a country boy at heart aren't you?"

"I suppose so," he said, as he gently chucked her under the chin with his finger.

She leaned back again and put on a little more serious face.

"Clearly, I'm in no condition to give advice because I've been at a stand-still since my husband died, it just seems to me that we should be doing what makes us happy."

"I have no idea what my life is going to be or what will make me happy in it. But if I can start with today, I'm doing what makes me happy right now. It's being in this moment, being honest with you, and sharing this beautiful day. That's all I can offer right now. I DO want to be happy. I've been a miserable son-of-a-bitch for three years and I don't even know why I still have friends or how my crew even works with me."

Gabriel was able to admit that and even laughed a bit. The skin he so terribly wanted to shed was full of darkness and pain, but it was slowly peeling back to reveal a more pleasant person. With Sarah's help, Gabe thought he could actually like himself again.

∽

How is it possible that this guy so clearly spoke her language? Sarah too, had found it hard to be nice. There had been so much pain and betrayal, even before her husband died. Bitterness was always brewing under the surface making it hard to hold conversations with most people, so she had taken to keeping her mouth shut. She lost sight of what a happy life could even look like for her, until now.

The both of them having to overcome so much made Sarah realize that this wasn't going to be easy. *THIS*, whatever they were becoming, was going to be anything but simple. They both had scars that they were only just beginning to share, and that were deeper than either of them were willing to admit.

She looked back up into his eyes, so full of tenderness. He was such a good guy, he deserved to be happy. It pained her to think that once he knew more about her, once all of her pain was on display, he would turn away from her. But for now, she could try to relearn what it meant to be happy. He reached over and brushed her hair away from her face and even that small gesture stopped her mind from the wheel of self-talk that was always taunting her with negativity.

"You know what I think?" she asked. "I think that the reason they are still your friends and the reason the crew still likes working with you, is because they see you for the great guy that you are. They must have realized that they needed to cut you some slack because you are this amazing guy who lost, basically, the person that meant the world to you. You were in pain and needed understanding.

Anyone who has eyes in his head can see you are a wonderful guy, unique, and caring. That kind of person is worth waiting for."

∽

Gabe sat stunned and thought how kind she was to find no fault with his surly attitude he admitted to. He realized at that moment, it was because she understood his pain. She too, was looking for the same empathy, and for her friends to wait out her mood swings and constant indifference, or resistance to invitations that made her feel uncomfortable.

They walked into the kitchen to dispose of his soda can and wash her tea cup. Standing there together, he ran his hand around her back and the other hand touched her jaw line, rubbing it with his thumb. It slowly weaved back through her hair and cupped her head to bring her lips towards his, while his other hand pulled her body closer until their torsos were pressed together. Gabriel kissed her slowly, feeling the plumpness of her lips. She didn't resist him and welcomed his warm mouth, opening to hers. It was a passionate kiss, each reaching for more, exploring tongues, and gasping in breath.

When they parted, Gabriel kissed her neck, then temple, and looked into her eyes for approval of his yearnings. He wanted to make sure he wasn't too forward or assuming in his feelings for her.

Sarah smiled and then buried her face in his chest while grabbing at his shirt. She then wrapped her arms around his waist and then looked up into his eyes.

"Well that was unexpected," she said, embarrassed.

"I'm sorry. I just couldn't help it."

"Don't apologize. I was a perfectly willing candidate."

"Sarah, I feel like a kid around you. I don't even know if that is a true analogy, because when I was a kid and liked a girl, I don't remember feeling quite this wound up. You make me want to be a better person. I don't even know if that makes sense."

"Gabriel Hart, I have a feeling this is going to be quite an adventure getting to know you."

The rest of the afternoon they finished his laundry, then went into town to a local deli to grab piroshkies and salads to take back to his apartment. They ate and listened to a comedy channel on the stereo, but mostly they talked and laughed. They even boxed up some things he never used to donate to the fire victims.

All of the seriousness from their earlier conversation was gone and they simply enjoyed each other's company. Before long though, it was time to head back. He was trying not to think of how he'd have to return to this space alone next time, without her. He was having trouble imagining being anywhere that she wasn't.

∽

During their drive back into Lake County, the countryside was dark so they didn't discuss the Valley Fire as they drove through the burned areas. Still, it brought questions to Sarah's mind.

"So how much longer do you have here, Gabe? I'm wondering for personal reasons now."

"I'm not a hundred percent sure, but it looks like this may be my last week. As a matter of fact, we might be done Wednesday."

She didn't even know what to say without sounding needy.

"Well, whenever you find out, let me know. We should get together for dinner before you go. I could cook," she offered.

Gabe exhaled quite loudly then for dramatic effect, whistled.

"She cooks too. I am intrigued. I'd love that very much," he said teasingly. "I am a great eater, not such a great cook I'm afraid. I can manage the BBQ alright, but I've a limited skill set."

"I'm told I'm quite a good cook, but you can form your own opinion if you like. All I need to know is do you have any food allergies or terrible aversions to anything in particular?" she asked.

"What, you mean, do I eat things like liver and onions or will I spit out lima beans into a napkin? Answers are NO, and YES. Other than that, I think I'm pretty much open to everything," he laughed.

"Got it." she laughed, "No liver and onions or lima beans. But I won't eat liver either so we are in agreement there. I'm sure I can whip up something suitable."

They were pulling into Lower Lake and as Gabriel parked his truck next to her red Honda, the town's Main Street was empty except for a couple of cars outside the bar at the end of town.

He turned off his engine and the headlights. The soft glow of the street lamp lit up the cab just enough to see the shine in Gabe's eyes looking back at her. Sarah's heart skipped a beat and fluttered into her throat.

"I hate to sound presumptuous, but what are you doing tomorrow? I know it's Sunday but didn't know your work schedule or if you had other plans, but I'd love to see you again," Gabriel said holding her hands.

Her heart swelled up and she smiled, looking down at their hands intertwined. "I haven't any plans at all. What do you suggest?"

"Anything! A walk, breakfast, a picnic, or whatever you'd like to do. I'm open to suggestions, so long as I can see you again."

Not wanting to sound too eager, she said, "How about you call me in the morning and we can discuss it. Maybe I can cook for you tomorrow instead of later in the week. We'll see."

"I cannot tell you what a lovely day I've had, spending time with you," Gabriel said humbly. "It's truly been the most awake and alive I've felt in years. I hope that's not too forward to say."

"No, I'm flattered. I've had a really great time too," Sarah said.

He leaned in to kiss her good night and she welcomed the advance. Feeling his lips lightly on hers electrified her, and she was aware of the pounding of her heartbeat, certain he could hear it outside of her chest.

He squeezed her hands before releasing them then turned to open his door and jumped out to round the truck and open her door for her. Sliding down the seat to the street below, she slid slowly down into Gabe's embrace. They hugged a minute and he kissed her forehead , then shut the door behind her to escort her over to her car.

When she had unlocked her door and set her purse on the car seat, she turned to meet Gabriel's gaze once more. They laughed at each other and their unwillingness to end the evening. At least it was a mutual difficulty, she thought.

"Well good night then. I guess I'll hear from you in the morning?" Sarah said.

"Yep. If not sooner," he laughed. "I told you, I feel like I'm back in high school or something."

She stretched up for one last quick kiss and then sat down in her seat. She turned the engine over then shut her door, and rolled the window down. They exchanged one last good night, as Gabe told her to drive safe, then he watched her back out and drive off into the night.

Sarah saw Gabriel hop back into his truck and she let out a sigh. She really was smitten and as she drove to her little house, couldn't help smiling to herself the whole way home.

As if reading her mind, a text message came through from Michelle, as Sarah was walking into her kitchen and reaching for the light.

Well are you home or do I have to send out the posse to look for you?

Laughing, Sarah decided to just call her rather than type it all out.

"Ok, Sister, spill it. I want details. Everything. Did you have fun?" Michelle interrogated.

Sarah plopped on her bed and smiled so huge she thought Michelle would know right through the phone.

"Well…it was quite nice. He's really something. Not only does he have that fantastic build and hypnotizing eyes, he really is amazing. He even boxed up some of his belongings to donate to the Valley Fire victims. Isn't that sweet?"

"Oh, my goodness yes. But get to the good stuff. Did you *do anything?* Did he make a move?"

"Michelle… really. We just met," she paused but then couldn't contain herself anymore and started giggling. "OK… we *did kiss.* Like a few times." Gabe wasn't the only one that felt like he was in high school again.

Squealing came over the phone line, Michelle voiced her approval.

"But that's all we did. Don't get any other ideas. Besides I have so much baggage he's unaware of…"

"Geez Sarah. Chill out. It was only a date. Now, *how was it?* The kissing? Was it fabulous?" she pressed.

Sarah rolled onto her side and squeezed her eyes shut smiling, "YES! Yes, it was fabulous."

"I KNEW IT!" Michelle laughed.

Just then, Sarah's phone vibrated and she looked down to see Gabriel was calling in.

"Oh my gosh. It's him. He's calling me. I gotta go, Michelle. I will call you tomorrow. I'm seeing him again tomorrow. I will talk to you later. Love you."

"Again tomorrow? Must be some kisser. You better call me. Love you, too."

Sarah sat up and smoothed her hair, as if Gabriel could see her through the phone, then she clicked over.

Answering with a laugh, Sarah said, "Hello? It's not tomorrow yet."

"I know. But I couldn't wait. I bet you are exhausted and I'm sorry to call already, but I had to tell you once again that I had a wonderful time today. Thank you for coming with me."

She twisted a strand of hair, "I did too, Gabriel. We should do it again sometime." she suggested.

"You bet. I guess I should let you go to bed. It's nearly midnight now. But that would mean it's tomorrow morning and then I guess we could see each other again." he teased.

"Unfortunately, I do require sleep. You wouldn't like the grumpy me," Sarah warned.

"Hmm…I believe I'd like you under any circumstance. But I will let you go to bed now. Good night Sarah McKinney. Sweet dreams."

She loved the way he said her name. "Good night, Gabriel Hart. Until tomorrow."

≲

Chapter Four

New Territory

"I'M HERE. SHOULD we meet in the lobby?" Sarah walked into the hotel and as she entered the high ceiling entryway, the elevator doors opened to reveal a handsome man, smiling at her with his cell phone pressed to his ear.

After a quick kiss hello they drove in Gabriel's truck to Main Street Bar & Grill. They were seated quickly in the very busy restaurant and given menus.

"Sarah? Wow. How have you been? I haven't seen you around in ages." Their server was a wild sight with bright make up, long acrylic nails, and over-dyed orange hair.

"Yeah, I've been busy. How are you Pamela?" Sarah wanted to crawl under a rock, but instead she plastered on a smile. She felt like a deer caught in headlights but hoped she was somehow pulling off calm and friendly. Pamela had no filter, never had, and there was no telling what would come out of her mouth.

"Great. Things are good. I mean, compared to everyone around here, I'm doing marvelous. Still have my house, the kids are great, I have my job, my health…you know, who can complain?…I mean, *I surely can't.* But who is this? Don't believe we've met," the waitress extended her hand to Gabriel while winking to Sarah.

"Um…Pamela, this is Gabriel. He's here working on the fire clean-up with a crew staying at the Best Western. Gabriel, Pamela Martin. She and I went to high school together," Sarah said giving Gabe a quick, alarmed eyebrow raise.

Gabe shook her hand while his smile made it clear he was enjoying Sarah's discomfort.

"Oh, my goodness. Gabriel? Well it's a pleasure meeting you. You're staying at the Best Western? Well isn't that something? You know, I heard the maids there sleep with a lot of the guests so be *careful of them.* Hussies will jump in the sack with just about anyone and they all have venereal diseases. My friend who works across the street at the clinic told me. Not that it's any of my business, but you should know anyway. Tell your friends." She let go of Gabe's hand, laughing hysterically.

Poor Gabe, his eyes were big as saucers. "Uh…yep. I'll tell them. Thanks."

"Maybe we should just order, Pamela," Sarah suggested, shaking her head in embarrassment.

"Sure, sure honey. What'll it be? We are out of the pepper bacon, but have regular, and the cappuccino machine is down so…"

"That's fine, I will just have the Denver Scramble with rye toast and an orange juice," Sarah said.

"And, I will have two eggs over easy with hash browns, and wheat toast. If you have Tabasco sauce that would be great. Just water and coffee to drink, thanks," he said handing her both their menus.

"Ok, be back in a jiffy." Pamela said sashaying away with a smile.

"I'm so sorry about that," Sarah said with a little laugh. "She is quite possibly the world's biggest gossip and I had no idea she was working here. She has always been like that. I honestly don't even know what to say," she giggled into her hand and kept shaking her head.

"Friend of yours?" he asked smiling and sipping his coffee.

"NO. No, I mean, I'm nice to her because, well…"

"Because you are nice?" he asked.

"Well, she's kind of like our town busy-body. I think every town has one. But it's gotten her fired from a lot of places. I thought she was working at a bar over in Clearlake Oaks, but I guess not," she laughed and sipped her coffee.

"Looks like she's a beauty school drop-out. You know, like in the movie *Grease*? Wasn't it Frenchy that had hair that color?" Gabriel asked laughing.

"Oh, here she comes. Quiet." Sarah warned trying not to giggle.

"Here's the O.J. and your water Gabriel. What was your last name?" Pamela asked.

"Hart. It's Gabriel Hart," he told her.

"Gabriel Hart. Sounds like a movie star or somethin'. Well anyway, sure is good you're dating again, Sarah. It's time you got out and enjoyed the living, you poor thing. Well, be back with the food shortly. You two enjoy," and she rushed off again.

"Oh my gosh! Seriously?" Sarah buried her face in her hands.

"Wow. Sounds like she just says anything that pops up in her head. You ok?"

Sarah peeked between her fingers to see Gabriel grinning at her.

"Oh sure. She's just not what I had in mind for today, but it's fine," she said waving her hand around, dismissing the whole thing.

"Good. Because it's going to be a good day," Gabe promised. "I am spending it with a beautiful lady."

She liked that about him. He was quick to find something positive. Sarah just smiled at him and sipped her coffee, wondering when he'd kiss her again.

❧

They managed to get through breakfast without too many strange revelations from Pamela, although watching Sarah blush every time she came to the table was very entertaining.

"I know you have been working the various fire sites while you've been here, but have you been to the lake?"

"What lake?"

"The one Lake County is named for! That settles it, we are going to the lake."

Gabriel paid the check and they walked out into the windy morning and hopped into his truck for a drive.

They left the area of Clearlake for a short stretch of highway that led them to a beautiful lake view drive. On Highway 20 heading west, the blue waters of Clearlake sparkled and danced beneath the huge dormant volcano of Mount Konocti. The large body of water wrapped around this mountain and all the county towns were nestled around the lake and it's nearby rolling hills.

"Wow, this is really beautiful, Sarah. And this lake is huge! I had no idea."

"It's the largest freshwater lake that's wholly in the state of California. My dad loves it for the fishing. It's been called the Bass Capital of the West, but the Catfish in there can get enormous. He's probably out there right now with one of his buddies. I just think it's beautiful."

They drove around to the opposite side of the lake and turned into Lakeport where Sarah guided him to a lovely park on the water and they watched children feed ducks and bass fishermen launch their boats. They drove further on to circle the lake, and headed to Highway 29, stopping in Kelseyville, where they poked into shops, and Sarah showed him the winery she worked at, but they didn't go in.

"I'm afraid they'd put me to work, so let's keep walking," she laughed.

It was such a quaint little town and had all the charms of his hometown of Pauls Valley, Oklahoma. Gabe could see himself living here. It would be a great fit for him, he thought, and squeezed Sarah's hand as they walked back to his truck.

"Well do you think I can take you to dinner or something tonight?" He was driving her back to her car at the hotel and he didn't want the day to be over.

"We could do that, or you can try my cooking. I mean, I could cook for you, if you would like that."

Gabriel smiled a huge smile, ignoring the way her words tripped over themselves. "I don't mind grocery shopping. What do you say?"

They made their way back into the town of Clearlake, as the skies grew darker. They shopped quickly for ingredients for dinner. Gabriel told Sarah to wait under the awning with the cart since it was raining when they stepped back outside, and he went to get the truck. They put everything in the back seat of the king cab and jumped in as fast as they could, but they were both quite wet by the time they were pulling away from the curb. Laughing at each other, Sarah reminded Gabe to drive her back to the hotel to get her car and he could follow her home.

It had been a great morning but as he watched her pull out onto the road in the rain, a sudden wave of fear struck him. His chest tightened, his breath came fast and it felt like his heart would pound out of his chest.

Gabe had to force himself to get a grip. He'd had some trouble driving right after the accident, but he'd never worried about someone else until that moment. She was starting to mean something to him and he was afraid of what would happen if he lost her. He shook his head at the thought and followed the red Honda into her town of Lower Lake.

Sarah lived out of town on a country parcel of about a half of an acre. He was very grateful for the few extra miles it took to get there because it gave him a chance to get his breathing back under control. As he pulled up the dirt driveway, he saw a little creek off to one side. Her house was bordered by a small lawn and stone walkway that was enclosed by a little white fence. She parked in front of the garage doors and waited for the automatic door to open. Gabriel parked just behind her and turned off his engine.

Before he got out, Gabe looked around and thought her place was very charming. It was a sweet little cottage of a house, and he was just a tad bit jealous of her lifestyle. Quite a contrast to his apartment living. He smiled and popped open his door.

They rushed the load of groceries through the rain, from Gabriel's truck to her garage and entered the house through the adjoining door that took them right to the kitchen. Sarah clicked the garage door shut then and they began unpacking their items.

Gabe immediately felt at home there. Her kitchen was in a U-shape with the opening facing the living room. There was a small dinette table in the kitchen area near the windows, and out in the small living room, he could see light streaming in from both the front window and the back sliding doors. It was completely different than his space. There were framed pictures and books on the tables, blankets on the couch, and extra pillows all around. It felt like someone lived there. It was a place he could see himself spending a lot of time in. A place he hoped he'd be welcome to come back to again and again.

∽

Anxiety had crept up on Sarah the entire drive to her house from the hotel. She had spent enough time with this man now to know he was pretty special. Still, bringing him to *their house* suddenly felt wrong. What the hell made her think she was ready to move on with anyone? Not that it would matter, no one would want her long term anyway.

She could do this. She deserved a little bit of happiness. She would block out those old memories, the reality of all the things she wasn't, all the things she would never be, and just breathe.

"Wow. This place is great Sarah," Gabriel said looking into the living room.

She saw him turn towards her out of the corner of her eye. She couldn't look at him, she would just unpack the groceries. And breathe. Don't forget to breathe.

"Sarah? Everything ok?"

He placed his hands on her shoulders but she still refused to meet his gaze. A small, nervous laugh escaped her throat and she shook her head. He put a finger under her chin and raised her face up to his so she would look at him. It was an internal struggle but his eyes were so sincere.

"Sarah, if you aren't ok with this, I don't have to be here. If we are moving too fast just say so. I can handle it. We can slow down."

"It's not that," she said. "It's just that...I just...Ugh. I don't really know how to talk about it," she squeezed her eyes shut to block him out.

"Take a breath and relax. You can spit it out and I can take it. Whatever it is, I can handle it," Gabe reassured her.

Jesus, this isn't how this was supposed to go. DECIDE damn it, she thought. She didn't want to lose him so out it came.

She took a big breath and let it go. She looked him square in the eye and said, "I haven't dated anyone since the death of my husband, and this is the first time a man has been in our house. I feel a bit strange, but I want you here. Does that make sense?"

"Absolutely it does. My apartment wasn't mine and Shelly's, I don't have any memories of her there. I can see how this might be too much. It's really up to you. I don't ever want to push you."

She smiled then and buried her face in his chest, wrapping her arms around his waist. His arms came around her and she felt him softly kiss the top of her head. The tightness in her was releasing and being in his embrace relaxed all her fears, for now. She was glad she told him, at least that little bit.

"So, what do you think? I would be happy to take you out to dinner, or I can head out on my own so you can have the evening to yourself. You can be honest," Gabe asked smiling back down at her.

She didn't have to have it all figured out right away, and she didn't have to tell him everything tonight. For the first time in years she was going to relax and go with the flow. "What I think is…I think…you should go build us a fire while I bake the caramel brownies I was going to make us for our dessert tonight. I will put on some music for us to work to."

Gabe's eyes lit up, "Yes, ma'am!"

And just like that, she found her smile again.

∽

Letting out a sigh of relief, Gabe realized how hurt he would have been if she actually asked him to leave, but still he'd have gone and respected her feelings.

Winters back home could be harsh and he got to be a professional at fire building. This time of year in particular he remembered the hearth full of his mother's decorations and then it dawned on him, Sarah didn't have any decorations up at all. Not that he did either, but he had been such a Scrooge since Shelly died.

"I bet it's been pretty hard for folks since Christmas is here and they are still trying to rebuild their lives. You've all been through a lot with that fire," Gabriel said.

"It's true. We did go through a lot around here. And for so many people, they are still going through it. I mean, look at Michelle and Caleb. They don't even realize what they are missing in their household until they go to use it and remember, 'Oh yeah, I don't have one of those anymore.' Stuff as simple as a rake for your yard, or a can opener, are just not there."

"That would be awful. Like a constant reminder. I really like them. Do you suppose there is anything I could do to help?" he asked piling up wood.

"Oh, geez, I don't know. I mean, just being around to help with stuff is what Michelle is grateful for. A couple of days after the fire, some ladies in Lower Lake organized a mass give-away of all kinds of products, both used and brand new, for the residents that lost everything in the fire. I went down to The Brick Hall and helped them organize things. I still felt it wasn't enough."

"I'm sure anything you did was a tremendous help to others," Gabe offered.

She stopped stirring the brownie batter and cocked her head, thinking back. "I helped Caleb and Michelle's sister in-law make food for the fire fighters so they would come back to the station to a hot meal. Still didn't feel like it was nearly enough. I gathered all the clothes I could spare and donated them to help out some of the women I knew who lost their homes, I bought blankets and pajamas… It never felt like it was enough. I still feel guilty that I have so much."

"You have a big heart, Sarah. You mustn't feel guilty though for anything. Helping when you can is all you can do. Time will pass and with it, most people will rebuild or relocate and you just have to pray they find peace again."

"I don't know if some of them ever will again. One of the ladies I know that lived on Cobb, she had her home paid for outright. Now the insurance company won't give her enough money to rebuild the same size home so she's going to have to take out a mortgage. She was ready to retire next year. Now she can't," Sarah shook her head.

"Yeah, that is unfair, that's for sure. That would be awful," Gabe agreed.

He lit the fire and stood back to watch the flames rising through the sticks. Briefly he wondered if those that lost their homes would ever be able to truly enjoy a winter fire in the fireplace anymore. For him, it was symbolic of romance, comfort, and family. And now, he could see a future with Sarah hanging stockings.

Then it hit him! "I have this great idea. What if you and I went Christmas shopping? I mean, for the families. You know. Give them Christmas decorations to make their homes festive since they lost all theirs in the fire. What do you think?" he could feel the cheesy smile plastered across his face.

"That's a wonderful idea, Gabriel. I think that would be fantastic, really. There are so many people I know we could help with that. What a great idea. When do you want to do it?"

"How about tomorrow after work? I can wait for you to call when you are available and I will just grab a quick shower after work, we can meet up, and you bring a list. How would that be?" he was so excited to finally have something he could contribute to these people's broken lives.

"I'd like that very much. Thanks Gabriel. You know, you're really a great guy," she continued to look at him in amazement, locking eyes with him until it must have made her uneasy, so she went back to her brownies.

∽

The afternoon moved quickly. While the caramel brownies baked and the beef stew simmered, they sat on her sofa. Gabe had asked about the people in her photos and after a little convincing, she pulled out some albums to tell him about her family. She flipped through pictures of her mother, Jane, and it made Sarah wish more than ever that she were still here. Having a mother to talk to about all her jumbled emotions over Gabriel would have made things easier.

Sarah kept struggling with just how much to let him in. Was it too soon? Would he accept her for who she was, with all her baggage? For all she was, and all she *wasn't*, would she be able to live up to this person he obviously thought she was?

"Your mother was lovely. You look just like her."

She smiled, "I was named for her. My middle name is Jane. My sister Maggie was named after our grandmother on my mom's side, Margaret, and my brother Joe was named after my grandfather, Joseph, on my dad's side. Names are pretty important in our family,

I guess. I think my dad and grandfather were just relieved when Joe was born to carry on the McKinney name," Sarah said.

"What, may I ask was your married name then?" Gabriel asked sounding apprehensive. "I assumed that McKinney *was* your married name since..." then he looked very apologetic he even brought it up but Sarah was already starting to think how to answer.

Sarah froze. She felt her chest tighten and for a moment wasn't sure how to take a breath. It was bound to come up eventually, like everything else would, but still it was difficult. She didn't want the day to be ruined with heightened emotions so she knew she'd have to quell his fears.

"Oh, I'm sorry Sarah. I really don't mean to pry. It was insensitive of me to even ask. You really don't need to explain. I was thinking out loud and didn't..."

She cut him off and put a hand over his, patting it to reassure him it was alright. Then took a deep breath. She could do this.

"Don't. It's ok, Gabriel, really. I just need... a minute I guess, but it's truly a fair question."

He sat there holding her hand with both of his, looking like a sad puppy and obviously feeling remorseful. He waited and said nothing until she had time to gather her thoughts. Grateful for the moment, she came up with the simplest answer she could. She just wanted to get beyond it and back to the two of them, and pretend for just one day, that her past wasn't real.

"Before my husband died, things with us weren't going so well." She choked out a laugh at that understatement. "No, that's not quite right. Things were actually quite terrible. We had decided to separate. I was devastated. He...well we... we were trying to buy a property near the lake to start a Bed and Breakfast and it needed a lot of work. We fought about that, among other things." Her stomach lurched at that. She was making it sound like they simply fought over curtain colors. "We...umm, we had very different ideas of what a happy marriage would look like. And then I found out, he was cheating on me.

And like an idiot she cried, even though she promised herself she wouldn't. Gabe gently pulled her into his arms and said nothing. He just held her and let her cry. She was mentally scolding herself for shedding tears in front of him and quickly tried to gather herself, putting up her tough front that guarded her heart.

"Oh, my gosh, Sarah. I'm so, so sorry. I'm sorry you have to go through this. I should never have asked such a thing. I'm so sorry you were reminded of this," and Gabe rubbed her arm.

She wiggled herself out of his embrace. She was going to be a calmer, stronger Sarah. She wiped her tears away and jutted her chin out, forcing a smile. "No, it's ok…I'm sorry I cried. I think that the worst part is not knowing if you were loved by the person who left. Now, I will never know. I have these stupid thoughts, they sound so insecure. When did he stop loving me? Why wasn't I enough? That's the part I hate." she admitted, stoically gathering herself.

"Sarah, I don't know you very well, I will admit, but I'm willing to bet my life that you weren't to blame. Some guys don't think and do stupid things. I have known my fair share. Even my own cousins have cheated on their girlfriends instead of breaking up with them, and I've always wondered why. Because I knew them and knew they really loved the girls they cheated on. For some stupid reason they got curious and did dumb ass things. I don't know the circumstances of your marriage, but one thing I do know, is that any man who could walk away from you is one foolish person. I have a hard time being away, just in the next room from you. You are an amazing person, Sarah. You have to know that."

Then the waterworks started up again and she was helpless to stop it. Tears spilled down her cheeks but she couldn't tell him the rest of the story. She couldn't explain why her husband didn't love her and how it was all her fault.

She again tried to gather the fragments of herself and wiped away the tears. Then Gabriel gently lifted her chin with his hand so she had to look at him. He gave her a stern look.

"Believe me, Sarah. He loved you. There's no way he couldn't have."

She stared deeply into his eyes knowing he couldn't possibly know that, but was grateful he'd said it anyway. She desperately needed to think that was the truth, but the way they'd left things before he died, she wasn't so sure. But Gabriel was here telling her such pretty stories, she felt completely weak and just wanted to be loved. Needed to be loved.

Without thinking, she leaned in and kissed him softly, the wetness of her cheeks shared upon his own. She kissed him for all he'd said to her and for all he made her hope for.

"Thank you Gabe. I guess I really needed to hear that," then she kissed his cheek and was up on her feet. "If you would excuse me for a minute, I think I'm gonna run to the bathroom to clean myself up."

Well she was really messing things up. Sarah wiped her eyes and blew her nose, then studied herself in the mirror. Shaking her head she decided she really wanted to spend time with Gabriel, even if he was certain to leave her eventually. She would grab any chance at happiness that she could and for now, she just wanted to enjoy his company and the comfort he brought her.

When she returned she walked by Gabriel, patiently sitting on the sofa, and she squeezed his shoulder on her way to the kitchen. She decided to get busy, as she often did when she became uncomfortable.

"It's too bad you didn't get your B&B. I could see you running a place like that." Gabriel offered walking into the kitchen.

"Well it is what it is, as my dad would say. I don't know what I would have done without my dad, or Michelle and Caleb, through all this. They were my life line," she said as she pulled the lid from the stew.

"I understand totally. When Shelly died, I didn't know how

to go on. Then I buried myself in work and that was *how* I lived. Then," and he smiled at her, "a few days ago, I started to live again. I met the most amazing people and they introduced me to the most spectacular girl."

She laughed at him and tossed her hot pad at his chest. They laughed together and it felt good. After being so raw with emotion, now being light hearted was a release. It was official, Sarah was hooked. And it scared the hell out of her.

CHAPTER FIVE

LEAVING

THERE WERE ONLY three days left to work in Lake County. Wednesday was their official date to pull out and head back to the Bay Area. There were only two more properties on the contract and they would probably not even need Wednesday to work on it. They'd simply been given the extra day in case of any hang ups. Gabriel's crew was elated, Gabe himself was anything but.

He had left Sarah's house right after dessert. He wanted to stay. He felt as if he could stay *forever*, but he knew Sarah needed her space and time. She needed to be able to sort her feelings out without him pushing.

The guys knew he'd started to date a local girl, but nobody had told their big boss, Tommy. Not that it was any big secret, but Gabe wanted to tell Tommy himself. If his relationship with Sarah continued to grow closer, as he imagined it would, then Gabe would most likely want to be moving on. It was going to be a delicate thing because Gabe still had some guilty feelings about letting Tommy down. Even though it had been three years and he knew Tommy would be happy for him, somehow he still felt badly about it.

At the end of the day, the guys were loading the equipment and Gabe helped chain it all and then handed them paperwork to sign.

They went over a few details for the next day and agreed to meet up at six a.m. in the lobby of the hotel. Gabe started towards his truck then, and said he'd see them all down the mountain. Barry winked at Gabe knowingly as he hopped into the water truck.

As soon as he got back to the hotel, Gabriel grabbed a shower to get ready to meet Sarah. The closer it got to his having to leave the more his nerves rattled him. Cleaning all the home sites from the devastating fire started out to be just a job. Now he was so much more sensitive to the issue. Driving to meet Sarah, and shop for her friends that lost everything in the fire, Gabriel hoped they'd help rebuild their lives during this first holiday season.

⤚

Sarah met Gabe in the parking lot of Walmart. It was dark and cold out when they entered the store, and Christmas music was playing inside. It was just the festive mood needed to spark inspiration for choosing gifts.

"What do you think about decorations for families? Did you bring a list?" Gabe asked.

"I did. There are four families I'd really like to get decorations for. Two are from my work, Walter and Christina. Walter and his wife Kelly are empty nesters but Kelly used to go all out for the holidays. Christina is single but she could really use the cheering up. She lived in the apartments in Middletown that burned. She was out of town when it happened and lost everything," Sarah said while they strolled down the isles.

"Poor thing," Gabriel said. "She's a good candidate then."

Gabriel pulled on a Santa hat from a shelf and then randomly started pushing buttons on some animated toys, causing some shoppers to look in their direction. He quickly pushed them again to silence them and stifled a laugh. He was playful and made Sarah laugh out loud.

"*ANYWAY...*" she was giggling, "there is a woman that Michelle knows that works at the school district whose family lost their home, and Caleb's cousin Laurie too."

"Ok, let's do this."

As they rolled down the Christmas wrapping isle, Sarah chose the shiny, sparkly gift wrap. She always gravitated to the shiny paper instead of the old fashioned Santa paper. Gabriel said it was a good choice and very festive. He grabbed lighted evergreen garlands, sparkly tinsel garlands, ornaments, window decals, and shiny beaded garland. Sarah grabbed wreaths, snowmen stocking hangers, stockings, and red bows packaged by the dozen.

Gabriel insisted they grab some household items to wrap for Michelle and Caleb. Bath towels, new sheets, and a kitchen clock, were all added to the cart. Sarah's smile lit up her face the whole while. Just being with him, and sharing this experience made her soften even more.

"How old are Michelle and Caleb's kids again?" Gabe asked.

"Sophie is 8 and Josh is almost 6. I was thinking something special for them. I'm like their aunt and they are pretty amazing kids. Great imaginations too." Sarah said.

"Are you thinking gaming system, or more like educational games? I was always playing in the dirt growing up, so I'm not sure," Gabe said.

She smiled, imagining him with Tonka toys, elbow deep in dirt.

"Well for starters, I really want to get them *The Minions Movie*, and maybe get them each new pajamas, a storybook, and a toy of some kind. Like a Barbie for Sophie and some kind of Lego thing for Josh."

Watching his enthusiasm, it made Sarah feel a tug inside of her. She could tell plainly that he'd make a great dad. They filled their cart with all the items for the kids, and as they did a small panic started to rise within her. She masked it as best as she could but suddenly she felt like fleeing.

"Hey can you take these up to the register? I've got to use the restroom real quick. Meet you up there."

Get it together! She walked fast to the bathrooms and found it empty. She stared at herself in the mirror and leaned over the sink. *This is not the time, so snap out of it! Don't screw this up!*

Within minutes she felt her heart rate slow. Sarah knew her time with Gabriel was limited and she didn't want to ruin it with being emotional so after talking herself out of a panic attack, she walked out and found Gabe at the registers.

The lines were ridiculous but they didn't care. Sharing in the Christmas Spirit made Gabe act giddy, and she relaxed while they crept at a snail's pace to the checkout.

Sarah started to contemplate her own house and lack of decorations. A tree wasn't such a bad idea after all, she thought. Before, she didn't feel like decorating at all, but now since Gabe was there, she thought more of it. Maybe she'd suggest it later in the week, if there was time.

They walked out to their vehicles and, like Sarah predicted, all the stuff didn't fit in the back of the cab in Gabriel's truck. They used both vehicles to pack up their treasures. He followed Sarah to her house, where they would store all the items in her spare bedroom, until she could sort them all out to distribute to the families.

It was 7:30 by the time they stowed all the Christmas goodies in her house, and they were famished. They found leftover stew from the night before and Gabriel lit a fire in the fireplace. Sarah doled out stew to put in the microwave and they behaved like it was any normal activity from any normal week night. It was easy. It felt right.

She didn't want the night to end and have Gabriel leave. Reality was creeping in as much as she tried to shove it away and ignore it. But sitting on her sofa, eating stew and watching the fire, a sinking feeling settled in and she knew his impending return to Danville was going to change everything.

❧

"I have to leave Wednesday morning. The others will be leaving Tuesday after work. I've been here 4 weeks, but now I don't feel like leaving," Gabriel said.

Sarah put her spoon down and gave him a thoughtful look. "Are we still going to keep this going? You and me?" she narrowed her brow.

He put his bowl on the coffee table. "I certainly hoped we would. I mean, I don't know anyone I'd rather spend my time with… and the fact that you willingly see me is a plus," he tried to joke.

But Sarah only gave a half-hearted smile and put her bowl down too. She looked at the floor then carefully formed words that slowly came out, like cold molasses.

"Gabriel… I live here and you live there. I know in the beginning it's going to be either me running to Danville or you running to Lake County, every weekend we have free. But then what happens when two or three weeks go by and neither of us can get away? Or when it becomes too hard? Won't you get tired of this back and forth thing pretty quickly? I'm just trying to be practical. Shouldn't we at least talk about it?"

Gabe was stunned. He thought everything was going so smoothly. He thought she was as enamored with him as he was with her. What did he miss?

"Sarah, I am willing to give it a try. I know there is nothing I want more. I am willing to do whatever it takes to keep seeing you. Don't you feel the same?" he pleaded.

"All I'm saying," she began, "is that it's not going to be easy. I don't want you to feel obligated. We need to be realistic from the beginning. I don't want to go down a path that will lead to ultimate destruction because we didn't see it coming. I… just don't think my heart can handle it."

There it was. Gabriel now knew it was because she was afraid of getting hurt. His chest filled with emotion that he simply didn't know if he could contain. He fought back from overflowing and scaring her away with too much, but he also knew, if he didn't proclaim his feelings now, he might very well lose her all together.

"I need you to listen to me very carefully, Sarah. I haven't had a reason to move on with my life for the last three years, until I met you. I realize this comes at a very close timetable for you in losing your husband. But if I learned anything at all from losing Shelly, it's that life can be taken from you in a single breath. We don't have a say in when we meet people or when they can be taken away from us. But I *do believe* that when a blessing is right in front of us and if we don't accept that gift, it may never come again. I am personally not willing to let you, my blessing, go. I can't. So I will promise you, that I will make every effort to prove to you how important this relationship is to me. If you feel anything close to how I do, then don't you think we owe it to ourselves to at least see where this thing goes?"

He studied her eyes, those beautiful windows to her lovely soul.

She stood up and circled around the coffee table and stood in front of the fire. She stared into it for a moment and Gabe let her think. When she turned back to face him his mind was racing with ideas to convince her. But before he had a chance to say so, she spoke.

"Gabriel, you are an amazing guy,"

Oh no! Not that speech. Not the, "let's just be friends" speech. He'd gotten that one from Danica Owens in high school, right after they'd slept together. His first. He wanted to jump up and run over to Sarah, and cover her mouth before she had time to ruin everything, but he was frozen.

"I didn't expect to meet anyone like you," she continued, "so my feelings for you are all pretty shocking."

Gabe suddenly realized her speech wasn't going in the same direction Danica's did.

"Yes." she laughed. "Of course I do. I just want to make sure we are being completely honest with ourselves in that a long distance relationship might be pretty difficult."

He stood then and rounded the coffee table to stand in front of her, pulling her body into his. Gabriel looked down into her soft eyes and kissed her slowly, passionately, deeply. He entwined his fingers into her hair, holding her head and pressing his body into hers. Their warmth was from more than the fireplace, and they each were grasping for the other, their need to live again. Their need for longing, yearning, and love.

"I know the risks, Sarah," Gabe said to her in a husky, eager voice. "I started falling for you the moment I laid eyes on you at the bar that night, before I even spoke to you. Something magnetic pulled me to you. Call it fate, call it divine intervention, but I wanted to know you. I just didn't dare approach you in a *bar of all places*. You would never have taken me seriously, and that's what I am, Sarah, serious. I don't play games, and I would never hurt you."

She laid her head on his chest and held onto him like a life raft. She spoke into his chest, the sound vibrating up to his ears.

"I don't believe you would, Gabriel. I just worry about letting my guard down. I had this whole other life, that I was so sure was going to be forever. It all unraveled on me and I was powerless to stop it. I don't know if I'm strong enough to go through such a thing again. I need to know you are up to the task. That you are strong enough to hold on even if it gets hard."

Remembering his talk with Max, the bartender, Gabriel thought to himself, *who wouldn't be strong enough to hang on to this girl?* Gabriel knew himself well enough to know a little distance wouldn't stop him from getting to Sarah. He would fight and move mountains to get to her. Holding Sarah tight, he felt anger brewing inside of him with the realization that she doubted him because of her ex being weak.

Gabriel pulled Sarah away from his chest to look her square in the eyes. He needed her to really believe him.

"I will *never* be that guy, Sarah. The guy that walks away. I will *always* be the guy that stands and fights. I'm not a quitter. It's not in my nature and I'm stubborn that way. I promise to be honest with you, always! So if you are worried I will walk out on you or end the relationship suddenly, without warning, it won't happen. Not from me it won't. If you decide this is what you want, then I'm all in."

He wondered if that was too much. He just put himself out there, exposed and vulnerable, but he didn't care. He wanted to. He needed to take the risk because if not now, he might not have the opportunity again.

✍

Sarah's head was spinning. She really wanted this man. But what if he knew the real truth about *everything*? Would he run like her husband? Could she risk it? Was Gabriel really that different that he could love her exactly the way she was? He was so genuine and gentle with her. He had pleading eyes and held her in those strong arms of his that Sarah grew weak, just melting into his body. Every cell in her screamed to just say, *yes!*

"I must be crazy." she laughed and shook her head. "We barely know each other, but ok. Ok, I'm all in too."

Gabriel picked her up, from around the waist, and swung her around before putting her down again. He laughed and kissed her on top of her head, then softly on her lips.

"Yep. We are crazy. But I think that's what makes this so great," he said. "You make me feel electric, maybe even a little irrational. Some people might feel it's too soon, but my grandparents met, dated, and were engaged all in the space of a month. Of course he was in the Korean War, and sometimes waiting wasn't all that important. They were married in 1952 and are still going strong. I think if it's going to work, it's about the people involved, not how much time you wait."

Sarah wasn't quite sure if Gabriel was actually talking about marriage already, but even with her mind swimming, she still clung to her decision to move forward with the relationship, regardless of her reservations.

She looked up at him then, smiling. He'd won her trust. She was sincerely happy, more than any words she could say.

"Well then, I guess we are in for a new chapter, Gabriel Hart. If you are willing to jump off into the deep end, then I'll jump too. Maybe you are right about the timing thing. Because I don't feel like I just met you. It feels like I've always known you. We can keep moving forward, and I will try not to analyze it. So it sounds like it's settled then? We're gonna have a weekend romance?" she asked.

"That's how it's going to start out. But I've a feeling it's going to be a whole lot more," he said.

"We'll see Mr. Hart. We'll see."

CHAPTER SIX

GOING THE DISTANCE

O N TUESDAY AFTER work, Gabriel took Sarah to dinner. He'd called Michelle during his lunch break to let her know he really wanted to have a nice evening with Sarah before he had to leave. Michelle said Park Place was one of their favorite places and always reliable, but to get reservations, so he called right after they hung up to set it up.

It was enjoyable but a little melancholy for them both. The reality of separation was setting in and they were both having a hard time with it. On the one hand, Gabriel thought it was a good sign they wanted to be together, but on the other hand, it proved Sarah right. It was going to be a difficult thing, dating long distance.

"How's your salmon?" Gabriel asked her.

"It's wonderful. Would you like some? It's more than I'm going to be able to eat after the soup and all that gorgonzola bread."

"Only if you try some of this pesto ravioli and we share," he said passing his plate closer to hers.

They both rolled their eyes at how good the food was and laughed, clinking glasses of wine together, toasting the evening. Gabriel marveled at how easy it was to be with Sarah.

"I gave out all the gifts that we bought last night, except for

Michelle and Caleb's family. I'm going to go over there tomorrow after work. I'm sorry you have to leave tomorrow. I know you really wanted to be there when we gave them their stuff," Sarah said biting into a piece of salmon and sautéed greens.

"I know, but it's more important that they get their stuff soon, rather than wait for me to come back on the weekend. I want them to be able to use the decorations and have the kids enjoy them, and see more wrapped presents under the tree. That's what's going to make their Christmas better. They will know it's from us, and that's good enough for me."

Sarah smiled and took a sip of her wine, looking sweetly into Gabriel's eyes.

"I like the way you say that. That it's *from us*. I know they will feel happy about that too. Michelle specifically, because she is taking complete credit for us getting together." she said with a laugh.

"Well I feel forever indebted to her for inviting me to dinner that night and putting us together like she did. I was so afraid I'd never see you again. Michelle is a saint as far as I'm concerned," he laughed.

"She will wear that badge of honor well. Saint Michelle, devoted saint of sentiment and affections. I can't wait to tell her," Sarah teased.

Gabriel reached across the table to hold Sarah's hand. He looked at her intensely, chest swelling with emotion he couldn't hold any longer.

"I think the sentiment she's accused of would be love. Sarah, I know it's probably too soon for you, but I'm falling in love with you, and there's nothing I can do about it. You have me so wrapped up and enchanted, I can't think of anything else. And before you say anything, it's not just infatuation. It's deeper than that. You are perhaps the kindest and sweetest person I've ever met. The way you understand people, especially me. You really look at people and know what they need and have compassion for their circumstances, without judgment. I knew I was attracted to you, but once I got to know you, I was right. You are exceptional."

She looked stunned. He thought maybe he'd gone too far overboard, but he couldn't help it. He felt that way, and since he was leaving the next day, he thought it was important he tell her how he was feeling.

"Wow. I didn't expect that. But...thank you, Gabriel. That's probably the sweetest thing anyone has ever said to me. You are a great guy. I'm pretty lucky to have met you," and she squeezed his hand, looking into his eyes.

Although the exchanged conversation was positive, she didn't use the word "love" as he did. Maybe he was right in his assumption that it was too soon for her. That was ok, though. He could wait.

⌘

Arriving back at her house, Gabriel hopped out of the truck and got her door. She was so conflicted with his leaving. He'd said he *was falling in love with her.* It nearly spun her head around. He grabbed her hand and walked her to the door in silence. When they stood under her porch light, Gabriel's gaze bore through her, awakening her yearning again.

He said nothing, just backed her up against the door. Pinning her there with heat building between them.

"I can't come in," he said in a husky voice. "If I do, I can't guarantee I'll be a gentleman. I'd have to stay."

She felt herself melting against his body, closing her eyes as he nuzzled her neck with his lips and cheek, his breath against her, hot and fabulous. *Dear God!* She almost grabbed him to take him inside when he pulled away from her.

"This week is going to be difficult, away from you Sarah. But I'm going to make you crazy for me. That's my master plan," and he winked then turned to walk to his truck.

Oh my, she thought to herself as she watched him jump in his truck. She slumped against the door, drunk from his touch. When he drove off and she was safely inside, all she could think of was how close she was to asking him to stay.

But she couldn't afford to be weak. There were things to consider. Maybe having some distance would be good for her to be able to gain some perspective. Still, he was so damn sexy it nearly drove her insane. It was very difficult going to sleep that night, and when she did, she dreamed of him walking up her drive.

❦

"Good morning, Sunshine!" he said softly over the phone. "I was wondering if you were awake yet. Hope it's not too early to call, but I wanted to say goodbye again."

She paused before speaking. "Unfortunately, I've been awake awhile. I couldn't sleep much."

Her voice sounded tired but somewhat preoccupied too. Maybe his attempt to drive her crazy backfired, he thought. Then she exhaled heavily, continuing.

"I'm glad you called though."

"You are? I was worried you were getting sick of hearing from me," he laughed.

"Of course not. I wanted to say goodbye again too. Drive carefully, ok? And text me when you get there. I will call you later tonight after I get home from work. I'm going to Michelle and Caleb's first though. I will let you know how it goes."

She sounded more interested in the conversation now and he thought maybe he'd read too much into it at first.

"Ok," he said. "Have a good day. Next time I see you, I'll be staying over and won't have to say good night at the door. I'll be thinking of you."

"Me too… Be safe," she said nearly whispering.

"Talk to you soon. Bye Sarah."

"Goodbye Gabriel. Call you tonight."

When he hung up, he looked around the room. As basic a room as it was, somehow he knew he'd always remember it. The place he lived for a month, where he was lost upon arrival, and found by the time he left. Gabriel Hart was a completely different person upon checking out of the Best Western Hotel in Clearlake, California, and he knew he'd be eternally grateful for that.

With his bags in hand, Gabe headed down to the lobby. When he walked out of the elevator, it was very early and extremely quiet. He turned and almost bumped into a guy walking the other direction.

"Oh, I'm sorry man. I thought I was the only one up around here," Gabriel explained. "How are you Max? I haven't seen you around."

"Yeah, well I wasn't on the schedule so I have been busy with a different job," Max said.

"Oh? What are you working on?" Gabe asked.

"Just organizing, right now. I've been constructing something pretty amazing," Max said.

"I knew you must be a contractor or something, because you seem like the outdoorsy, working kind of guy, like me," Gabe smiled.

"Yea, something like that. How'd it go with Sarah?" he asked.

Gabriel gave Max a quizzical look.

"I told you, everyone looks out for Sarah. You think I wouldn't hear about it?" Max laughed. "I'm happy she's been seeing a really nice guy. Just remember what I told you. She's fragile so treat her right."

"Absolutely," Gabriel said, extending a hand to Max. "I want to thank you for telling me what you did that night. It was important information to have and I am gonna take everything you said to heart. She's pretty amazing."

"Yes, she is. I'm glad you think so, too. Well… I suppose you are headed back to the city, huh? You going to do the long distance relationship thing?" Max asked.

"That's the plan. I didn't expect to get so attached to this place though. It's not just seeing Sarah, I actually like it here. But I have my job and…well, it's going to be interesting that's for sure."

"Good luck man. Maybe we will run into each other again, since you will be coming back a lot now," Max winked. "Anyway, I gotta go check the schedule before running off to my other job. You drive safe man. Take care."

"I will. Thanks again. Glad I ran into you. Literally." Gabe laughed.

Checking out was quick and he walked outside into the cold, overcast day. The wind was blowing, the sky was gray and his mood shifted to match. He had a three hour drive ahead of him, more if it started to rain, and when he arrived at the office he was going to have to tell Tommy why he'd stayed overnight. He was not looking forward to that conversation.

By the time he reached San Ramon, it was nearly eleven a.m. and pouring rain.

Dermont Excavating had offices in a small, modest building with a dirt equipment yard beside it. It didn't look like much from the outside, but it was Tommy's baby. He'd built it from the ground up and nearly lost everything more than once. Gabriel's willingness to dive in and work non-stop for the last three years had helped to keep the company afloat and competitive. At least, that's what Tommy had told Gabe.

After Shelly died, Gabe didn't want to socialize on the weekends, watch football, or go to bars. He slept, ate and worked. It gave him purpose when the rest of world was a dark a lonely place. The long hours meant Gabe built his skills, too, and was a damn good operator. He did bids and led projects on his own, more than doubling the jobs they could accept so Tommy was able to hire an entire second crew.

Tommy was a great boss and a great friend. But Tommy was also best friends with Shelly's brother, Alex. That's how he landed the job working for Dermont Excavating in the first place. Telling Tommy was equal to telling Shelly's family. It didn't matter that it had been three years since that terrible night, it still felt like a betrayal.

When Gabe walked in, his chest was tight. He wasn't looking forward to this conversation but knew he needed to do it anyway. Daryl was sitting at one of the secretary's desks, shooting the shit, and flirting as usual. Lucky for Gabe, Daryl was too engrossed in his conversation to do more than nod in Gabe's general direction. Gabe spoke to Diane, the lead secretary, and asked if Tommy was in his office. She was taking a phone call and just waved him to Tommy's door.

Gabriel gave it a quick rap and heard him holler to come in. Tommy looked up for his plans and his face lit up with a smile.

"Hey, man. You returned. I thought you'd be in earlier, but then Barry told me you were hung up one more night there. What's going on? You tired, ole man?" he teased.

Gabriel pulled out the chair in front of Tommy's desk and took a seat. He picked at the lint on his jeans wondered how to start. He was so bad with things like this, explaining his feelings to guys without sounding like a total pussy. He had to keep it simple and then dive straight into work talk.

"Yeah, I was detained I guess," Gabe started. "No... It's more than that, actually. I just didn't want to say until I was sure."

Tommy leaned forward in his chair then. "Ok, I'm intrigued now. Spill it."

Gabriel cleared his throat, uncomfortably. He opened his mouth then nothing came out, and he laughed.

"What the hell, Gabe? Why you all tied up? You are acting like..." Tommy paused then and got a knowing look. His eyes widened and he said, "NO!"

"WHAT? I mean. What do you think?" Gabe asked.

"YOU GOT A GIRL." Tommy laughed. "Right? I'm right aren't I?" Tommy laughed and clapped his hands. The weight that had been sitting on Gabe's chest the whole way home started to lift. He couldn't believe how happy Tommy looked.

"Ok. Ok. Yes, but it's…" he didn't even know what to say. Gabe hadn't expected a reaction like this. "So, you're not mad? I mean…I really like this girl. I didn't know how to tell you. I mean… I don't know what Alex is going to think and…"

"Hey, Alex is going to think, it's a damn good thing you finally found someone." His booming voice gentled, "Shit Gabe, nobody expected you to stay single for life. Look man, Shelly's been gone three years now and you've basically been a monk. I'm happy for ya, man. She'd be happy for you too, you know that?" Tommy got up out of his chair, rounding the desk to give Gabriel a hug.

Gabe stood and laughed. "Thanks for understanding, Tommy. I really think you'd like her. I also really think Shelly would too, strange as that sounds. But, she is in Lake County and I'm here, so it's going to be tricky."

"Well, you will have to bring her around. I'd like to meet her. What's this girl's name?" Tommy asked.

"Sarah, her name is Sarah," and Gabe smiled.

◈

At work, Sarah found herself a bundle of nervous energy. She was happy to be busy with orders and customers, but also had moments of preoccupation where her mind lingered on Gabriel and how he proclaimed his feelings for her the night before. She was still torn about how that made her feel, yet guilty feelings aside, she also wanted him.

When the day was done and they locked up, Sarah found her heart joyful again at the prospect of following Michelle to her house and giving them the gifts from her and Gabe.

"If you want to wait to bring the kid's gifts this weekend when Gabriel returns, that would be fine Sarah. I know how tired you must be and our place is so out of the way."

"Nope. I want to. Besides, I promised Gabe I'd bring them

today. He and I insist the kids have their presents under your tree as soon as possible. I will be right behind you."

On the drive, her mind went again to the memory of Gabriel's warm lips on her neck and cheek under her porch light. He *was* completely yummy and so incredibly sweet too. He made her feel alive in a way she hadn't for so long. But she also knew that reality had a bad habit of taking something beautiful and ruining it. She just didn't trust what she felt.

Pulling to a stop along Michelle and Caleb's sidewalk, Sarah decided to push all those thoughts aside and focus on making her friends smile. She jumped out and started to unload the presents. Michelle wanted to help but Sarah only let her carry the wrapped gifts to her kids. Sarah brought in the rest on her own, saving the decorations for last.

"What do we have here?" Caleb asked holding the door for the women.

The kids were squealing with delight at their Auntie Sarah, and the presents. They pawed at them under the tree until Caleb said they'd have to wait until Christmas.

"Oh, but I *do have something special for today*. Something you all can open right now," Sarah smiled, looking at all of their bright eyes staring at her.

"What do you mean?" Michelle asked narrowing her eyes.

Sarah walked over to the door and brought in the over sized Christmas bag filled with the decorations for their home. She really wished Gabriel could have been there with her to see them.

"Well come on kids, come look. It's for your whole family though. It's from Gabriel and me. Go ahead."

Sophie and Josh started pulling out the lighted garlands, the shiny beads, the stocking holders with the snowmen, and glittery window decals. Sarah looked over at her dear friend and saw her eyes filling with tears.

"We have more decorations, Mommy! Look at the stuff Auntie Sarah and Gabriel, got us."

"That is so *awesome!* Isn't it kids?" Caleb said winking at Sarah.

Michelle hugged Sarah and the two stood laughing and crying together while the kids and Caleb started opening boxes of decorations to hang up.

"You two are so unbelievably wonderful. This is the best, Sarah. Really. I can't believe you guys thought to get us decorations," Michelle said through happy tears.

"Well actually, it was all Gabriel's idea. I just provided him with a list of people I wanted to buy for and, well of course we did the most for my favorite people. You guys. There are some things under the tree to you and Caleb too. Not just the kids. We love you guys," Sarah said smiling over to Caleb and the kids, and squeezing Michelle's hands.

"Well, this *Gabriel*, has my vote. Right kids?" Caleb said.

The kids cheered as they continued to help their dad with the decorations.

Michelle pulled Sarah towards the kitchen and faced her with glassy eyes.

"Sarah, how do you feel about him? Is he *the one?*"

She couldn't suppress her grin. "He said he was *falling in love with me.*" Sarah giggled.

Michelle sucked in a fast breath, her hands flying to cover her mouth.

"I think I'm falling in love with him too but I just don't know. Still, I can't stop thinking about him. He's only been gone one day and I miss him already," she said.

"That's *fantastic,*" Michelle whispered.

"But what if he… I mean I don't know if he…"

"If he will understand?" Michelle finished her sentence. "Look Sarah, Gabriel is different. I knew it the night he came to dinner and you knew it then, too. Just take it one day at a time and stop over analyzing it all. Enjoy it, Sarah. Enjoy all of it."

From the next room, the kids ooohed out loud when Caleb plugged in the lighted garland they'd hung over the windows. The women went back in to see. Sophie and Josh ran to hug Sarah's legs, thanking her for the gifts.

∽

Their Thursday job was a simple residential driveway, and it went relatively quick. Other than a stop to check and see how it set on Friday, Gabriel was off until Monday morning, and by eleven o'clock, he was headed back to Lake County for the weekend, and to Sarah.

That afternoon, the sky was filled with puffy white clouds and later some rain was expected. No matter. Gabe still felt it was the start of a perfect weekend. He was going to be with Sarah. He parked across the street from the winery, on Kelseyville's Main Street. The large wrought iron gates were open to the huge wooden doors that reached about ten feet high. People were filing inside, shopping the gift area, and lining up at the bar for tastings. The soft sound of jazz music filled the air and the amber lighting was elegant. At the register was a man, ringing up customers, and behind the bar two women, pouring wine. One was Sarah. She was so lovely that a flutter erupted in Gabe's chest as he spotted her. She'd not seen him come in since she was occupied with her customers, so he stood back and watched her work in her element.

He just stood behind everyone, smiling to himself, arms crossed over his chest, and beaming with pride that Sarah was *his girlfriend*. She was a natural with people, smiling, soft laughter, and charisma galore. Her starched, white collar shirt and denim apron made her look so damned cute he could hardly stand it.

Then she looked up. From across the room their eyes met – her jade green eyes to his ocean blue ones locked and it spread a smile across both their faces, so much so that the others had to take notice.

She excused herself from her customers for a moment and made her way to him, "You made it."

To his surprise, she cupped his face in her hands and planted a sweet soft kiss right on his mouth. He was a happy man.

"I don't want to interrupt your work," he started.

"It's ok. I want to introduce you to the people we bought Christmas stuff for."

They walked together back to the bar, "Gabriel, this is Christina. Christina, this is Gabriel. He is the one who shopped with me for the Christmas decorations."

Christina put down a bottle of Zinfandel and wiped her hands quickly on her apron to shake Gabe's hand enthusiastically. She was a short, blonde, twig of a girl, maybe twenty-two or twenty-three. She was so happy and bubbly, Gabe could hardly believe she had just lost all her belongings just a few short months ago.

"Oh, it is SO great to meet you, Gabriel. I've heard such wonderful things about you from Sarah. Thank you for what you did. It really lifted my spirits. You both are so sweet to do that," Christina gushed.

Slightly embarrassed, Gabe put a hand over Christina's, shaking her hand with both of his, he assured her it was his pleasure. She was such a sweet kid. It made him feel like a big brother protecting his kid sister. He was really glad Sarah had picked her as one of the recipients.

Then, Sarah walked Gabe over to the register where a pot-bellied man in his forties was boxing up wine for a customer and said, "Walter, this is Gabriel, my boyfriend. He is the one who bought the decorations with me."

Walter thanked his customer, handed her bag over to her, then turned to shake Gabriel's hand, "Boyfriend?" Walter exclaimed.

Gabe winked at Sarah then said, "Yes, I like the sound of it too."

"Well, that's wonderful. Gabriel it's a pleasure." Walter continued. "I don't even know what to say, or how to thank you. You should have seen the look on my wife's face when I brought them home. She cried and I felt so happy that she was happy. You'll never know what a difference it made. Thank you." His smile waivered a bit, but his grip was firm.

Sarah popped back over to her customers, asking what pouring they'd left off with. She reached for a Cabernet Sauvignon and started pouring again for the crowded counter.

Most of the people left were at the counter sampling wine while the other shoppers hadn't made their selections. It gave Walter and Gabriel a chance to talk.

"I'm so sorry about your home, Walter. If there is anything at all we can do for you and your wife, please let us know. Sarah is very fond of you both," Gabe offered.

"That's very kind of you, Gabriel, thanks. We are managing but it's still hard some days figuring out how to get back to a normal life. I'm so thankful our kids are grown and they didn't have to experience this with us. Luckily, one of them lives only an hour away in Santa Rosa. We stayed with her for a month before finding a place to rent in Lakeport. I'm telling ya, it's hard moving into a house with twenty-something year olds. My daughter has two roommates and she was nice enough to give up her room to her folks and crash on the sofa awhile."

"I can imagine. That must have been rough."

"One of her roommates has a little brother in the Boy Scouts. His Troop out of Rincon Valley, ended up serving food to the evacuees at the Napa County Fairgrounds in Calistoga. Anyway, living with my daughter and her friends... they were all very sweet about it, but my wife Kelly and I felt very out of place," Walter said.

"Well the offer stands, Walter. Anything at all, just let us know. Sarah and I are on it," Gabriel said.

Gabriel ended up hanging out with Walter until closing. He

helped Walter in moving cases of wine around from the back into the front for stalking shelves on the displays. He carried wine boxes to customer's cars when they purchased heavy loads, and even drove to the intersection to bring in an A-frame sign that advertised it was *OPEN at Wildhurst*. Before Sarah pushed off for the weekend, she wanted to take Gabe back into the offices to see Michelle and meet her other friend, Stacy. She'd been with them the night at the hotel, the first time Gabriel had ever seen Sarah.

They walked into a small room where he saw Michelle and a blonde girl he'd seen the night from the bar. They both rose from behind their computers and the blonde, he assumed was Stacy, walked his way, while Michelle stood back waiting her turn. Stacy shook his hand vigorously, as Sarah introduced them, then Michelle approached him teary eyed, thanking him for the decorations.

"It's the least we could do, Michelle. I hoped it would bring y'all smiles. Sorry I wasn't there to see it. But I will take hugs anytime."

They all laughed and parted with Sarah saying she was headed out for the weekend, and did they have anything else for her before she left.

"Get out of here!" Michelle ordered. "Have a great evening."

As he and Sarah made their exit, they all promised to get together real soon. They were a very comfortable bunch to be around, Gabe thought. He was pleased he'd decided to make the drive to Sarah's work. It had been a long time since Gabe had felt even remotely sociable. It felt good.

Outside, in the twilight of evening, the streets of Kelseyville were busy with cars and people. The skies had grown very cloudy and a cold breeze was picking up to promise a full on windy evening. Sarah just concentrated on her joy that Gabriel had returned and she tried to see the charm of this town through his eyes. The street lights, the old fashioned pharmacy, antique stores, ice cream shop, and small town market made it all look very Norman Rockwell.

Next door to the winery was a rustic looking restaurant called *The Saw Shop*. It was only about 5:15 in the evening and already, people were pulling in for Friday night cocktails after work. Gabe raised his eyebrows, looking at it.

"So what's this place? Looks like an old farm house they made into a restaurant. Is it any good?" he asked.

"Uh-huh. It's quite wonderful actually. You want to give it a try for dinner? Everything is great there and I've never been disappointed with a meal. It would save us from shopping for food," she smiled.

She led him up the stairs. Inside, the wide-plank hardwood floors contrasted beautifully with the white linen table cloths in the candle-lit room. As they were led to a table near a window in the back, the hostess pointed out the locally made artwork on the walls and a table of blown glass vases for sale. Sarah watched Gabe's eyes survey the room and he smiled approvingly.

The hostess placed their menus on the table, assured them their server would be with them shortly and headed back to her station. Before Sarah could take her seat, Gabriel pulled her into an embrace, looked right into her eyes, then kissed her full on the mouth. The warm sweetness of him made her forget the crowd of people that filled the room.

"We didn't get a proper hello. I waited two days to do that," he said.

"Hello," she whispered back.

He pulled her chair out and they sat across from each other, staring goofily at one another. A short laughter then burst out of each of them before they took up their menus to see what to order. He made it hard to concentrate.

They decided to each order the specials and share both. Sarah ordered the duck in plum sauce with mushroom risotto, while Gabe ordered the sea bass with mixed seasonal vegetables and garlic mashed potatoes.

The waitress rushed away again to get their wine and Gabriel reached for Sarah's hands over the table.

"I missed you. How was the rest of your week?" he gushed.

"Wonderful...terrible. I missed you too. I can't believe how much," she giggled. "But seriously it was good."

Her heart was racing again and his touch made her feel elated. He was finally here. The rest of the world seemed to slip away as they talked quietly about nothing at all. His work, her work, Caleb and Michelle, but mostly they talked about how great this moment was together.

The wine gone, food demolished over cozy candlelight and mood music, Sarah felt more content than she could remember in a long while. She then started thinking how perfect the rainy night was going to be with him building them a fire later, then snuggling on the sofa.

The waitress arrived, snapping her back from her dream and they squabbled a moment over who would pay the check but ultimately, Gabriel prevailed.

"Sorry toots. My mother raised me to treat women like ladies and if I am on a date, which I most certainly am, then the man is to pick up the check. That goes with opening car doors, pulling out chairs, and bringing flowers to the house of your host when invited to dinner. What can I say? I'm a helpless romantic, old-fashioned guy," he said smiling.

"Well, remind me to thank your mother then," Sarah said. "In that case, I'm going to the ladies room and will return directly."

As she left the table, she could feel him staring after her and it made her feel confident, if not just a little sassy. It was incredible how high she felt. But in a short moment, all that was good in her world, felt pulled right out from under her.

❧

CHAPTER SEVEN

GHOST FROM THE PAST

HE COULDN'T HELP but smile as he watched Sarah walk away. He was a lucky man. A woman followed Sarah into the hallway, obviously intoxicated and bumping into the wall as she walked. She had just tapped Sarah on the shoulder and started talking to her when the waitress popped in front of him to ask if they needed anything else.

"No thank you, just the check."

Gabe was pulling out his wallet and noticed the drunk woman still had poor Sarah trapped in conversation near the opening of the bathroom. At least there was one thing for certain, that weird, drunk people were in all establishments that served liquor. Sarah was probably being nice and let the crazy woman talk herself out. Sure enough, as their waitress walked away with his credit card, Sarah came back to their table, but rather than laughing off the interaction she was visibly upset.

Standing up, Gabe said, "Sarah? What is it? What's the matter?"

"Have you paid the check yet?" her voice trembled.

"Yes, but she has to bring me back my card and I need to sign it. What happened with that woman?" he asked.

"Listen, I'm going to my car, ok? It's just across from yours and

I will see you outside, is that alright?" she said more of a statement than a question, then squeezed his hand and was out the door before he had a chance to say a word.

Sarah's red Honda was across from his truck on the opposite side of the street, just as she'd said. He could just see her through the wind and the rain in the driver seat, just waiting for him. He knocked on the passenger side door, making her jump, then she unlocked the door for him to hop in.

"What happened in there?"

When she turned to him, Sarah was crying and very shaken. He didn't know what to do except reach for her and hug her, but she shook him off. Something was definitely wrong. Gabriel sat back in his seat and waited for her to collect herself enough to explain. He didn't try to reach for her again, just sat patiently until she could talk.

"That *woman*. *That was HER*. The realtor my husband was messing around with. She was obviously drunk but that crazy bitch... She not only had the audacity to speak to me in the first place, but she happily pointed out that I was *dating so soon after my husband's death. AND, how maybe I didn't ever really love him enough in the first place or he wouldn't have needed to go looking for her.* What a horrid, evil, bitch." Sarah yelled through her tears.

"Oh, Jesus!" Gabe sat staring at her in shock.

"I'm sorry, Gabriel. I'm sorry I'm falling apart like this. I just really didn't need that. I didn't expect to see her... Like EVER. I have been pretty lucky that I haven't seen her in months. I was half hoping she'd moved to another community and I'd never have to run into her again. *But HOW DARE SHE.* You'd think that if she saw me she'd turn the other way, or at the very least, duck her head. She has NO SHAME about what she did to me or my marriage. And to suggest..." Sarah fell apart again, but this time, she reached for Gabe.

"Oh, Sarah," he said hugging her and stroking her hair. "That woman is stupid beyond belief and she's just lashing out at you because she knows the truth."

She leaned back in her seat and wiped her eyes. "What truth?" she asked.

"That you are a better person than she could ever hope to be. That you are more liked in this community. That you have more character…and that you absolutely were loved by your husband. *She can't handle the truth.*" Gabe said in his best Jack Nicholson voice he could muster.

She burst out with a laugh at Gabe's joke. Sarah turned in her seat to look at him and he brushed her hair from her face. The rain was washing down her windshield in ropes and veins of silver, with moments of golden light shining through from the street lights. Even in tears, this woman was a beautiful sight.

"Thank you, Gabe. I'm so sorry I lost it. I was just caught completely by surprise."

"Sarah, if the shoe were on the other foot, I'm not sure I'd have been able to handle it quite as poised as you did. I'd have probably decked a guy right in the restaurant, embarrassing myself and getting arrested. So you deserve an award," he laughed.

She smiled and shook her head while wiping tears off her cheeks. He had made her smile again so that was something.

"UUUGGHHH." she shouted and laughed. "I'm ok. I promise. I will get beyond it."

"You wanna get outta here?" Gabe asked clapping his hands together.

"YES. Yes I do. Want to follow me home?" Sarah suggested.

"It would be my pleasure," he said and leaned over to kiss her cheek and squeeze her hand. "Just let me get to my truck and I will be right behind you, and Sarah, drive careful, ok?"

"I will. I promise," she gave him a grin with tight lips.

It would have to do for reassurance, he thought. His truck fired up and he turned on the lights to pull out behind her. As he drove, his heart was heavy and he knew Sarah would be tense and upset from this episode most of the night, regardless of her strong front.

The downside of a small community where practically everyone knew each other, was never knowing who you were going to run into. Her close friends were happy for them, but he wondered how the opinion of others was going to impact their budding relationship. Maybe it was too soon for Sarah to be in a relationship. Maybe he had pushed for this too quickly. He tried to put those thoughts out of his head, but inside he knew that timing was everything.

∽

The twenty minute drive alone was a good thing for Sarah. She was reeling from seeing that terrible woman. What Gabriel said he'd have done occurred to her many times. She'd fantasized about pummeling that woman to pieces but when given the chance, she resorted to what? Running off in shock. She'd not even said one of the things she'd rehearsed in her head. She barely got out, "Go to hell," before making her escape. At least that was something. Not nearly what she deserved, but something.

Now, Sarah had a choice. She could roll up in her grief again and let her sad past ruin her, or she could reach for her future. He was right behind her, making sure she was safe. The struggle was nearly killing her though because as much as she wanted Gabriel in her life, she knew there was a part of her he might not be able to accept. She knew what caused her husband to stray and she didn't know if Gabe would do the same.

When they pulled into her driveway, the rain in Lower Lake was lighter. She opened her garage door with the remote and Gabe parked behind her. He got out and offered to grab more wood for inside to build a fire. She smiled weakly and nodded yes, then said she'd put a pot of tea on.

She worked methodically on filling the pot with water and wondered, what the hell she was going to do. How was she going to mask her emotions now and enjoy the evening with Gabe? Surely she had ruined everything. He gave her space in the kitchen and she could hear the snapping of kindling as he worked to build the fire, while she poured hot water over bags of Earl Grey into large mugs.

Sarah brought the mugs into her living room and sat them down on the coffee table. They sat, sipping slowly in front of the fire. Awkward silence.

"Hey, I have to go grab my bag out of my truck still. I just want to put this out there... I don't expect to sleep with you tonight, Sarah. I'm just so happy to be here with you. After what happened, I would expect you to feel strange about the whole thing. My being here, the thoughts rolling through your head after running into that woman, it's probably all too much. I'm sorry the evening turned out like this, but we are still us." He reached a hand up to tuck her hair behind her ear, "We can just take it slow. I'm not going anywhere. I will sleep on the couch. I will even head back to the Best Western, if that is what you want."

He really is amazing, she thought. *Don't screw this up, Sarah!*

Sarah smiled and put her cup down. "Thanks, Gabriel. Truth is, I don't know what I feel right now. I was having such a great night until she popped in and ruined it. Now I'm a bit depressed and wondering what everyone else is thinking of me. Am I jumping into a new relationship too soon? Is it disrespectful? But my real friends seem so happy for me. I even told my father I was dating and he smiled. He smiled at me. Oh, by the way, we have to meet him for breakfast Sunday. He wants to meet you," she squeezed his hand and tried to see in his eyes if the prospect was uncomfortable.

"He wants to meet me? That's good, I hope," Gabe said.

"Yeah, it's good... But I am a bit messed up from what she said. I can't lie. It hurt me to think I could be hurting anyone with my actions. I don't want to disrespect my marriage by jumping into a new relationship too quickly... But you should know, when I looked up today from the counter at the winery, and I saw you standing there… my heart leapt. I was so happy to see you."

Sitting there, with him gathering up both her hands and kissing them, Sarah's heart leapt again. Michelle was right. She just needed to take it one day at a time and give Gabriel a chance.

❧

Oh, thank God, Gabe thought. She wasn't kicking him to the curb. She wasn't having second thoughts about him, only their timing and what others would think.

"Let me ask you something, Sarah. Do you think of me when I'm not here?"

"Of course I do." she said.

"Ok. Do you like the time we spend together? Do you feel we are good for each other? I mean, do we complement one another?" he asked.

"I believe we do," she said.

"Alright, are you happier with me in your life or out of it?" he asked.

"Gabriel, in it of course. I'm much happier now."

He smiled at her. "Then you just answered all the doubtful questions you have. All the people you truly care about are happy for you. So why wonder what the gossips will say? They will chew the fat on something else besides you soon enough anyway. Am I right?" he asked her with pleading eyes.

"I suppose you are right. Even as a kid I would get too caught up in what others would think. Gabe, I really am happy you are here and want you to stay," she said leaning in to kiss him softly on the lips.

"Ok then. Do you want to watch some TV?" Gabriel asked in hopes of helping Sarah to relax.

"I have no idea what's going to be on. Friday nights are not usually good TV nights."

Gabe put his arm around her and took the remote. They clicked through a number of channels like Discovery Channel, National Geographic, and History Channel. Nothing really caught their eye.

"What would you be turning to if I weren't here?" Gabe asked Sarah.

She smiled then said, "Honestly? I would either be reading with the music on, or I'd be baking cookies, or watching HGTV for some home makeover show. I'm a sucker for home renovations."

"Well then let's check it out." Gabriel said turning to HGTV.

The mood lightened as they both laughed at Chip, on *Fixer Upper,* jumping through some drywall on demo day. When Joanna revealed the final product of the renovation, Sarah declared it fabulous.

"I just love her style. I watch all these shows but her rehabs are my favorite," she said before standing and then said, "I think I'm going to go change ok?"

"Sure, I have to go grab my bag out of the truck."

When he returned to the house, Sarah had put on her pajama pants and a camisole. She wore a light sweater over the camisole and had socks on her feet. She looked adorable and he smiled at seeing her so relaxed in her home.

"I know, not very sexy. But this is me. I'm not really the lingerie type," she tugged her cami down and pulled her sweater a bit tighter around her.

He advanced to her standing by the fire, smile spread across his entire face like a wide eyed child. "You are adorable and *I* get to be the guy with *you*. There is nothing sexier than that."

Gabriel grabbed her around her hips and pulled her into him. She pressed her torso into his, wrapped her arms around his waist, and laid her head against his chest, each feeling the other's heart beat. They stood there like that in the firelight for a few minutes, just feeling the tension drain out of them from the last hour. Gabriel stroked her hair and kissed the top of her head.

A growing yearning returned in Gabriel that he wasn't so sure was something he should act on. Sarah was feeling wounded and he didn't want to take advantage of her. But GOD, she was so attractive and he loved her more each time he held her. Every touch, every look, gave him more cause to fall deeper. It was going to be a difficult evening, he thought.

He kissed her nose and then her forehead, "Sarah, there's no place I'd rather be than with you. I can watch TV with you, walk with you, cook with you…or anything else we decide to do," he winked at her. "But just sitting by this fire with you all cozy in your pj's… I'm just really happy to be here. When you are ready for anything else, it will happen naturally. Television is fine with me, so long as I get to be with you."

Sarah got tears in her eyes, pulled on his neck to pull him close to kiss her. She softly planted moist, light little kisses onto his mouth then leaned back to look up at him.

"You are so good to me. You are truly the sweetest man. Thank you for understanding me. Thank you for just being you. And Gabriel…I love you."

"I love you too, Sarah. More than you could possibly know."

❧

Gabriel convinced Sarah he was perfectly ok with sleeping on the sofa, although he'd have much rather spent the night feeling the smooth, softness of her naked body curled up against his. Patience is something he knew would pay off in the long run. Then around one o'clock in the morning, Gabe heard a sound coming from Sarah's room. As Gabe sat up to look, Sarah was padding down her short hallway. She stopped just short of the couch and looked pleadingly at Gabriel.

"You ok, Sarah?" he asked.

"I couldn't sleep, knowing you were right out here. May I lie here with you?" she asked.

What a question. He'd dreamed of her lying with him *anywhere* since the day he met her. Gabriel threw back the blanket and sheet that Sarah had fixed him up with, and scooted his body as close into the back of the couch as possible. Sarah lay down on her side, facing Gabriel, throwing her leg across his and placing her head gently on his bare chest. Sleeping in just his underwear, Gabe thought it was a damned good thing that Sarah had on her pajama pants because he might have exploded if she'd have come to him in much less.

"Thank you Gabriel. I needed to be close. Good night," Sarah whispered.

"Good night, Sarah," Gabe said, kissing the top of her head. "Sweet dreams."

But sleeping was difficult, at least the first hour. Once Gabriel relaxed, he slept quite comfortably. Feeling the rhythm of her breathing made Gabriel nod off and before he knew it, it was six o'clock in the morning and he needed to pee.

When he got back from the bathroom, Sarah was very much awake. The sun was barely peeking out from the horizon and the rain had stopped. Their fire had died to smoldering embers and it put out a faint glow and just enough warmth. With the curtains mostly drawn, only a pale light came in from the sunrise.

Sarah sat up pushing the blankets aside, and swung her legs out from under them. Her bed head hair was a tossed mess, and the flush of her cheeks made her skin glow. Gabe thought she'd never looked more beautiful.

As he approached, Sarah's eyes never left his. She had a penetrating stare that was immediately arousing. When he sat next to her, she didn't say a word.

Moving dangerously close to his naked torso, Sarah kissed Gabriel's collar bone, then his neck, then her lips stopped just short of his mouth.

"Are you sure?" Gabriel whispered.

She answered by kissing him, long, slow, and wet. Pushing

Gabriel back against the sofa so that he lay down on his back. Sarah laid on top of him, intertwining her legs with his. There was no time for conversation now. She'd given him the green light and this time he wouldn't hold back.

Running his hands up under her camisole, Gabriel found her breasts, soft and heaving with every breath. He pulled the garment up and over her head and tossed it aside onto the floor. Skin to skin, their bodies were warm with passion. How he'd longed to feel her like this. Gabriel's head was spinning that the moment was real.

He grabbed her hips with one hand and her upper back with the other, and in one quick turn, Gabriel flipped Sarah onto her back on the couch. As she lay there, looking up at him with desire, he kissed her neck, then breasts, then stomach. Slipping his hands around the waistband of her pajama pants, Gabriel effortlessly pulled the pants off her hips, down around her knees, and Sarah pushed them off with her feet.

Reaching for his pants that lay on the arm of the sofa, Gabriel retrieved a condom. He knew he was presumptuous in buying some, but he was still a guy.

"What's this?" Sarah asked.

Gabriel just answered with a raised eyebrow and, "Protection. Just being responsible."

She laughed a little then said, "Umm…someone was feeling pretty confident."

"No. Not at all. Just hopeful."

Gabriel's yearning wouldn't be denied much longer. All that stood between them now were her lace panties as he lay on top of her. They kissed ravenously, and before long, the last of her apparel was lost to the ground. They found each other in a union more explosive then he'd ever felt.

Waiting, although they'd known each other only a short time, had felt like an eternity. He was very glad they'd waited until morning, rather than fumble through a forced obligatory meeting the night before. Being together without guilt or stress, had made their first time the best love making Gabriel had ever experienced.

When they were both spent, and heaving to breathe, Gabriel kissed Sarah ever so softly on her eyes, her forehead, and her cheeks. Then he looked into her eyes and found a look of love he'd hoped for.

"I love you so much, Sarah. Being with you is the most amazing thing I've ever felt. You truly make me want to be the best man I could possibly be." he said.

She lifted a hand to his face, "I love you like I've known you all my life. I'm so happy we met. I cannot imagine my life now without you."

❧

They showered together, sudsing each other up and laughing. Sarah felt so much energy around him. Her very basic bathroom had a tub/shower combo and a simple curtain. Sarah liked her cozy house and smiled at how Gabe was so relaxed there. She couldn't imagine him now going back to his lonely modern apartment. Being in this little cottage with Gabriel felt like something out of a fairytale was happening to them, and she never wanted it to end.

Drying off, Sarah wrapped a towel around herself then another around her head to dry off her wet hair. Gabriel put one around his waist and they went to the kitchen to make coffee. While Sarah got the coffee out of her freezer, Gabriel washed the pot out and placed a filter into the basket. It was all so natural and easy. The two of them together were like a couple that had synchronized movement from spending decades together, and it was wonderful.

While the coffee brewed, Gabe grabbed Sarah around her waist and pulled her close to him. He kissed her nose and looked into her eyes with a smile that spread across his face ear to ear.

"We should get dressed. We are gonna freeze soon," Sarah declared.

"I'm too worked up to be cold right now," he said.

Sarah laughed and placed both her palms on his chest, rubbing his skin up towards his shoulders while looking up at him with a smile.

"I don't know what made you decide today was the day, but I couldn't be happier," Gabriel said. "In fact, I cannot remember ever being happier in my life than I am today."

It's because I didn't think at all, she thought. *I stopped analyzing. Thanks Michelle.*

They engaged in a long kiss and then Sarah was the one to muster up the energy to pull away first.

"Listen," she began, "We have to decide what we are going to do today. It's nearly eight o'clock. Come to think of it, I usually sleep on weekends until eight, but since you were here…" she trailed off with a sexy smile.

"I know, I know. I messed up your schedule," he laughed pulling her closer again.

"Seriously. We should try to see if Michelle and Caleb are busy. Maybe tonight we could get together? And don't forget tomorrow morning we have breakfast with my dad. You are gonna love him." Sarah gushed.

Everyone loved Don. She was just the teensiest bit nervous to introduce them, but her father was the hero of her life. He was the one constant, true north of her existence so it was important to her that they like one another.

"I can't think of anything I'd like to do more…well maybe one thing," he laughed, squeezing Sarah.

The morning hours slipped away with the two of them sipping coffee at the kitchen table and enjoying pancakes with real maple syrup. No artificial syrups in her house. Only the best was worth all the calories pancakes packed on. Once they cleared the dishes, Gabe wanted to take a walk around Sarah's property and the adjoining areas.

Fresh smelling earth wafted into their nostrils from the previous night's rain storm. The ground was starting to firm up again and the dewy moisture on the foliage was invigorating. By ten in the morning, the sky was clearing and the sun shined on all the wet grass and leaves. Sarah loved where she lived. Closing her eyes, breathing deeply, she felt peaceful.

"This reminds me of Oklahoma. The only difference is if it *were* Oklahoma, it would be either near zero in temperatures in December, or so humid if it were spring or summer, that steam would already be rising. I'm loving these mild northern California winters." Gabriel laughed.

Walking out towards the main road, Morgan Valley Road was a paved, two lane road that many residents driveways came out onto. Sarah's was lined with tons of live oaks and pine trees. Out on the paved road now, walking with Sarah in front and Gabe following her, they stayed just right of the white painted line on the street, walking through pine needles, rocks and dirt. Not widely traveled as it was years ago when the mine was out that way, the road was quiet this Saturday morning, but for a few cars here and there.

"Before the Valley Fire wiped out most of Cobb Mountain and Middletown, the Rocky Fire was just out that way," Sarah said pointing northeast. "It started out on a road called Rocky Creek Road, about ten miles from here. It took out a little over fifty homes I think. Anyway, we thought that one was the worst thing we were going to see. Boy were we wrong." *Very wrong,* she thought.

Gabriel was quietly walking behind her a ways before he spoke. "I can't believe how much tragedy has hit your area. The people are probably drained from the stress."

"Well, it can really take a toll on ya, that's for sure. I wasn't personally hit, but I did have to evacuate for that one and it rattles your nerves pretty badly, I'll admit," Sarah said.

Suddenly, a hand was on her shoulder and Gabe was closer behind her. She turned to look back at him and gave him a half smile before moving on.

The day was proving to be quite lovely and they walked about half a mile to Bonham Road and turned right to walk out that way. The homes there were of eclectic styles. The first was a mid-century modern home that had a pool under a covered patio, tennis courts and a run-down yard. In its day, Sarah remembered, it was quite nice and still could be with some TLC. Next, on the right, was a rambling ranch with a modular home at the end of a long driveway. Then on the left was her favorite, a cute two story Tudor style painted white and with some cobblestone around the base.

"I use to play with a girl that lived there when I was small. My family lived out here until I was ten and I road bikes up and down this road a million times, with all my little friends. Amanda Parker, I think, was her name. I loved this house. It was small inside, maybe fifteen hundred square feet in all, but I remember how cozy and friendly it all felt," Sarah said, smiling at her memories.

"I can see why you'd like it. It is really a cute house," Gabe agreed.

"I imagined coming back here one day as an adult and buying it, fixing it up, and living here. Funny thing is I've never once seen it go on the market for sale, yet many families have come and gone from here. The owners must just rent it out," she said.

They walked on and Sarah told Gabriel stories of her youth, pointing out her bus stop as a kid, naming all her friends and pointing out their houses down Quarter Horse Lane. Passing the corner of Quarter Horse and Bonham, they continued out Bonham to a small driveway that ran off to the right of the road. Small houses lined one side of the shared dirt driveway, and a small walnut orchard stretched along the other.

Walking along the drive, some homes were single-wide mobiles, some tiny cottages, but then the road curved to the right where a huge hedge of bushes blocked the view of what lay ahead. As they walked around that corner, the land opened up to a half-acre parcel, complete with another small walnut orchard, oval shaped lawn, and a circular gravel driveway. The house was brick red and very tiny. She took a deep breath upon seeing it and smiled with nostalgia.

"This was my childhood home. It's pretty run down now, but my dad had it so darn cute. Over there," she pointed to the detached garage, "our garage was built over the creek. It is about a twelve foot drop over the edge to the creek bed floor, and it literally sits like a bridge, right over that creek. In the winter, if it rained a lot, we'd always wonder if the creek would flood and wash it away." she laughed.

They walked a bit closer but stayed out of the yard. There were cars there so they could tell people were home. Sarah had told Gabe where her tetherball pole use to be, and where they had a chicken coop, until her dog started terrorizing the chickens and they'd gotten rid of them.

"And which room was yours? Point it out for me so I can imagine it," Gabriel asked.

"To the right, along the side of the house is a sliding glass door. My room was in there, along that side of the house for a while. Then I traded with my brother for the one at the very back that faced the back field. My whole south facing wall was four tall, old windows. You know the kind with a metal handle that you wind and it opens outward, and if you wind it back the window swings closed inward again? It was pretty old, but I loved the charm it had. My room was the smallest but I didn't care. I liked it. My sister had the bigger room that my dad had to add on, but I was happy to not share."

"You weren't ever scared to be alone then huh?" Gabriel asked.

"Not really. I liked my privacy even as a small kid."

"Sounds like you had a great childhood. I can see these people probably don't care for the house as well as you guys did, but I'm picturing it now. Why did you guys leave anyway? Why did you move?" he asked.

"Because my dad wanted to give us all a bigger house," she said. "Mom wanted to have a bigger kitchen and more space to entertain.

We loved having parties. Mom was a wonderful cook. And she made this yard right here a fairytale garden that you wouldn't believe. God, she could grow anything. That tree over there, the huge oak in front of the house, she had ivy growing up it and below was a large flower garden with dahlias, poppies and zinnias. Oh, I loved it. And all around the lawn she had flowers growing too. Not just pansies like you see most people plant. She'd buy exotic bulbs from everywhere and plant tulips, iris, foxglove, bluebells, I mean she had an extraordinary yard…" Sarah trailed off, hung her head, and turned to walk back out.

They walked a minute back past the hedge and down the lane towards Bonham Road, the way they came.

"You miss her terribly, don't you?" he asked putting his arm around her shoulders and pulling her into him as they walked.

If he only knew just how much.

"Yah, I do, some days more than others. She was truly amazing. She was everything to me. I wanted to be just like her when I grew up. Then one day, she was just gone. Cancer. I was fourteen years old, going into that terribly dramatic time of high school and my freshman year, and suddenly I was motherless. Now, with my life having been turned upside down with a failed marriage, then being widowed, and then finding happiness most unexpectedly," she winked at Gabriel, "I really wish she was here to talk to about it all."

She forced the lump that was forming in her throat to relax and she shook her head.

"She's here," he offered. "Just not in the way you'd like, but she's here."

She playfully nudged him, gave a weak smile up at him, and as they walked, she thought how she loved him for saying that.

ᔐ

CHAPTER EIGHT

SHARING

B Y THE TIME they'd made it back to Sarah's house, it was nearly noon. Sarah called Michelle to ask about a get together for that evening. As it turned out, Michelle was having her brother-in-law and his wife for dinner and was thrilled Sarah and Gabriel could make it to join them. It all sounded festive and with Christmas right around the corner, Gabe and Sarah were happy to go see what they'd done with the decorations they had bought for them. It sounded like fun.

"What do you think we should bring?" he asked. "More Sauvignon Blanc?"

They exchanged a snicker, then Sarah said she wanted to make this jalapeno cheese bread she had a recipe for, and wanted to stop by Gregory Graham's for a bottle of Viognier.

"Who is Gregory Graham?" he asked.

"It's not just a who, but a what. Gregory Graham is a winery off Point Lakeview Road. The wine will pair perfectly with the spice in the bread."

After running errands, changing and dressing for the evening was challenging for them both. Gabriel kept trying to undo what she'd put on and Sarah wasn't putting up much of a fight. Soon they were nearly ripping off their clothing, mauling each other like teenagers. Gabe tried for the bedroom but Sarah pushed him to the living room sofa again. He didn't care the location. He was just interested in the final outcome.

Later, while curling her hair, Gabriel sat beside her on a dining room chair he'd grabbed from the kitchen to talk with her while she got ready. He was halfway into the hall because the bathroom was too tiny for the chair and both of them, but with the door open, music playing from the living room, and watching Sarah in the mirror, he felt like his life was made.

He tried to lean over and kiss her, then she drew back and pointed. "This iron is hot."

"I'm willing to take my chances."

She pointed it at him playfully, wielding it as a sword. Gabriel swiftly grabbed her wrist, then gently took the iron and set it aside with little to no protest from Sarah. He then pretended to bite into her neck and growled like a ravenous dog while making her giggle and squirm away from his grasp.

This was fun, he thought. She was sweet, but funny. She was tender, but exciting. Sarah was gentle and fierce all at once and Gabriel loved that.

By six it was dark and Gabe and Sarah were pulling into the driveway of Michelle and Caleb's house, next to Michelle's minivan. Sarah handed the tray of stuffed French bread to Gabe and she carried her purse and the bottle of wine. They walked to the door and Sarah opened it without ringing the bell or knocking. Obviously, these people were family to her.

Once inside, a trail of children, none over 10, came running towards them and screeched to a halt when they saw Sarah and Gabe had let themselves in. "It's Aunt Sarah and a man," yelled a little girl.

"Sophie, this is Gabriel. Gabriel, this is Sophie, her crazy brother, Josh, and their cousins, Taylor and Sam. Everyone say, hi," Sarah said.

"Hi!" the kids yelled and then ran off towards the kids' room.

"Wow. That felt like déjà vu. Just like me and my cousins when we were kids, totally running amuck." Gabriel laughed.

"Hey!" Michelle and Caleb came around to greet them both with hugs and smiles.

"Jimmy, get Gabe a beer. Come on in guys. We've been waiting for you. Michelle and Angie have been cooking for an army and Jimmy and I have been doing our part by drinking beer. Come in. Come in." Caleb said.

The tree was lit and with plenty of presents under it, sparkling from the light dancing off the packages. The windows were dressed in festive garland, and they even had country Christmas music playing in the background. Gabe smelled the fabulous aroma of pork roast and cherry pies coming from the kitchen and he was immediately overwhelmed with the sense of family and belonging. He knew he'd really hit the jackpot in finding not only Sarah, but the people in her life that surrounded her. The smells and atmosphere reminded him of home, and it felt good.

⋙

The introductions went swiftly, Jimmy and Angie both meeting Gabriel, and just like Caleb, Jimmy was thrusting a beer into Gabe's hand and insisting he join them at the table for one more hand of cards before dinner. The kids were squealing in the back of the house, playing with their cousins, and Martina McBride sang out White Christmas. It was like a Hallmark card and beer commercial wound into one. Sarah prayed it wasn't all too overwhelming for Gabe, but he smiled broadly and allowed himself to be carted off to the testosterone table.

As the ladies poured wine and checked the roast potatoes, Sarah looked over at him and Gabe winked at her, causing her to break into a huge smile.

"Tell me what you've both been doing all day, Sarah?" Michelle asked loudly.

Sarah just pushed Michelle playfully into the counter and unwrapped her breads. They finished up a salad while the bread cooked and the roast rested. Angie was checking the kids when Michelle leaned over to whisper to Sarah, more discrete this time.

"I can tell by your behavior that you've *taken this relationship to the next level.*" Michelle teased. "It's about damn time I think. I mean Jesus, Sarah. Just look at that boy. He's a hunka burnin' love. I'd have had that the first day. But that's just me. I'm a slut." Michelle laughed at her own joke.

Sarah only laughed with her but said nothing more of it. She certainly was the good girl when it came to kissing and telling. Still, Michelle knew her better than anyone in the world, and from the looks they gave one another, it was apparent Gabe and Sarah were in love.

"Gin!" Caleb yelled.

"You freakin' cheat, Caleb. How the hell did you have that ace all along?" Jimmy yelled back, laughing and throwing his hand onto the table in defeat.

"Well I wasn't anywhere near going out," Gabriel said with his full hand of pitiful cards.

"Clear the table of those cards now boys. It's almost time to eat," Angie ordered.

"You are lucky I'm such a good sport and we've got company tonight," Jimmy teased. "Caleb here is notorious for having a mysterious card pulled out of thin air just when he needs it. Never trust him at cards, Gabe. Just like our grandma, he cheats."

They laughed and cleared the table as they were told. Angie pulled out some festive linen holiday placemats with pictures of Christmas trees on them. Michelle hugged her and then Jimmy, too.

"Oh, I love these! You guys are all so wonderful. Caleb don't we have such a wonderful family? Sarah and Gabriel getting us and the kids all the decorations and presents, and Angie and Jimmy helping us with so much. We wouldn't have been able to set up house without you guys." She was smiling as happy tears rolled down her cheeks. Sarah had a napkin for Michelle's eyes, as Angie wrapped her in a hug.

"Nobody is more deserving than you guys. Now stop crying or you'll get the food all wet," Angie said playfully.

The kids had a card table set up near the adult table and they had their own table cloth and sparkling cider, to feel special. They passed around food and Michelle and Angie passed the kids their plates before they all sat to start. Jimmy raised his beer and cleared his throat loudly to get the attention of everyone.

"I am usually very corny and love to poke fun at my little brother, but today I just wanted us to raise our drinks to toast him and his beautiful wife, Michelle, and their great kids. I love you guys and pray for your new start to be promising, full of hope, love, and fun. Mostly fun, if I have anything to say about it." Jimmy said.

"Here, here." Angie and the rest said, clinking glasses and cans. Even the kids were toasting each other giggling at their own table.

"Eat up now guys. But save room for pie. I baked all day," Michelle ordered through her tears.

Sarah surveyed the room and kept watching how Gabriel was reacting. The only thing she saw was a look of contentment in those twinkling blue eyes of his. When their eyes met, he gave her a reassured nod, and smiled. He fit with their group, just like a glove.

Gabe thought the food was amazing and Jimmy and Angie were equally as wonderful as Caleb and Michelle. He was happy to spend time with them.

Jimmy was very close to looking like Caleb's twin, maybe a little taller and slightly smaller frame, but still very muscular, and had light hair and skin. Angie was tall, with a thin athletic build, had long reddish blonde hair and wore little to no make-up. She was quite pretty, in the girl next door kind of way. She obviously was very comfortable in her own skin and carried herself confidently. They both had a great sense of humor.

Before the table was cleared, Gabriel got everyone's attention.

"I just wanted to add real quick y'all, that I am very honored to have made everyone's acquaintance, and thank y'all so much for making me feel so welcome. I'm so sorry for the hard times you and your town has seen, but if there is ever anything I can do to help, I'm not going anywhere," he said grabbing Sarah's hand and kissing it.

"Well that's good news man, cause I'm planning on planting some sod in the spring." Caleb teased.

"Hey, I'm your man." Gabriel laughed.

The guys decided to help clean the kitchen since the women did all the cooking for such a lovely meal. Most of the plates, silverware, and glasses were just put into the dishwasher. For the pots and pans, Jimmy washed, Gabriel dried, and Caleb put things away. The brothers teased about it being like old times, growing up and having to do the dishes together. They said they fought the whole time. Gabriel laughed at this.

"You have brothers to fight with Gabriel?" Jimmy asked.

"No, I didn't. But my cousins lived only a few miles away and we were pretty close growing up. Fighting didn't usually last long though because they'd go home and I couldn't really fight by myself," Gabriel laughed.

Jimmy threw the wet sponge at Caleb. "Little brother here used to rush to get done so he could go watch TV, and half the dishes would be put away mostly wet. Mom would be so pissed."

"Hey, I had my priorities." Caleb laughed snapping the wet dishtowel towards Jimmy's legs.

"Well, looks like you both survived it," Gabriel said, folding his arms across his chest looking at the brothers. "You guys actually still seem to like each other so that's good."

"True," Caleb said. "Honestly, I don't know what I'd do without this guy, but don't tell him that. His head is big enough already, being a bad-ass fireman and all."

"That's right. You are the fireman. I almost forgot Caleb and Michelle had told me that. Wow. You have been busy this season huh? Must have been pretty hairy." Gabriel said.

Jimmy raised his eyebrows and shook his head, unable to properly put it into words. "I can't even tell ya how hairy. I fought along veteran guys that had thirty plus years in and it puckered their asses pretty good. We'd never seen anything so unpredictable. It's a freakin' miracle more people didn't die. Total miracle."

"Hey anyone want another beer? One more Gabriel? Jim?" Caleb asked walking towards the door to the garage.

Jimmy nodded and gave a thoughtful pause. "When I realized how bad it was blowing up, my stomach churned. I told Angie to keep calling. Michelle and Caleb weren't picking up and luckily we had the kids with us. People were screamin' on the radio for help. All departments were scrambling. I still don't even know how we managed as well as we did. Cal Fire was so damn stripped because of multiple wildland fires all over the state. It still feels like a bad dream."

Jimmy's voice took on a more serious tone, eyebrows furrowed, and his eyes seemed distant. Caleb walked in then and handed them each a beer and they sat down at the table. All three took swigs off their bottles before Jimmy started back up.

Some of the kids came around the corner and Michelle followed them in. Gabe saw Caleb slightly shake his head at her and she took the cue to steer the kids away so they could talk alone.

"When I left the house, I heard radio traffic saying, 'Shelters are deployed with firefighter entrapment.' I knew right then it was the thing we all feared would one day happen. A fire storm was hitting the Cobb area and there are only a few ways out for all those residents. I had no idea it would end up engulfing Middletown and then it hit Hidden Valley too."

Jimmy took another swallow off his beer, hand trembling.

"There was a helitack crew that got overrun by the fire. They had to deploy their fire shelters. That's usually really freakin' bad. Luckily, all survived. The worst was their crew captain who lost some fingers being the last to get into his shelter. He wanted to make sure his guys were in before he got into his own. They flew them to U.C. Davis Burn Center and they were there awhile. They were so damn lucky. But meanwhile, the Division Chief of Cal Fire was screaming for help. She ordered up twenty engines, twenty crews, twenty dozers, and said she'd augment that all with forty additional engines in the next ten! That's why I knew I had to leave my kid's party and run my ass to the station. All hell was breaking loose."

"Jesus," Gabriel said. He stared at Jimmy, whose face was pinched now with painful thoughts. Looking to Caleb, he too rubbed his forehead uncomfortably then looked down to peal the label of his beer bottle.

"Our district was stripped. We sent all we could afford, including medic units. I was sent to Cobb on a strike team our chief Willie was assigned to. I ended up running an engine that felt like a damn ping-pong ball, moving everywhere and anywhere we could help. They had us doing structure protection but that moved so much. For awhile it was like a living hell, with houses going into spontaneous ignition like in a freakin' movie. All we could do then was help evacuate. We worked with Highway Patrol, Sherriff, State Parks, and Fish and Wildlife. All we could do was get people out. It was no longer as important to save structures as it was to save lives. We had engines with evacuees on board. Some of those engines got trapped up there momentarily and it looked like it was all over. I have no idea how they managed to get out.

"The head split around Boggs Mountain. Anderson Springs was devastated. It headed to Middletown and the mayhem continued. Night fall made things worse and in the light of day, you got disoriented because everything was almost unrecognizable because there were no land marks. When I ended up on highway 29 from the Middletown, to Lower Lake corridor the next day, I saw burned out cars abandoned everywhere, on the sides of the road, but some right in the middle of the highway. Where were the people who were driving these cars? How did they get out?"

Jimmy's voice was nearly a whisper, like he wasn't talking to them anymore but reliving the nightmare and questioning the universe. His focus was on his hands, wringing themselves and squeezing with white knuckles.

Caleb walked around to the back of Jimmy's chair and put a hand on his shoulder. Jimmy seemed to knock the cobwebs off then and wake up from his trance. He was talking out loud but his mind was back there at the fire.

"I didn't know for certain, until that next morning when I called Angie, that my kid brother and his wife were ok. When I heard they were ok, I cried like a baby," Jimmy said tearing up again right there at the table. He looked up at Caleb, who with tears as well, squeezed his big brother's shoulder for support.

Gabriel didn't know quite what to say. He decided to stay quiet while the brothers had a moment. Then Caleb took over the story.

"Michelle and I drove straight to Jimmy and Angie's house for our kids. We didn't know what else to do. We ended up staying there for several weeks. Jimmy didn't come home for three days straight. I was kind of happy for the job of taking care of the women and kids while he was gone so I didn't have to think too much about how my house just burned up with all our stuff in it. We had our kids and our dog so that was all that was important. Still, when things settled down and we had to deal, the shit got pretty real pretty damn fast." Caleb said.

"Holy shit, man. You guys have been through the ringer." Gabriel said.

"The fires burned over 35 percent of the county. The damn thing started September twelfth and the containment wasn't 100 percent until October sixth. It went into Napa County, too. You could say, our crews are spent." Jimmy said with a smirk.

"I'd say. Jesus, Jimmy. I bet you are pretty damn happy fire season is over," Gabe said.

"Understatement," Caleb said raising his beer bottle.

The three raised their bottles to each other and drank up what was left of their beers.

They sat in silence a minute before Jimmy broke the quiet and said, "Listen man, I don't want you guys to think I'm a mess or anything. I just haven't really talked about it much yet and Angie always says I spill things in increments. During an incident, I go into work mode, then I suppress it, then it bubbles up slowly. I regurgitate a little at a time until it's out of me. This one will take awhile, I'm afraid. Especially since I had my own family to worry about. Our cousin, Laurie and her husband lost their home too, in Middletown. Thank God none of you guys were hurt." Jimmy said to Caleb.

Caleb just nodded. Then he walked over to Gabe and said, "Bet you are glad you landed here in Lake County, huh, Gabe? We are all a mess and most of our property stinks like a wet campfire. We are usually much more fun than this, I swear," he laughed.

"Listen," Gabe started, "You guys have ample reason to complain. Like I said before though, I would like to help anywhere I can, really. If there is anything I can do, just let me know."

"Well, you've done plenty, just making Sarah happy," Caleb said. "She's been so lonely, and sad, and dark since…well, you know. Seeing her so happy is like a damn Christmas miracle."

"True dat." Jimmy said patting Gabriel on the back, as both he and Caleb laughed.

"Well if that's all you guys wanted from me, then I have the easiest job in the world. She's pretty amazing."

And just on cue, the girls rounded the corner into the kitchen and Michelle said, "Who wants pie?"

They ate cherry pie with vanilla ice cream and laughed. It was an amazing evening. Enlightening for Gabriel about just how much this family had been through and still it was pleasant to be in their company. They were all such positive people and they shared a bond so strong that Gabriel felt honored to be a part of their pack.

That night when they entered into Sarah's kitchen from the garage, they were laughing and fumbling for the light. She said she was going to go change and would be right back. But when he started to follow her, she kind of turned back like she was going to say something, paused, then smiled and shook her head, walking back to her room without a word.

"What? What did you want to say?" he asked.

"It's... no, it's just..." she put her hands on her hips and shook her head, looking at the ground instead of at him.

"Sarah?"

"You must know why I haven't had you into my bedroom right? Why we've stayed out on the sofa?" she said.

"I have a suspicion," Gabe said.

"I have never been with anyone except my husband in that bed. I kind of felt weird about it I guess. To be honest... I'd never slept with anyone but my husband, before you," Sarah admitted to a spot on the floor.

Gabriel needed to be close to her. This woman had shared something special with him and he didn't even realize it. In some ways she was still grieving but had allowed him into her heart to fix what was broken, to help her feel whole.

"Sarah. Wow, I mean...I will do everything I can to do right by you. Thank you for telling me," he said kissing her gently.

"But," she said, grabbing his hand. "I think maybe tonight we can make other arrangements."

She smiled up at him then, pulling him by the hand, and led him down the hall.

❧

CHAPTER NINE
HOLIDAY CHEER

THE NEXT MORNING, Sarah took Gabe to her father's house in Clearlake. It would seem that this was the weekend to formally announce their becoming a couple. Gabe was being such a trooper though, and didn't act like he minded at all. He actually appeared eager, smiling all the way. Still, lingering in the back of her mind, she knew in a few short hours he'd be heading back to Danville. She tried not to think of that.

"Nervous, are ya?" she asked teasing.

"Huh? No! Oh, I am happy to meet your father. I'm sure if he's half as wonderful as you've told me, I have no reason at all to be nervous. Right?"

"Yeah, except that I don't think you know how much of a Daddy's girl I am. He treats me like his favorite. I always told my brother and sister that I *was in fact his favorite.*" She laughed at the memory.

"Oh so you play like that, do you? Well, I will remember I have competition for your affections. Daddy always comes first, boyfriend second. Now I know my place," he teased back.

"Seriously Gabriel, my father is a pushover. He will love you. You'll see," she reassured.

They pulled into the driveway of a residential neighborhood

called Burns Valley. It was near the foothills of Mount Baldy in Clearlake, California, and in close proximity to the town. Her father had a half-acre parcel out in a walnut orchard and his dirt road driveway was shared with multiple other residents. The house was two stories, had an attached two car garage, and sported a small lawn in front. The charming blue house had a small front porch, complete with rocking chairs and there were potted plants along the porch edges, although they were withered with the oncoming of winter. It was a very country-looking home and Sarah adored it.

Gabriel walked with Sarah up the stairs to the front door and she walked right in, pulling Gabriel along with her.

"Dad? We are here." Sarah announced.

The house smelled of sautéed onions and coffee brewing. Sarah suddenly became aware of how famished she was. Her father walked around the corner from the kitchen at the back of the house to greet them.

"Finally. I get to meet Gabriel Hart. The man my daughter has been boasting about. Well, look at what we have here. Tall, dark, and handsome. Should have known, kiddo," he winked to Sarah as he reached to shake Gabe's hand.

"It's a pleasure to meet you, Sir," Gabriel stated with a hardy handshake and wide smile.

"Please, call me Don. We McKinney folk are very informal. Besides, the pleasure's all mine, Son. It's great to meet you. I hope you're hungry because I've been cooking up a storm. Sarah, I've made your favorite egg and sausage bake. I used sourdough bread and everything. Just how you like it. Come on in and take off your coats."

Watching the ease of her father moving through the house warmed Sarah, even if it pained her, knowing her mother wasn't there with him. They removed their coats and hung them in the entryway, following Don to the back of the house and into the kitchen.

The house was very homey and even for a single older man, Don kept it as if her mother still lived there. Sarah's mother's touch was still everywhere you looked. The furnishings were warm tones with lighter colored throw pillows. The walls were painted a sandy color with white trim and family pictures everywhere. It looked lived in and very comfortable.

"I have coffee ready or if you are feeling particularly adventurous, I have mimosas." Don said.

Both Gabe and Sarah laughed at Don's enthusiasm. In the end they each decided on coffee with vanilla cinnamon creamer that Don offered. All three settled around the dinette table in the corner kitchen window. The sun was bright even if it was cold outside. Don had birdseed in the bird feeders just outside and they were able to see the birds battle over territory while they enjoyed their coffee.

"I feel like I'm in one of those country-fantasy Hallmark Movies that my mother always watched. Everything is so perfect here," Gabriel said.

Don and Sarah laughed.

"Not so very perfect, but I try, thanks. So tell me something about yourself, Gabriel. Sarah tells me you work at an excavating company in the Bay Area," Don said.

"Yes, Sir. I work as a foreman and I am an operator. I live in Danville right now. It's a good job and I'm good at it. I'm just not sure it's where I plan to stay, Sir," Gabriel said.

"Don. You can call me Don. Well, it's a great profession, being able to operate heavy equipment. I just wonder if being three hours away isn't going to drive you two crazy eventually. I sure am glad you made the trip this weekend to come see us, but maybe next time you will be able to meet Sarah's brother, Joe. He will be coming home from school next week and sticking around until late January," Don informed them.

"Joe's coming home next week? Good." Sarah said. "I bet he is ready to sleep in his own bed by now."

"Well, I'm ready to have someone to watch the games with

and someone to cook dinner for. It's been hard having him away. You girls are so grown up and now my boy. I need my buddy to come home."

They went on talking of football, how both Don and Gabriel each played in high school and some college. They spoke of cooking, recipes, and Sarah's mother's pies. They drained the coffee pot and when the breakfast casserole was ready, they ate with laughter over fishing stories, and childhood milestones. Don told stories of Sarah's upbringing such as her first perm and how she cried. Her dance classes and how cute she was, the first fish she'd caught with her dad, and mostly of how much she made him proud.

"Sarah's a father's dream." Don said. "I've had three kids. I know. Don't get me wrong, I don't have favorites, but as kids go, Sarah was the easiest to raise and the one I worry about the least. She's a real fighter with a heart the size of the great outdoors. My Sarah is hard working, good with her money, and very self-sufficient. Always has been. The only thing I would ever worry about is her getting hurt." Don gave her a knowing look of sympathy and squeezed Sarah's hand. "She wears her heart on her sleeve. But I have always said, if you risk nothing, you gain nothing. Love is the greatest risk. I loved my Janie with all my heart. She left us too early and shattered my heart in a million pieces, but I wouldn't change a day I spent with her. She was the love of my life and we were blessed to have her with us as long as we did. You two should be so lucky as to have the kind of love my Janie and I had," Don beamed.

"Sarah has told me a lot about her. She must have been a very special woman," Gabriel said.

"Yes, and beautiful too," Don said. "Why, look at Sarah Jane, here. She's the spitting image of her mother and you won't find a more beautiful girl in the world."

"Oh, Daddy." Sarah protested. "You are embarrassing me."

"Well he speaks the truth, Sarah," Gabriel said. "You are

spectacularly beautiful, even if you don't know it." Then Gabriel kissed her hand.

Looking at the two of them, Sarah couldn't have hoped for a better situation. They got along beautifully.

After clearing the dishes, flipping through old family photo albums, and walking outside to see the walnut trees and property, it was time for Gabe and Sarah to leave. It was nearing 12:30 in the afternoon and Gabe needed to head back to Danville after taking Sarah home. She hated the thought of it.

"Well, thank you Sir, I mean, Don. It was very nice to meet you and the food was great. I look forward to coming back and meeting Joe. It's really great being here," Gabriel said.

"Ok, now. Don't be a stranger. Come around as much as you like. Maybe next time you're here we will put on the game and burn some steaks on the barbeque," Don said.

"I'd love that, Sir. Thank you," Gabriel said.

They pulled out in Gabe's truck as Donald McKinney stood waving from the front porch. He smiled at them enthusiastically, but it felt sort of sad leaving him all alone in that big house. Sarah told Gabe that when Joe was home, all his college friends came home, too, and filled up the house with guys for weeks. It was like a frat house when Joe came home and her father was in heaven at the barbeque. Just telling Gabe this helped her feel better, thinking of her father being happy like that.

"Right after the fire, my dad had some of our friends stay with him for a month until they found a place to rent. He was doing them a favor but in reality, they were doing him a favor, too. He had someone to cook for and visit with every day for a month. They were a middle aged couple, same as my parents, and they lost their home in Middletown. He works in the Napa Valley at Pine Ridge Winery and she is an employee at Safeway where my dad used to work. Luckily their kids were grown and gone but they lost their cat. It was very sad but my dad was more than happy for the company," Sarah said.

"Geez, Sarah. It's like everyone you know was hit somehow. That's terrible," Gabe said.

"Well, over a thousand homes and businesses burned so in a small community, that's a lot of people. Everyone knew someone who was hit hard," she said.

They eventually pulled into her driveway, and even though the day was sunny and bright, Sarah felt like a dark cloud had parked over her head, looming just above her and dampening her spirits. He was leaving soon.

Neither one wanted to talk of his departure, but they knew they only had a few precious hours left together before he'd have to leave. They both knew it would go by in a flash.

Walking inside, they barely had the door shut behind them when Gabriel pulled Sarah into his embrace. They stood forehead to forehead, arms wrapped around each other. The weight of their inevitable separation was heavy in their hearts. The moment was desperate and sad. It was not at all how either of them wanted to be.

"This is silly. We can't start this out by moping every time we have to part. Right?" Gabriel said. "What are we going to do about us? We're a depressing lot aren't we?"

Sarah forced a small laugh. She knew he was right, of course. Only how was she to pretend she wasn't sad? It was a struggle for sure.

"Do you want to go watch some TV or something to get our minds off of it?" Gabe asked.

"We could do that," she said. "Or…" she put both her hands up under his shirt, rubbing his magnificent chest, "we could do something else to pass the time."

They kissed, warm and passionate, then before she could say anymore, Gabriel scooped her up and carried her down the hall. She threw her head back and laughed out loud.

≈

The next two weeks flew by and each weekend, Gabriel drove to Lake County to be with Sarah. She said she would make the drive to Danville, but he insisted her house felt more homey than his apartment. He agreed that after the holidays she could drive down and meet his friends.

At Sarah's house, they'd decorated a tree and put it in the corner of her living room, by the north facing window. It was just far enough away from the fireplace, but just in case, Sarah purchased a humidifier so it wouldn't dry out. It was darling with colored lights and Sarah had all sorts of shiny glass ornaments and beaded garland. Gabriel thought it looked like something out of a country cottage magazine.

Back in Danville, Gabe didn't even have a wreath, much less a tree. It was all very sterile looking and, at Sarah's house, it was lived in and comfortable, with festive holiday touches. She had lighted garland around her windows and she burned candles that smelled of Christmas cookies, or cinnamon sticks. It made him feel warmed from the inside out.

Since Christmas was on a Friday, Tommy had given the entire company Thursday through Sunday off. Gabriel had driven to Sarah's house on Wednesday night and was grateful for the long time they'd be able to spend together. He was also excited to give Sarah her present. It would be hard to wait until Christmas to give it to her.

"When do you open your presents?" Sarah asked Gabriel as they lay in her bed Thursday morning.

"Well, growing up, we were able to open one present on Christmas Eve then the rest were opened on Christmas morning. All my cousins and I would get together at my Grandparent's house to open presents and if it snowed, which it often did, we would stay outside having snowball fights until our fingers were numb. Christmas dinner was then usually spent either at our house with my uncles and their families over or we'd go to one of their houses. We kind of took turns. We kids spent the whole time playing with our new toys and basically messing up whatever house we were at."

"That sounds nice," Sarah said. "Well at our place my mother would make this elaborate Christmas dinner with the whole works. Turkey and all the trimmings were her specialty. We had the best desserts too. But presents we opened one on Christmas Eve, which was usually new pajamas or a book, and the rest in the morning, just like you. Not so many cousins though," she laughed.

"So how do you want us to open presents?" Gabe asked with a sneaky grin on his face.

"Why? You can't wait or something?" she teased.

"I think we should compromise and open our presents at midnight tonight, Christmas Eve. That way it's sort of Christmas Eve *and* on the day of Christmas too. And since we have to go to your dad's house in the morning, it will save time in the morning. What do you think?" he asked with a puppy dog look on his face.

"Oh, ok fine. You win," she laughed, tickling his ribs.

They spent the day working around her house and grocery shopping for things they'd need over the weekend. Sarah was to bring a dish to her father's Christmas morning so she needed items for that as well. Her brother Joe was home and Gabe was going to meet him and one of his college friends he'd brought with him for the holidays. It was a most unexpected family style Christmas. Gabriel never imagined in a million years that he'd be this happy to celebrate. Life had taken a wonderful turn.

"When are you going to call your mom?" Sarah asked while they unpacked the groceries. "I don't want to occupy your time so much so that you forget to call your family."

"Around four o'clock," he said. "My dad will be home by then and I will get to talk with both of them. It will be six o'clock in Oklahoma and just before they get ready to go over to my Uncle's house, so no worries."

Sarah stopped from folding up a paper sack and turned to Gabriel. "Do you miss them terribly? I know if I were so far from my dad I'd be so homesick."

He set down the cans of pumpkin and looked at Sarah thoughtfully. "You know, I did. I mean, I still do miss them." He searched for the words. "After Shelly died, I use to feel like, *what the hell am I doing here?* I somehow felt I owed it to Shelly. That if I went back to Oklahoma, I'd somehow be abandoning her, if that makes any sense. I think my guilty feelings of surviving the crash made me feel like it was my *duty* to stay in California. Besides I couldn't stand my family feeling sorry for me and the looks I'd get, and my mother coddling me. It would have been so much worse. I threw myself into work. I took every job Tommy could find, worked late, got up early. It got me through the rough times. But NOW..." he said grabbing her around her waist, "now, I have a wonderful understanding why I was meant to stick around. If I had left and went back to Oklahoma, I'd never have met you."

They kissed sweetly and he held her a moment in his embrace, feeling thankful for how the planets just all seemed to line up for them. It was a feeling of utter contentment, yet still so fresh and new that she made him feel like a little kid.

There was to be a Christmas sing-along at the Methodist Church in Lower Lake that night. All the children of the community were performing and Sarah wanted to go see Michelle and Caleb's kids. Sophie was excited but Josh couldn't have cared less about the singing. He just wanted to get to the part where the Santa Claus came and gave each of the kids candy canes.

"You don't mind going to watch a bunch of little kids sing Christmas carols do you?" Sarah asked Gabriel after they put all the food away.

"Of course I don't mind. It will be cute. Besides, it's Christmas Eve so we should be with our friends. I really like Caleb and

Michelle. They have made me feel welcome and part of the gang. I haven't felt like that in a very long time," Gabriel smiled.

The program started at seven, so after talking to his parents on the phone and grabbing a quick bite, they set off for the church.

The parking lot was packed and once they found a spot and got inside, it was nearly starting. The pianist began with introduction music and the small church was busting at the seams. Caleb and Michelle were seated in the middle of the church by the aisle, waving their arms at Sarah and Gabe to join them. The four of them sat tightly together and waited for the children's presentation. Gabe glanced around at the stained glass windows and was reminded of his own home town church back in Oklahoma.

After a complete rendition of the Nativity Story, where Sophie played Mary and Josh was a lamb, the children broke into a sweet version of, "Silent Night." After that, there was an entire choir of kids in costumes, standing to sing, "Gloria," "Oh Christmas Tree," and of course, "Jingle Bells."

The grand finale was when Santa Claus came in and the kids sang, "Santa Claus is Coming To Town." Everyone stood up and cheered. Gabriel and Sarah truly had a great time watching these munchkins perform and afterwards, the entire congregation walked over to the social hall to enjoy refreshments of coffee, cocoa, and cookies. It reminded Gabe so much of the small town Christmases he'd spent with his family.

In the Hall, Caleb helped Josh out of his costume while the rest enjoyed refreshments. As Josh was released from his lamb costume, he bolted for the cookie table and they all laughed. Some of the other parents gathered around and they all shook hands, sharing some laughter over how cute the kids did in their performances.

Visiting on Christmas Eve was fun but the children needed to get to bed before Santa arrived. With the goodies mostly eaten and the coffee and cocoa all gone, everyone said their goodbyes and wished each other a Merry Christmas.

There was a full moon out when they arrived back at Sarah's house, but a cloud cover was heading in, causing the moon to play hide and seek. It looked as if rain was coming. There were warm glowing coals still in the fireplace from earlier that evening, so Gabriel stoked the fire back to life while Sarah opened a bottle of wine that she'd saved from their first trip through the Napa Valley together. The 2012 Grgich Hills, Cabernet Sauvignon would be perfect to share by the fire she'd said. She poured two glasses and took them into the living room.

Gabriel offered Sarah a spot next to him and pulled a blanket off the back of the sofa to cuddle under. He threw it over their legs and took the glass she offered him. Between the crackling sounds of the fire, they could hear soft rain drops starting to fall on the window as the world beyond faded away.

"That was fun," she said. "What did you think of our little town church? You go as a kid?"

"My mother was raised Catholic," Gabe told Sarah. "I was drug into church a lot as a small kid and did the whole Sunday School thing. I'd never have admitted it, but I actually enjoyed going most of the time. When I got older though, we just stopped going. My dad was never really into going and I guess my mom decided I'd been introduced to God enough to make my own decisions by then. Still, we went most Christmases to Mass and Easter Sunday, too. We became what my dad called high-holiday church goers."

Leaning over to look into his eyes with her penetrating stare, Gabriel felt his heart turn to Jell-O. Her lips softly grazing his with little whisper kisses, nearly did him in. She then looked up at him and said, "I love you Gabriel. I'm so glad you are here."

THAT PUT HIM OVER THE EDGE.

His desire was such that he didn't think he'd be able to hold out much longer, but Sarah then sat back with her wine and took a long, slow sip. God. He was completely under her spell. He had no choice then but to just do as Sarah did, and sit back a moment and sip his wine. *Easy there, Cowboy.* He was talking to himself in his head because he didn't want her to think he was some sex-crazed maniac. But it was hard for him to not be totally obsessed with this woman.

They stared into the fire a moment then Sarah started asking questions about his home in Oklahoma. It was a good distraction for him and it slowed him down from wanting to maul her, so he was grateful for the conversation.

"So what's your hometown like?" Sarah asked.

"It's pretty much like a post card picture of Small Town U.S.A. Pauls Valley is small but we have a beautiful, old downtown with brick-faced buildings and your typical coffeehouses, retail shops, barber shop, and hardware stores. It's about 6,000 plus people but everyone still tries to get into everyone's business. The big Amtrak called The Heartland Flyer runs right through there on its daily route from Oklahoma City to Fort Worth, Texas. It's pretty cool," Gabe said sipping his wine.

"Oh my gosh. That sounds really great. And your parents have a cattle ranch?" Sarah asked.

"Yep. My Dad's dad bought it in the 50's because he always wanted to be a real cowboy. It's about eight miles out of town. He got a herd of cattle, started growing grass hay and alfalfa, and never looked back. It has its bad times though because farming can be a bitch, but the cattle end up making them money on the lean years so it's usually alright," he told her.

"And what did you do as a kid for fun?" Sarah wanted to know.

"I mostly played in the dirt," he laughed.

"Really? That was it?" Sarah laughed too.

"Well, I mean, from the time I can even remember my dad and grandfather put me on tractors or I played with Tonka Trucks. By the time I was a teenager I was helping cut hay and driving the tractor out with the feed trailer for the cows. My uncles were both heavy equipment operators, and my cousins were rodeo kids or just plain ran around the ranch. We got dirty."

"Sounds like a great childhood," Sarah said putting her head on his chest.

"It was. I ran around town at night with my buddies and if we weren't playing football, we'd sneak out and climb the water tower in town, drink a few beers, and pray we didn't get caught," Gabriel laughed at the memory.

"The proverbial water tower huh? I guess most of those old towns have one. We never had one here. You know, like the ones you guys have out there that you can see from everywhere in town. Did yours say Pauls Valley?" Sarah asked.

"Nope. It said *PANTHERS*. It was our high school's mascot. We wore red and black and we were famous in every coffee shop, town bar, and barber shop in Paul's Valley. All our pictures were up and newspaper clippings were on display for everyone to see. We take our high school football pretty serious out there," Gabriel said giving Sarah a teasing nudge.

She laughed at him lovingly then said, "I bet you were wonderful. I wish I could have seen you play. I bet your folks were so proud of you."

He smiled thoughtfully. "I suppose. But it would really have been great if I had a high school girlfriend like you cheering me on in the stands."

Staring at her with his head back against the sofa, it was difficult to even think of any other time than the moment he was in, being right here with her.

෧

Sharing in Gabriel's past was helping Sarah to get to know him better, and she loved how he painted the picture for her.

"I'm pretty certain being the parents of Gabriel Hart, was an easy task, if you were as easy going as you are now," she coerced him forward.

"Well, being an only child, I guess dad was happy I was a boy because he loves football. I played the first year in college too, but then it was just beating the crap out of me and I was done with that part of my life by then. It wasn't like I wanted to play professionally anyway, so I stopped. But it was great while it lasted."

Sarah stiffened a bit. *He was an only child. Good thing he was a boy.*

"It's nice to learn more about your life," Sarah said smoothing out the blanket across her lap and breaking eye contact with him.

Gabriel leaned to set his glass of wine down on the coffee table and then turned his body to face hers. "You can ask me anything you want. I want you to know me, Sarah. Before long, we are going to know *everything* about each other," and he pulled her chin towards him to place a kiss on her lips.

EVERYTHING? What if he didn't like what she had to say? When she finally tells him, will it *ruin everything?*

Before she could allow her freight train of thoughts to ruin the evening, Sarah put her wine down on the table and concentrated on the moment. It was Christmas. She gave her full attention to Gabriel then. She wrapped her arms around his neck and pulled him into another long passionate kiss. The fire's glow and Christmas tree were the only light in the room. The romantic quality of this first Christmas Eve together was nothing short of amazing and almost dreamlike.

Their lovemaking was slow, each touch so sensual. They explored each other's bodies and it was nearly midnight before they were spent in each other's arms. Lying on the living room floor wrapped in a blanket in front of the fire, Gabriel rolled out from under their love shelter to grab Sarah's present he'd placed under the tree. His naked body reflected in the firelight was lean and muscular. She watched him the whole time, adoring him more.

"What do you think you are doing? Is it really that time?" Sarah asked.

"Time flies when you are having fun," Gabriel teased. His smile was that of a child, so excited to open gifts at Christmas.

"Well then you better grab yours too while you are there. If we are going to do this you need to grab the one I got you too," Sarah said.

She sat up, pulling the blanket up to cover her bare breasts and she fixed the pillows they'd pulled off the sofa to lean against the hearth, so she could lay against them. Gabe sat back down, pulling the blanket over his waist and faced Sarah with his gift. He sat the one she'd gotten him in his lap, and laid the one he got Sarah in her lap. He was truly childlike with enthusiasm.

"Well, how do we do this? You want to go first?" Sarah asked.

"No, no I want YOU to go first. I've been dying to give you this since I first bought it. Go ahead, open it."

Suddenly, she became nervous. She smiled coyly but inside she felt crazy butterflies banging the walls of her stomach and chest. She pulled the white ribbon off the edge of a silver wrapped box and set it aside next to them on the blanket. Once the wrapping was off, a black velvet box was revealed in a rectangular shape. Her eyes met his shining blue ones and he pointed at it, motioning for her to continue. Flipping the velvet box open, Sarah saw the strand of perfectly sized pearls lying on the pink satin lining. She looked up at Gabe in amazement.

"My gosh, Gabriel. These are beautiful."

"Do you like them?" he asked beaming. "I hope you don't already own a strand of pearls, but I think they are timeless and elegant... like you."

"They are lovely, Gabe and no. I don't have pearls but I *love them.*" She said staring down into the little box.

"Let me put them on you," he said reaching for the box.

"Really?" she laughed, eyeing their nudity.

"*YES, really,*" he insisted, gently pulling the blanket away from her breasts and leaning to kiss her collarbone.

He took the box and pulled the gleaming white beauties out from their holder, then while Sarah turned her naked torso sideways and pulled her hair up, carefully fastened the clasp behind her.

Sarah turned around and dropped her hair again, giving Gabriel a smoldering look and asked, "Well, how do they look?"

"Spectacular." he said, and they sealed it with a kiss.

"Ok, Mister, now it's your turn. Open the box." she ordered.

Gabriel picked up the box wrapped in navy metallic paper with a silver bow and he tore into it like he'd waited all year for just this one gift. The little box was shaped much like the one he gave her. She hoped he loved it as she loved her pearls. Buying for men was nearly impossible so she tried to find something to signify how she felt for him.

With the paper set aside, he held a small wooden box, sanded with a matte lacquer. It was gorgeous on its own, but she had another surprise for him inside. Gabriel rubbed it and each grain of the wood stood out with different shades of tan, gold, blonde and brown colors.

"It's oak made here in Lake County by a friend. He carves and creates these boxes and sells them. I mean it's beautiful, but look inside. There's more," Sarah urged.

Pulling open the box, Gabriel found a metal Celtic Trinity Knot pendant hanging from a black leather necklace with a metal clasp attached at the back. It was a beautiful piece of art.

"Do you know what it is, Gabriel?" she asked him.

"Sure, it's a Celtic Knot. These are supposed to represent some kind of protection right? It's amazing Sarah," he said lifting it from the oak box.

"Another friend of mine made it. She creates one of a kind metal works and all kinds of jewelry. I asked for this because of my Irish heritage. It's also called the *Triquetra,* or Trinity Knot. The Celtic Christians celebrate everything in threes. The three stages of life, past, present, and future; and also the three domains, earth, sea, and sky. And if you believe, it also represents The Father, The Son, and The Holy Spirit. The single continuous line of the design symbolizes there is no beginning and no end. I like it. I thought it would bring you luck and keep you safe."

Gabriel looked at it, turning it over in his hand smiling. He held it up then in the firelight and studied it more closely. Sarah reached for it and put it around his neck, fastening the clasp behind him.

"I love it, Sarah. You are amazing. Thank you," Gabriel said kissing her again.

"I'm so glad," she said. "I was hoping you wore jewelry. Some men won't. I mean, some don't like it but this is masculine and symbolic at the same time so I was hoping you'd like it."

"I do, and I love you for thinking so much of me. I'll always wear it," Gabriel said.

Relief washed over Sarah, that he did, at least he appeared to, love the gift she'd given him. Their night ended with a walk into the bedroom where they fell asleep in each other's arms. Their first Christmas together had proven intimate, pleasurable, and joyful beyond their expectations. It was a new beginning for both of them. Neither could have imagined that love would walk into their lives after so much tragedy.

But something was lurking silently. A secret was being hidden that could threaten, maybe even shatter, their fragile love.

᪥

CHAPTER TEN

OMISSIONS

CHRISTMAS MORNING AT Sarah's father's house, the frat boys were up and loudly helping in the kitchen. Sarah and Gabriel were official bartenders and mixing everyone mimosas with an assortment of juices to go with their champagne. There was orange of course, plus pineapple and mango to choose from. Don said Jane started that tradition of mimosas on Christmas morning and he wasn't about to change it now.

Joe had brought home two friends from college and they were all wearing frilly aprons that use to belong to Sarah and Joe's mother. They were scrambling eggs, frying bacon, and Don was supervising the operation, telling Joe's friend Teddy to put refrigerator biscuits on a cookie sheet into the oven. They spoke loudly over music coming from the living room stereo. Christmas music from some cable station was cranking out "Jingle Bell Rock" and the boys were all dancing around in their aprons while cooking away. Gabriel and Sarah laughed at the spectacle.

As the gang was beginning to eat, accompanied by the loud Christmas music, Don leaned over to Gabriel. "How you doing, Son?"

Gabriel raised an eyebrow, quick swallowed a mouth full of eggs, then turned to Don.

"I'm better than I could ever say. This has been…" he searched for the words, "unexpected. I'm grateful," and Gabe nodded in Sarah's direction.

Don smiled, understanding, and patted Gabriel on the back before winking over to his daughter.

The guys went to play Foosball and Sarah and Gabriel did up the dishes so Don could enjoy a moment with Joe's friends. Taking the entire scene in, Gabe was in heaven at being surrounded by an energetic family again, just like back in Oklahoma. He couldn't believe how comfortable he felt with everything and everyone associated to Sarah.

"You having a good time, Gabriel?" Sarah asked.

"Are you kidding? The best."

He bent over to give her a kiss just as Joe and his friends ran through the kitchen and Joe shoved a baseball glove into his chest.

"Let's catch!"

Sarah laughed at him and pushed him towards the back door. He obliged and followed the college brood outside. Don and Sarah sat chatting on the back deck as Joe's three friends and Gabe tossed the ball around in a diamond, four way.

Although it was a great time, Gabe couldn't help but notice, the seriousness of the conversation Don and Sarah were having on the deck. Their faces lost their smiles. Just as they were finishing up playing ball, Gabe saw Sarah wipe a tear from her cheek, then she turned and caught him watching. She forced a smile and gave him a nod of reassurance. He wondered if they were talking of her mother. He guessed Christmas must be hard on all of them. Gabe waved and smiled at her.

"Have you told him, Sarah Jane? Does the boy know yet?"

"Daddy I... I haven't been able to yet. It's too soon. Anyway, our relationship is too new and I don't think..."

Her father interrupted. "Sarah, a real man works with his partner through hard times. I think you will have to give Gabriel a chance to be that man for you. I'm willing to bet he will stick around for the long haul," and he patted her hand.

She shook her head slightly and then tilted her head, questioning her father with tears filling her eyes. He just continued to smile at her, that smile of pure love, and patting her hand. When she looked up, Gabriel was starring at her from the orchard. She knew she had to pull it together quick.

When they finally left it was nearing two in the afternoon. Joe and his friends had settled into the living room with the movie *Old School*, on the big screen TV, and her dad stood on the porch, waving her and Gabe goodbye as the truck drove off down the dirt road.

Sarah was thankful to Gabriel and told him she was so happy he shared Christmas with her and her family. The only thing missing was her sister Maggie and her family, but they would be up on another weekend. They were spending Christmas with her husband's family.

She was torn because she truly was feeling like Gabe was a perfect fit. Like they were meant to be together. She watched him driving and he turned to look at her and grabbed her hand. Still, she knew eventually she'd have to tell him everything. Her father made it clear it was probably time. She just didn't want to ruin Christmas.

The weekend flew by, as they feared it would, and before they knew it, it was Sunday morning. They agreed to a brunch at Caleb and Michelle's house where they were hosting an after-Christmas get together with several of their friends and family. Sulking a bit, not talking much, and nearly avoiding eye contact with him, Sarah was feeling down. Gabe didn't ask much about it. Sarah couldn't explain it anyway, how she was becoming increasingly paranoid, and agitated about his upcoming departure.

On the drive over, Sarah continued her silence and the quiet was palpable. Gabriel kept giving her strange glances and furrowing his brow. They arrived at Caleb and Michelle's to a full crowd that she hoped would snap her out from under her gray cloud.

Don't screw this up, Sarah!

Sarah knew she had all weekend to tell him. Now everyone that knew would be crowded into one house. What if somehow it got out before she could tell him herself? What if Michelle was wrong and he *didn't understand?* What if she lost him?

They set down the food they'd brought onto Michelle's counter. Giving Gabe a little squeeze on his shoulder, Sarah smiled up at him, that tight smile again, then walked over to say hello to her friends. She'd left him to his own devices, no words were shared because she didn't know what to say. He gave her a quick, wrinkled brow look, but she looked away. She just had to try and get into a better mood and pray none of the guys would say anything.

≈

What the Hell is going on? Sarah's behavior had completely turned around from happy and loving to surly and distant. Gabriel stood in the kitchen a moment, watching her walk into the living room, wondering if he should talk to her or leave it alone.

"Gabe! Merry Christmas my friend." Caleb was pulling Gabriel into a guy's conversation with his brother Jimmy and some of their friends. They were headed into the garage, or as Michelle called it, Caleb's Man Cave. He'd set up a heater, poker table, and Jimmy had brought over a TV so everyone could watch the game. They had a pool started from the brewery in town, hanging on the wall.

"Does Gabe want any of this action?" a guy named Kraig was asking. "I could call the brewery and see if these last two squares were bought up."

"Yea Gabe, you want in? They are $25 a square. There's a pay off at the end of each quarter. What do you say?" Jimmy asked.

Gabriel wasn't sure what to say but he knew he'd better get into the spirit somehow so he answered with feigned enthusiasm. "Sure, if they are still available, I'll take a square."

Being included in the day's events made Gabriel feel a bit better, and it distracted him from his upcoming, late night drive, and Sarah's strange mood.

The six men sat around the table and Caleb dealt them all in. The guys were good natured and fun loving. Gabriel found himself actually relaxing and enjoying his time. Beers were flowing, kids periodically came running through to harass their dads, and the TV was loud with Sunday Football. It felt very familiar to Gabriel of days in Oklahoma at his cousin's house. He won a few hands of poker, lost a few, and then said he had to go use the bathroom. Gabriel excused himself and the other guys agreed to take a break and raid the house for food.

Walking in to say hello to the ladies, Gabriel locked eyes with Sarah and said he and the guys were taking a break. She had an unusual look about her that teetered on the irritated side. Maybe he was reading too much into it. He wasn't so sure anymore.

"I'm gonna go use the restroom and look back in on y'all before we resume the male testosterone fest back in the garage," Gabe laughed. The ladies laughed. Sarah just smirked.

Awkward.

When he returned from the bathroom, Sarah was sitting on the couch with some of the ladies. He gave her a quick kiss before resuming his poker game. She obliged but was quick to pull away. Definitely something wrong. He left them and started back towards the garage when he saw Michelle near the door talking with one of the guys he was playing with and his wife. They paused their conversation when they saw Gabe. He felt maybe he was interrupting, so he just smiled and walked into the garage.

Jimmy was offering him another beer. Could he use one? They also had a huge score of food piled up. Gabe just stood there feeling sick, wondering about what was up with Sarah. Still he decided one more beer would be fine. He had several hours before he had to leave. *Let it go for now.*

They got through the afternoon and were all eating dessert inside and wrapping the party up. Gabriel knew he had to get Sarah home and start back to his apartment. It was something he hated the thought of. But more than dreading the drive back, he dreaded the obvious conversation they were going to have to have before he left.

They said their goodbyes to everyone there then walked back to his truck on the street, silent, not holding hands and feeling the steel wall between them. He needed an explanation for sure and there would be no getting out of it. He felt sick inside though, and his heart raced like a panicked bird.

They both buckled up in his Dodge and he turned to her.

"Sarah? What the hell is going on? I mean, I can tell you are upset about something. You have been distant from the minute we pulled up here today. Did I do something or are you upset because I have to leave?"

She looked down at the floor, or her hands, but diverted her eyes away. She was tearing up a bit but he didn't reach for her, waiting for her to explain. It was killing him but he stayed patient.

"Just drive us to my house Gabriel. We can talk there. I don't want to talk here in the truck."

So he drove them to Sarah's house, pulled into the driveway, then killed the engine, and they both sat there in the cab motionless. After a minute that felt like an eternity, Sarah exhaled, then pulled up the door handle and opened the door to slide out. She closed it and walked towards her house without any words to Gabriel. It was understood though that he was to follow her.

They sat down on the couch and felt the terrible tension creeping into their guts. He couldn't imagine they would already be having a problem. Whatever it was, he was prepared to fix it and move on. There was no other option, for him.

᠅

What can I say? What can I say? Shit! Don't screw this up, Sarah. You just had Christmas, for God sake! Think.

Gabriel sat there staring at her, waiting for an explanation for her tears. Her crazy switching mood. It was so much simpler to be alone and not have to worry about getting your heart shattered. But her father's words kept ringing in her head.

No risk, no gain, Sarah Jane.

And she did love him. She didn't want to lose him. So she did what she had to do.

"Look, I'm no good at this. I guess the whole Christmas thing being perfect, us moving so fast. I think I just got scared when I realized you were leaving today and I… I don't want you to. I am torn between trying to be this brave, strong girl, and being in a relationship where I'm supposed to be open, and trusting. I don't like feeling so vulnerable I guess. Can you understand?" There. It was an explanation. It just wasn't the whole truth and she felt the lie in her bones.

He smiled at her then and reached for her hands, rubbing them with his thumbs. "Sarah I completely understand. Sure, this is really going fast. I was worried about that. But I can't take back the fact that I love you. For that matter, you love me too. But yes, I know it's going to be an adjustment. Just don't push me away. When you feel like you need time, just ask for it. If you are sad I'm leaving, you can say it. I'm going to miss you too." He kissed her fingers.

Gabriel was so understanding, she felt enormously relieved. He made everything easy, and she felt like a total pain in his ass. But he'd heard her and accepted what she'd said.

"I'm sorry," she said to her feet. "I didn't mean to be so distant. Old habits I guess. It's a default from my past. I get afraid of my feelings and I sort of put up walls. I'll work on it, ok?"

"No apologies. I'm just glad you told me. Let's just promise to talk about what's bothering us. I hate the wondering."

Promise? Oh geez.

She forced herself to smile and nod her head.

"Good," he said.

Gabriel pulled her into him then and held her. She could feel his breathing and heartbeat. She hated not being honest but it wasn't the right time. They'd just celebrated Christmas and he was about to leave. All she wanted to do was stay in his arms, smell the scent of his cologne and feel the warmth of his body next to hers. It would have to wait. She wasn't ready to lose him just yet. She needed more time.

⁓

The week drug on, but now that Gabriel had convinced Sarah they were in this together, come what may, he at least felt better about that. Work was distracting enough to occupy his mind because they'd been awarded two big jobs that Tommy was hoping to get, and Gabe was helping go over the plans needed to put them both into motion. They were going to be very busy.

In Livermore, Tommy's crew was starting a wine caves job that was going to be huge. It would carry the company for months. Gabe's crew would do a tear down and clean up job at a strip mall in Pleasanton. Gabe couldn't afford any distractions now and he knew it.

"Look man," Tommy said, "I know I'm putting a lot on ya right now. If you don't mind though, I need you to bid these other jobs, too."

"You want me to bid all these, Tommy?" Gabe asked quizzically. "There's like six here man, and the Country Club is always your domain. They want a whole new event center. What are they gonna think when I drive out there?"

"Shit, no that one's mine. Yeah, it's gonna be big too." Tommy said grabbing the papers back on the Country Club. "But I would like your opinion so if you could go out there with me when I meet with them, that would be great. I'm heading there Friday afternoon. We could grab a beer after."

Gabe wrinkled his brow and rubbed his chin. "What time? Sarah's coming to town Friday and I'm gonna take her out for New Years Eve."

Tommy's eyes widened, "Sarah's finally coming here huh? Wow. Well, maybe you should take her to the Country Club for dinner and dancing. Besides, I get to meet her right?"

"Hold on cowboy. I mean, yeah I want her to meet you for sure, but what did you have in mind? I don't want us all givin' her the full court press on the first night," Gabriel laughed.

"Oh, I'm a perfect gentleman, you know that. Anyway, what time do you think she'll be getting to town?" Tommy asked.

"She's working only half day and has to grab some stuff from her house… then there is Friday night traffic. I'd guess she'll be getting here around five maybe."

"Perfect." Tommy exclaimed. "Just in time for us to grab drinks and then I will leave you two love birds to your quiet dinner. Where do you wanna meet? We can wrap the Country Club meeting up around four and go get cleaned up. What do you say?"

Gabriel raised an eyebrow then squinted his eyes at Tommy as if to say, *behave yourself Tommy.* "Oh, ok. But not too much harassing. I want to take her to The Farmer's Wife. She's a country girl, Tommy. The County Club in San Ramon is just too hoity and I think she will like the barn floors and Mason jar lighting at The Farmer's Wife. It's more us and I will request the booth in the back with the big window. Don't you need to ask Gwen first since it's New Year's Eve?"

Gwen was Tommy's wife of three years and the only thing that tamed his wild streak. Before he met her, Tommy was quite a man whore. After only dating about a month, Tommy knew he had to marry her. Gwen only met Shelly a few times before the accident, but Gabriel remembered they seemed to really like one another.

"Nah. I will let her know tonight. We weren't sure of any plans. She will jump at the chance to meet your lady and have some girl talk instead of listening to me ramble on about backhoes, excavators, and playing in the dirt." Tommy winked.

By Friday morning Gabriel was as giddy as a school boy waiting for the day to come to a close so he could see Sarah again. She'd called at 1:30 to say she was going to get her car gassed up and be on her way. Gabriel couldn't stop smiling.

Tommy and Gabriel drove in separate trucks to the Country Club in San Ramon. Gabe wanted to be able to leave as soon as Tommy felt he didn't need him there any longer so he could go back to his apartment to shower and change before Sarah arrived. His anticipation was building up so much he felt like he'd burst.

It was a clear day when they drove out to the site. The event center was going to be enormous. The site plans showed it would sit on the edge of a cliff, overlooking a valley of California oaks, meadows, and soon a man-made pond and walking trails. They hoped to break ground in the spring. This would work out just perfect for Tommy with him finishing up the Livermore wine caves just around then. To be awarded this project right behind the wine caves would put Tommy's company, Dermont Excavating, in one of the top three excavating companies in their area of the East Bay. It was huge.

After walking around the area, looking over plans and discussing it with their chief developer and contracting foreman, Tommy said he would finish talking it over with them and fill Gabriel in later. Tommy thanked Gabriel for being there and winked at him before pulling him aside.

"I think we've really got a good shot at this one Gabe. I'll talk with you more later on, but I see huge things in Dermont Excavating's future. You are going to be a very busy man. We are going to have to talk money soon, you and I, but go see your girl now. I will catch up with you at The Farmer's Wife."

"Yea, ok Tommy. Thanks for letting me in on this one. See you at the restaurant. I made seven o'clock reservations for four so see you then. And plan on staying for dinner. It would be weird if you guys just left after drinks," Gabriel said before walking over to shake hands with the others from the Country Club project.

He rushed home, threw off his clothes and set them on the washing machine before jumping into the shower. Having shaved that morning, he just put some cologne on and combed through his dark hair after pulling on an aqua blue, button down shirt and fresh jeans. He was brushing his teeth when his cell phone rang. Looking at the screen, he saw the picture of Sarah and her beautiful eyes staring up at him, signaling it was her calling in. His heart skipped and he smiled knowing she was almost there.

✍

"Hey You. Where are you?" Gabriel answered.

"I'm downstairs trying to decide where I can park and not get us into trouble," she said.

"There is a visitor parking area on the left side of Building D. Just drive around to the left of where I park my truck. I'm heading down to you. Be right there," he said.

She hung up and did as he said. As she turned off the engine and opened her door, she saw Gabriel jogging around the corner of the building just as she was stepping out of her little red car. The anxiety of the week turned to relief and an outbreak of joy flooded her veins upon the sight of him. He wore a smile so wide, he was beaming. She started to laugh out loud at his eagerness.

"You didn't have to come down. I could have managed my one suitcase," Sarah laughed.

He didn't wait to reply. Gabriel grabbed her purse right out of her hands, tossed it back onto her seat of the car, and pulled her swiftly into his embrace. He kissed her long and passionately right there in the parking lot. He weaved both his hands into her hair, pulling her towards him gently and stroking her cheeks with his thumbs.

"Maybe we should at take this upstairs," she whispered.

He laughed from deep in his chest and she felt the vibration through her whole body.

Upstairs, they closed the apartment door behind them and Gabriel set her suitcase down in the entryway. He had a boyish smile plastered across his face, unable to erase it. Sarah laughed and put her head onto his chest.

"You keep smiling like the cat that caught the canary," she giggled.

"I heard what you were saying," he laughed. "Light traffic for a Friday. Work was busy today. You stopped for iced tea. Now, can I please make love to you?" Gabriel asked running his hands up her sweater to find her breasts.

She laughed at his persistence then asked, "Don't we have to meet your friends soon for dinner?"

His breathing was ragged and fast. "We have plenty of time. But if I don't have you now I will surly explode, Sarah."

He grabbed her and scooped her up quickly. She put her head on his chest as he carried her back to his bedroom. It was just like some romantic movie and her pulse quickened. Her body tingled. Dropping her slowly onto his bed, he started undressing. She followed his lead and undressed herself watching him all the while.

Their lovemaking was insatiable and aggressive. She grasped for him like she couldn't get close enough and dug her nails into his back as she reached the heights of her yearning. In the end, they were a tangled, sweaty mess in the sheets, each laughing as they tried to catch their breath.

As they lay together, he played with her hair that cascaded down the pillow. The only way they could look upon each other was to stare. She felt stronger and better just lying with him. Gabriel was the missing part of her soul that had returned to her, reinforcing her. She knew now she could never give him up.

They jumped in the shower, Sarah's hair up, trying to keep it dry, before they quickly drove into town. They arrived at The Farmer's Wife with five minutes to spare. Their table was ready and the place was crowded.

"Do you like it?" he asked her.

"Oh yes. It's wonderful, Gabriel." Sarah chimed.

The restaurant had wide, barn plank floors, and high, open beam ceilings with rustic chandeliers turned down to amber lighting. The dark wood of the building and huge tresses above, were complimented by white washed rustic booths with tan upholstery, and quaint Mason jar lights on each table. The open tables in the center of the restaurant were farm style and were accompanied by cowhide chairs. It was like a restaurant set in some fabulous old barn but the smells coming from the kitchen were more divine than the animal smells of a traditional barn. Sarah loved the rustic-chic feel of the place.

They arrived a little ahead of Tommy and his wife so Sarah and Gabe ordered drinks while they waited.

"I'll just have a glass of wine if you have a list," Sarah said.

"Of course, Miss," the waitress said handing her the wine list.

"I will have a Coors Light in a bottle please," Gabriel said. "I don't need a glass."

The waitress nodded and looked to Sarah for her choice.

"I will have the Flowers Sonoma Coast, Pinot Noir," Sarah a said.

"Certainly. I will be right back with your order," she said and quickly ran off to the bar. The place was loud and hopping with everyone in a festive mood.

They sat in a large, round corner booth that had a huge window behind them looking over a garden that crawled up a hillside directly behind the building. Winter had only slightly put the foliage asleep, because there was still ivy and cyclamen in pink and white with an outdoor light shining onto it so the patrons could enjoy the beauty through the window. Sarah sat smiling and looking around. Gabriel smiled back, reaching for her hand.

"I love this place." Sarah said. "It would be a huge hit in Lake County."

"I knew you'd love it. I found it by accident one day and ate here on a Friday after work with one of the guys on my crew, Barry. We just ate at the bar but it was so cool I knew I had to bring you here. They have fantastic food too. Wanna check out the menu?" he asked grabbing two of the four the waitress left on the center of the table.

Just as they were reading aloud items that seemed intriguing, Tommy and Gwen walked up. Tommy's grin was infectious and both Gabriel and Sarah set down their menus and smiled right back at him, standing for the introductions.

"It's about time I get to meet this gorgeous creature you've been hiding from us, Gabe." Tommy said reaching for Sarah's hand with both of his. "Sarah, we've been so excited to meet you."

"I'm just as happy to meet you both," Sarah said reaching for Gwen's hand. "Gabriel speaks so highly of you two, I feel I already know you.

"Well Gwenny here is a saint but if Gabe said anything good about ME he must have been talking about someone else." Tommy teased.

Tommy was a little older than Gabe but equally good looking. Another tall, dark, and handsome, her father would have said. Gwen was petite and blonde with a perfect figure. They both beamed upon meeting her and it felt very welcoming.

They all sat down and the waitress arrived with her and Gabe's drinks, then quickly took Tommy and Gwen's order and ran off to fill it.

"Wow. Busy tonight huh?" Gwen said smiling.

"Yes. Isn't it great? I was just telling Gabriel that I'd like to see it in my area. It would be hugely successful there. I love the rustic charm."

"I've never been to Lake County. Tommy says that's where you are from."

"It's pretty sweet. I grew up there. It's agricultural with wine grapes, walnuts, and pears. All the small towns are separated mostly by wilderness and family farms. The county isn't that large, you can drive around the whole lake in little over an hour, but it's beautiful."

"Sounds lovely," Gwen said.

The waitress returned with their drinks and took their orders then scurried off again. The conversation was lively and every once in awhile, Gabe would look over at Sarah and wink at her. She gave him a warm smile to reassure him that she was doing just fine.

"So the Country Club job is as good as ours, ole boy." Tommy boasted. "The owner, old man McElroy, told me *he looked forward to working with us.* He hadn't even seen our bid yet.*" and Tommy held up his beer to toast Gabriel.

Sarah looked over at Gwen with a raised eyebrow and the girls laughed. But Sarah's was more out of nerves than anything. That would mean a lot of work for Gabe. She knew Tommy counted on him a lot, but this sounded like he'd be busier than before and it concerned her. "What do ya think, Gabe my boy? We are going to be in the top three excavating companies in the East Bay Area. You are going to be getting a huge freakin' raise man." Tommy nearly yelled above the crowded room.

Gabriel met eyes with Sarah and she sipped her wine, looking over the rim of her glass at him, trying to hide any emotion. He seemed to hesitate then turned to smile at Tommy. He toasted him and kind of shook his head wide eyed.

"This is amazing Tommy, really. I don't even know what to say."

Studying him, she could tell Gabe was less than enthusiastic, what with his fidgeting and hesitant responses. She watched him lie to Tommy though, and pretend to be happy for the ensuing work load. Then she wondered if he was feeling guilty because he was going to let Tommy down…or feeling guilty because he knew he was going to let *her down instead.*

Regardless, the four of them went through the evening laughing and joking. They ordered dessert and stayed late as the crowd got louder and they ordered a round of champagne to celebrate. Gabe had stopped drinking and only accepted the glass for a toast.

"It's New Year's Eve for Christ sake! Hey, to us," Tommy said raising his glass. They each raised theirs to his. "A bottle for the four of us. Thank God there are no more of us!"

Laughter erupted and Tommy laughed the loudest.

"We are going to stop by my sister's house after this. Would you two like to come?" Gwen asked. "She's having this small get together that Tommy and I said we'd pop by for. You know, ring in the New Year. What do you say?"

They looked at one another. Gabriel had his mouth open like he wanted to say something and Sarah waited. These were his friends so she didn't want to step on toes or appear to be the controlling type. But truth was, she really wanted him to herself.

"Um, I think we are going to take a rain check, Gwen. Sarah and I are probably going to have a quiet rest of the night and,"

Tommy cut in, "and do the romantic thing. Hey we get it. You two love birds need alone time. We get it, don't we Gwen?"

"Of course, of course. We are just happy to have spent some time with you guys tonight," she agreed.

A weight was slightly lifted when Gabe spoke up. She didn't feel like being amongst strangers tonight, even though Gabriel had been perfectly willing to be around all her family and friends. What did that say about her, she wondered. Maybe he was a better person than she was. Maybe she was an insecure person and more needy than she'd like to be. Either way, she'd not said a word and it was his choice. She was greedily glad for it.

The bill was picked up by Tommy and although Gabe protested,

Tommy agreed that next time he'd let him pay, since he'd be making oodles of money.

"On that note, you two love birds should excuse us while I have my wife take me to bed or lose me forever." Tommy laughed.

"He's watched *Top Gun,* one too many times," Gwen laughed, "and he forgets we are going to my sister's."

She thanked Gabriel and Sarah for joining them for dinner.

"Well *Ice Man,* you can be my wing man anytime," Gabriel told Tommy.

They all walked to the door and Tommy and Gwen said their goodbyes and left them standing in the glowing amber lighting out in front of The Farmer's Wife. The evening was clear and cool, with a light breeze. It had been a very long week. Still they had the rest of the weekend to look forward to being together. Gabriel scooped up her hand and walked her to his truck with the stars hanging above them. She breathed in the moment deeply.

Once they were headed down the freeway, Sarah turned to him.

"What's going on with this new Country Club job, Tommy was talking about? Seems like you were a bit hesitant," Sarah said.

He continued to look ahead, pursing his lips and stalled.

"I don't know, Sarah. I mean, before I met you, I would be jumping at this opportunity. Not for the money, but for the job. The distraction from living my life. Now…" he paused not knowing how to proceed.

"Now you have me," she said simply.

"Yes. Now I have you."

He left it there. Sarah wasn't sure if that was a *good thing* or if it was a *bad thing.* Having her. But he pursued the relationship. He said he loved her first. She tried to remember that. Still, what if he were having second thoughts? She tried to stop thinking of it. They had two more hours before midnight and she wanted to make this New Year's Eve special. She decided to be like Scarlett O'Hara and think about it tomorrow.

⁓

Tommy's plans for Gabe's future were in the back of his head the rest of the evening. He had never told Tommy no, or even put on the breaks before when it came to work. Now, Gabe just wondered if all this moving fast with work was what he wanted anymore. There was Sarah to consider now, and he wanted to spend more time with her. He just didn't know how to talk to Tommy about it. Gabriel knew Tom had always been there for him so he didn't want to let him down. This Country Club job was going to last well into the summertime, he thought, and that meant Gabe was going to have to make some pretty important decisions in his life real quick, before he committed anything more to Tommy.

Back at his apartment, Gabriel shoved his anxieties down deep and tried to focus on what was right in front of him. Sarah.

She'd disappeared into the bathroom so while she was gone he lit some candles, turned on some instrumental music and poured them each a glass of champagne. The lights were turned down and he waited for her on the sofa.

When she returned she stopped and put her hand to her mouth.

"Aww, Gabriel. This is so nice," she said.

"I thought we'd need something at midnight. Here," he handed her a glass.

She sat down and they touched glasses, each taking a sip.

"Sarah, I am so glad you made the trip today. I hope you liked my friends. I know they loved you."

"They are really sweet. Of course, I loved them."

"Good. I'm glad that all went well. I was anxious about it all week."

She set her glass down, wrapped her arms around his neck. She leaned in to kiss his throat. Gabe felt his pulse quicken and skin electrify. Immediately, the conversation from the evening at dinner left his mind and all he could think of was her. She kicked off her shoes and put her hands under his shirt to rub his torso and pull him closer. Gabriel's heart raced and quickly he scooped her up and carried her to his bed again, where they made love without rushing this time, slowly, exploring, and sensual. Just before midnight, he ran to grab more champagne and brought it to bed. He held it up counting down the seconds.

"5, 4, 3, 2, 1, Happy New Year, Sarah."

He kissed her softly then they each sipped more bubbly and slumped against his head board. It really was a *happy* New Year for them. He hoped the beginning of a new life.

"All week, being away from you, whenever I close my eyes, you are there," he said. "I'm beginning to think I'm obsessed."

"I feel the same," she said. "This is uncharted territory. I don't really know what I'm going to find but I'm so intrigued, I have to keep following to see where it leads. It's like a drug. I need you," she said.

He needed her too. Gabriel clung to her then and held her all night, feeling the warmth of her next to his body.

By the morning, the night's very important conversation he planned on having with Sarah was left in the back of his mind for another time. There were details to work out but not yet. They would have to discuss the future whenever it arrived.

❧

"You never told him?" Michelle hissed quietly on Monday at work. "Sarah, honey I know you don't want to talk about it, but you said you were gonna tell him. What are you waiting for? You need to know how he's going to take it. Your future depends on it."

"Don't you think I know that?" she fired back. "Look, I couldn't. It was too perfect. It was New Year's Eve. Besides, his boss was all talking about big changes in the company, yada, yada. I couldn't pour more on him then... but I will. Soon."

She worked on new strategies for marketing the winery that

week. The first of the year they always held a meeting for new ideas. Plus the owners were hosting a big party in a few days. She tried to focus on her tasks, but it was difficult with her jumbled mind.

Each night she talked to Gabriel. The gushy newness of their romance was comical, but in the back of her mind, she was troubled. Michelle had made her feel pressured to put a timeline on *full disclosure*. It couldn't be done on the phone for sure, so when she spoke with him during the week, there was no inclination of a problem.

She had so much to work through. She knew she could do it, but she wasn't about to lose Gabriel in the process. She knew she had hang ups. She knew her past and her healing process was much like the county's that she lived in. It had a huge scar and she was counting on that scar creating strength.

"We have a party to attend this weekend. I hope you will be up for it. Our owner's wife is having a big birthday party and the whole winery is invite. Don't worry though. Nothing fancy. It's casual," she said.

"If you will be there then I'm in."

The tear down in Pleasanton was taking all Gabriel's concentration so thinking of Sarah was not a luxury he could afford at work. Less than twenty feet from the strip of buildings he was taking down was a new structure that the land owner *did not want to be touched*. With all the water and electric turned off, the crew began the process with Gabriel working as the excavator operator on the job. As Tommy had said, it was far too touchy of a job to let any of the other guys run it.

They got the first part of the complex tore down the first day and started hauling off loads of debris to the landfill. The second and third days were just as busy and Gabe figured by Friday they'd have the entire strip mall tore down and hauled off, so clean that you wouldn't even know it had been there.

Tommy was thrilled he didn't have to worry about it because

he was out at the Livermore wine caves job getting started at the same time. He didn't have time to worry about anything additional. Gabe was happy to take the pressure off his boss but was struggling inside about when to discuss his wanting to leave. He'd realized he belonged in Lake County with Sarah, even though he'd never talked to her about it yet. The other thing was, Gabe didn't know where in the hell he'd get work in Lake County. It was something he would need to discuss with Sarah when he finally got there. There seemed to be a lot of details he'd have to work out.

On Friday, when Gabriel was knocking down the last of the rotted building, he took extra care to watch his clearance around the detached building to save. The guys were in awe of Gabriel's technique and total control operating the CAT 330BL. He was a natural and the building came down without so much as a scratch to the adjacent building. By the day's end they had it all cleaned up and hauled out.

"Helluva job today, Gabriel. Just like Tommy. You got skills, man." Barry said to Gabe as they were all getting ready to load up and head back to the yard.

The guys had all the equipment on the trailers so Gabriel headed to his truck. He just needed to drop by the office real quick before heading out of town. He was going to get a much later start than he'd have liked, but there was nothing to be done about it. Friday night traffic had already started.

When Gabriel got to the yard, he walked into the office to find it a crazy collaboration of guys milling around waiting for their paychecks. Tommy walked in right after Gabe had sat down at his desk to go over paperwork the girls had put in his box. It looked like getting out early really wasn't going to happen now. There was a bunch of calls that had come in for Gabriel to call back on, and jobs to bid for the following week he needed to at least look at before Monday. Scratching his head, he was feeling annoyed.

"Gabriel, my boy. How the hell did it go today? You guys finished, right?" Tommy hollered over the voices in the office.

"Of course. It's done and no damage to the next door building. Slick as shit." Gabe said.

Tommy laughed heartily as he meandered over to Gabe's desk.

"Listen, I imagine you are heading out soon, but I wanted to tell you on Monday I want a meeting with you at four. I will be back in the office by then and we need to go over some business. Diane told me you have some call backs Monday and there's that Dublin pave job, but nothing huge on your books next week. It'll be perfect timing for you to start going over the plans for the Country Club job. I want you dialed into that job as soon as possible." Tommy said with a huge smile and pat on Gabe's back.

Before Gabriel could really comment, Tommy was walking towards his office and into the sea of construction men. Gabe realized it was senseless to try and talk to him at all now about how he might not want to stay in the Bay Area, so he just let Tommy go and focused on organizing his paperwork so he could get the hell out of there.

By the time he got into his truck, it was sprinkling rain and dark. He picked up his phone to dial Sarah, but before he finished dialing, her number came up ringing through his truck speakers on the hands free system. He answered on the second ring.

"I was just about to dial you. I'm on my way."

On the other end, Gabriel heard a panicked Sarah, voice trembling and scared.

"Are you coming? It's my Dad. Gabriel he's had a stroke."

CHAPTER ELEVEN

BENEVOLENT HART

TEARS RUNNING DOWN her face, Sarah sat in the waiting room barely able to hold onto her cell phone from her trembling hands.

"They gave him something that treats the brain. Some kind of drug that breaks down the blood clots that could cause a worse kind of stroke, I guess. I tried to understand what they were saying but it all happened very fast. They took him for a CT scan then everything was a blur after that. I'm just waiting now for them to come out."

"Ok, well listen. Was he able to talk to you at all? Could he walk?" Gabriel pressed.

"Well not at first. I mean he came inside from the back porch and I was getting us some tea. He sat at the kitchen table and had a strange look on his face. He couldn't really talk to me or tell me what was wrong. Then after a few minutes, he said some jumbled things that didn't really make sense, but yes, he was talking."

"GOOD. That's good, Sarah. He probably had a mini stroke, or TIA. My Grandpa had several of those and if it is what I think it is, he might be ok. Usually within twenty-four hours they know. I hope that's the case. Just keep praying. Have you called Michelle? Would you like me to call her?"

"No. I didn't call her yet. I just called you because I...I just needed to cry to someone. My sister is on her way from Sacramento. We decided to wait until we know more before we call Joe at school. We don't want to disturb his classes if Dad is going to be alright. I'm just scared, ya know? I already lost my Mom. I don't want to lose my Dad too," she said weeping softly.

"Oh, honey. You can't think like that. We don't know anything yet," he said.

She started to feel foolish for bothering him with all her concerns. "I'm sorry, Gabriel. I'm really mostly ok. It's just I'm here alone right now and scared. But Maggie will be here soon."

"Listen, stop apologizing to me. You have every right to be concerned. I'm on my way but I'm getting a late start out of here and it's already raining and traffic is bad, so it might take longer than usual. You sure I can't call Michelle for you? She would be great company so you wouldn't have to be alone."

"She's got the kids right now so no, but thanks. I will be ok. I'm sorry I called all upset. I will be ok," she insisted.

"You call me back as soon as you hear anything or if you just want to talk. I'm worried too. I'll be there as soon as I can."

"Drive careful, please. We are at the community hospital here off of Highway 53 in Clearlake. See you soon. I love you, Gabriel," she choked on the words and muffled her cries as she did.

"I love you too, Sarah. All there is."

She gathered herself and recomposed before anyone could see her falling apart. Hospitals. The horrible smell of them with their sterile, slightly metallic taste it leaves in the back of your throat as you breathe in, brought back memories of waiting for answers about her mother. Answers about her husband. Answers about what was happening to her when they had brought her in. The answers were never good ones. Sarah hated hospitals.

᷉

Slightly soggy from the rain, Gabriel walked into the hospital and the smell of it immediately brought back bad feelings and he felt a flutter in his chest. The last time he'd been in a hospital was after his car accident. He woke to find Shelly was gone and everything in his world went black. At his insistence, and after a huge fight with her family who said it would be too painful for him, Gabriel was granted permission to see her body. He wouldn't have been able to accept she was gone until he saw her.

Shaking the cobwebs from his mind, Gabe looked at the directory board. The corridors were silent and lights were dimmed. The directory guided him to the left and then another left and right, to find the Family Waiting Room at the end of the hall. He walked quietly along the tile floors as he went to find Sarah.

There was a woman sitting inside but it wasn't Sarah.

"Maggie?" he asked.

She pulled her hair to one side and looked confused.

"I'm Gabriel. I thought I'd find Sarah here."

After Maggie shook his hand and said how great it was to meet him finally, she told Gabe that Sarah took a walk to the vending machines. Sure enough, leaning over to study her choices, Sarah stood exhausted in front of the machines.

"I'd go for sugar about now. What do you think?" Gabriel said.

She looked up slowly and the shock on her face was both startling and pained at the same time. As she walked to him, with each step, her face twisted into a frown before the tears came pouring out. She buried her head into his chest and wrapped her arms tight around his waist. He knew for certain then, that his coming was the right decision and he wasn't intruding on a family thing. She needed him.

"You are here. You are here," she kept saying.

"Told you I was coming, Babe. Where else would I be?"

"I love you so much. Thank you for being here."

After hugging her for a minute, he convinced her to buy the cookies and they walked back to the Family Waiting Room together.

"You met Maggie already?"

Both Maggie and Gabe smiled and said yes simultaneously. It got a quick laugh from them, but then they were back to the business of talking about Don. They all took a seat.

"Thanks for coming up for our Dad," Maggie said.

"My girl was sad. I couldn't stay away. I'd never have been able to sleep anyway knowing what was going on here, so I thought it would just be best to drive here to you guys. If Don goes home, he might need some help getting up his stairs of the house so I could be of assistance," he said putting his arm around Sarah's shoulder and giving her a squeeze.

They ate the cookies and drank some awful coffee Maggie got from the ER Waiting Room. Just as they were settling in watching TV Land, a doctor came in to talk with them.

"Hello, Sarah? Maggie? I came to see how you both were doing and give you an update on Don. Who's this?" he smiled at Gabe.

"Doctor Wilson this is my boyfriend, Gabriel. He just got here from Danville."

"Well, it's nice that Don has such a great support system. I was just coming to tell you girls that he is resting so well and his vitals are all good. If all continues like this, he will be discharged most likely tomorrow at some point. He probably won't have any more issues tonight. You are all going to have a long day tomorrow and for the next few weeks. It's a good idea to go home and get some good sleep, if you can. " the doctor asked.

"He's really going to be ok?" Sarah asked.

"The medication we gave him worked beautifully and with your quick response to getting him help, I have a feeling Don will be just fine. Of course he will need to follow up with a neurologist, and his family physician to monitor him closely for the next few months, but I think he's mostly out of the woods. We will go over any dietary changes and medications upon his discharge. But you all should try to rest."

Maggie shook his hand and Sarah came in next, thanking him for the news. Doctor Wilson walked out and Sarah turned to ask Maggie what she wanted to do.

"I think you should take Gabriel here back home and you two should sleep while you can. I know when I go home, you will probably be staying with dad. I will stay here tonight. It's my contribution since I live so far away and will be going home after we know for sure he's going to be ok. You, on the other hand, will be waiting on him hand and foot, and probably making him dinner, and fussing like you do. I know you Sarah. You won't rest. So let me take this shift, please. Dad is going to be just fine. We are going to have to make him change his diet and see his doctor more regularly, but he will be ok. I know it," Maggie said.

Sarah started to tear up again and looked up at Gabriel unsure of what to do. "It's up to you, Babe. I will do whatever makes you feel most comfortable," Gabriel said.

"NO. I'm telling you guys. Go. I've got this and you really need to sleep. I actually can use this like a short vacation. Being away from the kids and Ronnie for a few days and alone with a TV, uninterrupted. Wow. I'm telling you. Just go home for a few hours, Sis. You really need it. Gabriel, tell her," Maggie bossed.

He laughed at her take charge kind of attitude. "I don't think we have much of a choice, Sarah."

He looked into Sarah's tired eyes and knew then that Maggie was right. The whole ordeal had really taken a toll on Sarah and she could use the rest.

"Honey, I think if your sister can promise to call you if *anything* changes, then you could use the rest. It's her dad too and I'm sure she's right about you fussing as soon as she leaves. But if you really don't think you could rest, then I'll do whatever you want.

We could set up camp here and have a slumber party if you want. I'm all in," he said.

Sarah looked from him, to Maggie, then defeated, Sarah decided they were both right and she agreed to go home.

"But only until like... six in the morning. I will come back at six and then you can go to Dad's to sleep. Ok? Deal?" Sarah asked her sister.

"Whatever, deal. But wait for a coffee house to open and bring me a mocha latte. Is *that a deal?*" Maggie demanded.

Sarah laughed, "Ok, you've got a deal, Sis."

Arm in arm, Gabriel escorted his girl out of the hospital and down to his truck. They drove off in what was left of the night to her house in the hopes of getting some rest. Although Don wasn't his father, the thought of losing him was surprisingly arresting to Gabriel. He was relieved to know he'd have plenty of more opportunities to get to know the sweet man.

❧

She was mostly silent on the drive to her house. It was about 2:30 in the morning by the time she excused herself into her bathroom to get ready for bed. She left Gabe to lock everything up and closed the door, quietly locked it, then sat onto the closed toilet seat to cry. She wept quietly, shoulders shaking and head in her hands. The sobbing was intense and she tried the best she could to stay silent, drawing her feet up under herself, knees to her chest. It came from deep inside of her, the anguish she felt. Even though she was undeniably grateful for the good news about her father, she was overwhelmed by what nearly happened that she couldn't contain it.

Orphaned, is what she'd have been, had her father died. Is a grown woman still called an orphan if she loses both parents, or is that title reserved for children?

Maybe it was the exhaustion that took over, leaving her so distraught, she thought. She reached for tissue to blow her nose.

"Sarah?"

Just outside the door, he softly knocked. She bolted upright and tried to gather her emotions, wiping her nose and eyes.

"In a minute."

When she opened the door, she found he was in her room, sitting on the edge of her bed waiting patiently for her. She sat down next to him and leaned into his shoulder.

"Are you ok?" he asked.

"I will be."

"You will. I will be here to help."

She crawled into bed and was thankful for his warm body, holding hers. She allowed her body to relax for just a minute and that's all it took before she was fast asleep. Before she knew it, the alarm was going off and it was time to go fetch Maggie's coffee and head back to her father.

Walking into the front of the hospital that morning was quite different than the night before. There were people at the front desk and also in the waiting reception room. The corridors were beginning to have staff hustle about and the voices echoed from down the halls. She didn't even notice the hospital smell anymore. She was just anxious to see her dad.

"Maggie," Sarah said as she entered the waiting room. "We brought coffee and muffins. Any word yet?"

It was around seven and the staff was getting ready to change shifts. Maggie said they'd be able to go in and see Don shortly as soon as the morning shift was debriefed.

"Doctor Wilson said he'd be turning everything over to a Doctor Prager, or Trager…something, soon. They did decide though that it was just a TIA. It sounds like Daddy will be going home today," Maggie said sipping coffee.

Relief filled Sarah as she felt her body's tension release and she smiled up at Gabe. It was going to be ok. She squeezed her eyes tight and smiled, shaking her head in a nod of gratitude.

"Did they give any indication as to when?" Gabriel asked Maggie.

"No, unfortunately. If it looks like it's going to be awhile, I'll go to Dad's and sleep but if it's sooner then I will wait."

Just then a tall, male doctor in green scrubs walked into the waiting room. He was thinly built and had long fingers when he shook their hands.

"Hello, I'm Doctor Trager. I am taking over for Doctor Wilson in caring for your father, Donald McKinney. We are getting ready to move him to a regular bed until his tests can be done this morning and if they all look good, he can go home."

"That is a relief!" Maggie said. "Any idea on how long that might take?"

"I'm guessing by late morning or early afternoon. I wish I had an exact answer for you. But for sure no later than one o'clock. We are still waiting for neurology to get back with us, too. I will keep you posted. Until then, do we have everyone's cell phone numbers?"

They nodded.

"Ok, you can go in and see him. He will be moved in the next hour to free up the bed in ICU. We will keep you posted."

He smiled at them and left. Sarah felt Gabe squeeze her hand.

"You two go. I'll wait here," Gabe offered.

They looked at each other and nodded. The girls left their coffees with Gabe on the table and Sarah kissed him quickly, whispering a thank you to him.

As they walked into ICU, there was a nurse's station to the right and straight ahead were several rooms with large, glass sliding doors to each. Their father was in the room to the far left. Sarah could see him through the glass, sitting up in a hospital gown.

The door slid open and a nurse holding a clip board smiled at them, moving aside. Sarah recognized her as a friend of Walter's, from work, named Ashley.

"Hey Ashley. I didn't know you worked in I.C.U."

"Yeah. Hey Don's doing great. I will let you guys talk. I'll be just outside if you need me."

She walked out as they each took a side of the bed and stood above their father. Sarah locked eyes with him and she tried her best to keep from tearing up but failed once she saw him.

"Hey, we only have good news here, Sarah Jane. No worries kiddo," he said.

"Daddy, we had quite a scare," Maggie said. "But yes, the docs all said you were going to get to leave soon. Just a few more tests."

He reached out to squeeze both their hands.

"I wish you two wouldn't fuss so. I feel fine. Just tired of being here."

He really was going to be fine, Sarah thought. She started to realize how fortunate she was then. She adored her father beyond words, she had the very best sister and little brother, and Gabriel was there for her without even being asked.

They left him to be moved into the regular ward and Maggie went to get some sleep. After she was gone, Sarah turned to Gabriel.

"I need to call Joe so he will come home this weekend. He might be pissed I didn't call him last night but he will get over it. Now he can drive back safely and I won't have to worry about him on the road alone and freaked out. You wanna go for a walk outside?" Sarah asked.

The air outside was fresh after the rain. They stood at the top of the hill just outside of the hospital main doors, looking over the rolling hills of Oak trees, Manzanita, and in the distance were vineyards in their dormant slumber. Gabriel stood at the railing just breathing and listening to the soft whirl of traffic below them as Sarah talked quietly on her phone to her brother.

When she was finished, Sarah joined Gabriel in the peaceful moment, breathing the clean smell of wet earth and foliage filling their senses. Another deep breath taken in, then Sarah was putting her hand along his shoulder. Gabriel turned to her and wrapped his arms around her. They both were exhausted from the emotional roller coaster but surrendered now to the welcome peace. They stood holding each other, trying not to fall asleep like standing horses, before Gabe turned and stood with one arm around Sarah's shoulders.

"When I was in with my dad, a woman Walter and his wife Kelly introduced me to, was my dad's nurse. Her name is Ashley. It was good to see someone we knew caring for him. She's had quite a bit of trouble in her own life though. She and her daughter lost their home in the fire too."

Gabriel looked down at her with a furrowed brow. "More loss. Gosh that's terrible."

"Well it was pretty dreadful," Sarah began. "Walter told me at work that Ashley and her daughter Marisol who is 15, left for the day. That Ashley had taken her dog on a short walk that morning before they left, and normally they would take him places with them. That day Ashley thought it was too hot for him to go on their trip and thought he'd be more comfortable at home. They were gone when they'd received a call about the fire. Ashley drove over Mount Saint Helena like a mad woman, passing, tailgating, honking, and crying trying to get home to save her dog, two cats, and a guinea pig. She and Marisol were sick with fear trying to reach them in time. I guess they got within five miles of their house when the road was blocked to through traffic, and the highway patrol officer told her it was too late. Too late. They couldn't save them. They would never see their house again, or any of her family heirlooms that her house held. All their family history was in that one house, because it originally belonged to Ashley's father. It was all burned. They lost everything. They lost their animal family and have to live with those visions in their heads of how they all died. It just breaks my heart."

Gabriel turned her towards him again, kissed her forehead, then pulled her into him. He said nothing. Just held her like that for a few minutes until she pulled out and turned to look at the view again.

So much around her in the last year had gone wrong. For her and her whole community. With Gabriel now in her life, she was hoping things were turning around. He made her feel safe and loved.

She looked out across the valley then poked Gabe in his ribs, pointing out in front of them. "Look! It's a rainbow." A complete arch was forming from one side of the vineyard to the other and was spectacularly bright. They stood staring and let its splendor fill them with hope.

"It's a sign of things to come," Gabe said. "My grandmother use to always say, 'If God leads you to it, He'll bring you through it, Gabriel.' Maybe she was right."

Sarah took a deep breath, staring at the brilliant rainbow. She certainly hoped he was right.

*

They got Don home later that day. He seemed just fine, besides being slightly moody. It appeared Don's pride was hurt the most. He didn't like everyone fussing over him. He said it was his job to take care of them and he didn't like the turn of events. He especially didn't like Maggie and Sarah lecturing him about his diet and the need to begin regular exercise.

"Geez girls. I'm fine. You can stop hovering now. Tell them, Gabe. A man doesn't need babysitting." Don said, trying to get masculine support from Gabriel.

"Daddy, Gabriel came all this way to make sure you were ok. I don't think he is going to sabotage our efforts to get you well. *Are you Gabriel?*" Sarah said.

"Hey, with women, we are *always* outnumbered, Don. Face it. They have us beat. Might as well get use to it. They win. Just agree and save yourself the frustration of arguing," Gabriel advised with a laugh.

Don laughed for the first time all day. His stern face softened to the smiling eyed man Gabriel had first met.

"You know Sarah? I like this guy. If I ever had any doubts before, and I'm not saying I did, there is no doubt now. This one is a keeper." Don told her reaching out to squeeze her hand.

"Daddy, I just told him what had happened and a few hours later, he was here. Gabriel is the sweetest thing ever." Sarah boasted.

"Ok, you two. You are making me blush. So what can I do to help about dinner? We all have to eat." Gabriel asked.

"I have it all handled," Maggie said. "When you two were with Dad at the hospital, I came home to sleep awhile then I went to the store. We are having chicken breasts, steamed veggies, and a salad, Maggie style." She smirked.

Joe arrived just as they were about to sit for dinner and grabbed a plate. He left his duffle bag at the entryway and sat right by his father, staring at him for a moment.

"You trying to check out on me, ol' man? The girls scared the shit out of me. But you look good. Tired, but good," Joe stated.

Don put a hand on his son's shoulder and looked him square in the eyes.

"Aw Joe, do you really think I'd check out when you are going to owe me big money when your Panthers lose to the Broncos in the Super Bowl?" Don smiled.

The serious vibe in the air was immediately broken. Dinner was relaxed and conversations turned from Don's health to sports, Maggie's kids, and Valentine's Day.

"Your mother loved Valentine's Day, kids. Remember all the decorations and special treats on the table first thing in the morning?" Don said. "She would leave you kids boxes of chocolates right with your breakfast and put a toy or balloons at the table every year. My Janie was always excited for every holiday. She went all out." Don remembered.

As the others began to talk about special recipes Jane would cook, Gabriel leaned over to Sarah and asked her if she would like to do something special for Valentine's Day. He suggested they celebrate with the family and include Don.

"Well, Caleb and Michelle were talking to me last week about a Valentine's Day dance to raise money for the high school's sports. Also, it will be a good thing to get the community back together and celebrate something positive since the fire and all. What do you think? We could all go. Maybe Joe would even come home and bring a date. Sound too cheesy?" she asked wrinkling her nose at him.

Gabriel smiled big and leaned over to kiss her. "It sounds perfectly cheesy and great. I love that idea. Will Jimmy and Angie be going too?"

Sarah smiled at him with love in her eyes that pierced his heart. She reached up to touch his face and just stared at him for a moment.

"Where in the world did you come from, Gabriel Hart? You have turned my life completely around." She said.

"I'm from Pauls Valley, Oklahoma, Girl. My daddy taught me to work hard and take care of my loved ones. My momma taught me that when you love someone, you do everything humanly possible to show them how much they mean to you. You hold on tight and never let go. I'll never let you go, Sarah," he whispered grabbed her hand to kiss her fingers.

"Well that's a good thing. Because I don't ever want you too far away," Sarah said.

Gabriel took a chance and said what was on his mind. He decided that considering what had just happened, now was as good a time as any to bring it up.

"What do you say to the idea of me *never being far away again?*" he asked.

"What do you mean?" she asked.

Gabe scooted a bit closer to her and leaned over to talk quietly while the other three talked on about Maggie's daughter's recital.

"I'm talking about moving in with you, here in Lake County.

What do you say to that? Is that moving too fast for you?" he asked. "If it is, that's OK. I will wait until you think it's right."

Sarah laughed out loud. She put her hand over her mouth and tried to quiet herself but Don looked over to her and the rest stopped their conversation, staring at Sarah and Gabriel.

"What are you two love birds talking about over there, and what's so funny Sarah Jane?" Don pressed.

Sarah looked at her father with tears of joy in her eyes and smiled from ear to ear. Gabriel realized she was not against the idea and he, too, was grinning at her reaction.

"Daddy, Maggie, Joe, we want to tell you, Gabriel is going to move in with me and live here in Lake County. Won't that be wonderful? I think that will be wonderful." She announced and turned to hug Gabriel as she laughed.

They three turned to look at one another and each slowly began to smile. Joe raised his glass of Coke and Maggie and Don their iced tea glasses. Seeing it was a toast, Sarah and Gabe each lifted their glasses of tea as well.

"Here's to my baby girl and her suitor. May they be truly happy in each day together," Don toasted.

"I just want to say, that I don't remember a happier time in my entire life, than I am being a part of Sarah's life and enjoying her friends and family. I intend on making you all a permanent part of my family. Nothing would make me more proud, or happier. Thank you for welcoming me so openly. All of you." Gabriel toasted back.

And just like that, it was settled. Gabriel and Sarah sat staring at each other realizing their decision was real. They'd said it out loud and all that was left were the details. Gabriel was ecstatic. His heart was full and he couldn't wait to tell his mother when they next talked. She worried about him so much.

Since Maggie and Joe stayed with Don that night, Sarah and Gabriel were sent home.

HOME.

It was going to be Gabe's home soon as well. He was so excited that night that as Sarah lay next to him with her slow steady breathing, sleeping soundly, he was wide awake. Staring at the ceiling, he imagined himself in a new life, in a new town. Now he had to tell Tommy.

Chapter Twelve

House of Cards

I KNOW, I HAVE to tell him. What if he wants to get married? Damn it, Sarah. How are you going to tell him?

The plethora of thoughts that filled her brain continued to haunt her. Racing thoughts that ran a series of mind movies, all with terrible outcomes, played over and over again in her head. She didn't even want to talk to Michelle about it. She couldn't face the lecture, but she knew it was long past time to tell him. He deserved to know. She just didn't want to lose him.

Her insecurities were not attractive, and she knew this. If she could only feel as strong as everyone thought she was. It's not that she had a poor vision of herself. She knew she was smart. She knew she had great friends. It's just that Sarah was not the strong and confident person that a lot of people envisioned her to be. If she were to lose Gabriel now, after she'd completely surrendered her heart to him, Sarah was certain it would be the end of her. She didn't think she could pick up the pieces one more time. And now that she'd waited and basically lied by omission to Gabriel about her circumstances, she wasn't even sure she deserved him.

Honesty was something she expected from others, so the guilt she was feeling festered. She promised herself she would tell Gabriel before he moved in with her. No more excuses. This time she knew she had to come clean.

⋲⋗

The time was now. Gabe had to tell Tommy about moving. He'd decided to finish up the Country Club project and have that be his last gig at Dermont Excavating. That would give Tom enough time to find a replacement for him. A few months to, actually. Gabe felt he owed Tommy that. He owed Tommy everything.

Gabe had driven down that morning after helping Sarah with Don all weekend. Their job for Monday was a pretty easy one, so the crew could handle it without him. Tommy was due back in the office that afternoon to handle paperwork and customer calls. Every mile layered on his concern for how to tell his friend he was leaving the company he had helped to build. As he sat in his truck staring at the office, Gabriel thought he'd have a full blown anxiety attack. How could he tell Tommy he was leaving him? What could he possibly say to Tommy that would convey his gratitude and love for the guy all the while telling him he was leaving the company? Gabriel felt like the world's biggest asshole and it nearly brought tears to his eyes. He shook his head to clear those thoughts, *don't be such a pansy-ass man. Suck it up dude.*

Walking up the ramp to the office, Gabriel opened the door to the warm interior and found both secretaries were gone from their posts. It was nearly silent spare the soft sound of water running in the back of the building. Someone was in the bathroom using the sink.

Gabe walked to his desk as quietly as he could so the possibility of him going unnoticed was good, or so he thought.

"Gabriel?" she asked.

He took a deep breath then let it out again. It was Diane. She was back from lunch and of all people for Gabe to have to confront, she was the best possible person he could think of, and he was sort of relieved.

"Yes. It's me, Diane. I'm sorry. I thought I was alone in here," he lied.

"Well that's alright. I thought I was too. You must have just returned then. Most of the boys won't be back for quite some time now from Tommy's crew, and yours are all done until tomorrow. I gave Laci an extended lunch so she could make the bank deposit for me," she said.

Gabe avoided looking directly at Diane. He felt ashamed and torn. The guys, Diane, and especially Tommy, had become family to him. He didn't really think he realized just how much until that very moment. But still, his mind was made up.

"Well I won't keep you. I am just going over some plans here and making more calls," Gabriel told her.

Diane furrowed her brow and parked herself in his cubicle.

"Ok Slick, what's up? You aren't yourself and after a weekend with Sarah, I thought you said her dad was going to be alright. Did something else happen?"

"Don is home and he's going to be fine. I had a wonderful time. Really, I can't remember being this happy. Sarah is the most amazing woman, and I really feel at home with her," Gabriel began.

"I think I am beginning to understand," Diane said with a crooked smile.

"You do? I mean, what do you understand?" Gabriel stumbled over his words.

"You are in love with this girl and she lives pretty far away. The distance thing is getting to you, isn't it?" Diane asked. "You are thinking of moving aren't you, Gabriel?"

Gabriel exhaled loudly. He hadn't even realized he was so tight in the chest from holding onto his breath so much.

"Yes. Yes I am going to leave the company and move to Lake County to be with Sarah. I just don't know exactly when, but I'm thinking as soon as we finish the Country Club job."

"I see," she said looking out the window.

"I hope I can find a way to tell Tommy without killing him. It's already destroying me. I think about letting that guy down and it ruins me. I hate hurt feelings and hate it worse if it's because of me. My mind is made up, but the guilt is tearing me up. I hope he will understand," Gabriel said nearly pleading with Diane to give him some advice.

She laughed lightly. "Gabriel, all we ever wanted for you was for you to be happy. I'm sure Tommy will understand. In fact," she said looking over her shoulder, "I think he half way expects it."

She winked at him and left him to finish up his business. He sat there with a slight sense of relief, but getting himself all worked up left him feeling like a twisted, wet rag. He was exhausted and hadn't even told Tom yet.

When Tommy came in that afternoon, Gabriel was waiting in his office for him.

"Well what are you doing in here, Hoss? Waiting on me?"

Gabe gave him a tight lipped grin and nodded. "I just have a little something to talk to you about before we go home today."

"Ok, well lay it on me," Tommy said setting his water down on the desk and walking around to his chair.

"You see..." Gabriel began as he nervously sat in the chair opposite Tommy's desk. "I have made a few plans that you need to know about."

"Plans? Ok, what sort of plans?"

"Well, as you know, Sarah and I have become extremely close."

"That's great, man. Congratulations."

"Let me explain." Gabriel took on a more serious tone. Gabe could see the confusion in Tommy, as this was not the behavior you'd see in a guy who had a new love. "We are planning to live together. But... we are not going to live here... I'm leaving to move to Lake County. In fact the Country Club will be my last job. I just didn't know how to tell you."

Tommy leaned back in his chair and rubbed the dark stubble

on his chin with his hand. His brows were furrowed as he looked out the window. Gabriel knew Tommy would be mad. He knew it and it was killing him.

"Say something man. This has been eating me up. I have felt like talking to you a few times about it but I couldn't bare hurting you or disappointing you. I mean, you have been there for me in every way, after Shelly died, and I can never repay you for all you did. This job, letting me push hard at work, giving me something to live for. You saved my life Tommy. I didn't know how to tell you I was leaving." Gabe had tears in his eyes.

Tommy stopped rubbing his chin and looked Gabe straight in the eyes. Then a slow, but definite smile spread across Tommy's face that pulled some of the weight off Gabe's chest.

"What the hell man? Are we breaking up? Getting a divorce? Stop worrying. You think I didn't see this coming? I knew you were headed north a month ago. You had a look, man. I will find someone, don't you worry your pretty little head about it. In fact, I already have someone in mind. I just didn't want to tell you until you spilled you were leaving. Actually, once we get underway, you might not even need to stay for the whole Country Club job. Unless you want to that is. We can talk about it. Anyway, stop fussing about me. I love ya, man. No hard feelings. Don't get your panties in a bunch over what I'm gonna do here without you. We will manage."

Tommy stood up and walked around his desk to Gabriel. Gabe felt the tension leave his body, as he rose to hug his friend. They gave each other a loud pat-pat on the back as they hugged it out. Tommy was the one friend Gabe knew was just as emotional as he was and their bond was very strong. Tommy had been more like family to him than anyone in California since Shelly died. It would be very strange to not see him all the time.

At least that was over with. Now he just needed to decide when the best time to leave would be. Soon, he hoped.

৵

"Hey you guys need to come to this fire department dinner thing with me and Caleb this weekend." Michelle was talking to Sarah as they stocked the shelves with more wine. "Angie called last night and told me to ask you guys. We'd all be Jimmy's guests. It sounds like fun. What do you think? Will you be able to leave Don yet?"

She was planning on coming clean with Gabriel that weekend, but having a little fun before dropping her bomb might soften it, she thought.

"Sure. Maggie and the kids will be here with him. Sounds good. I will talk to Gabriel about it tonight when he calls."

Just thinking about telling her secret knotted her stomach. She avoided Michelle's eyes in case she could read her face. Sarah didn't need another lecture from her friend on how badly she'd screwed up on not talking to Gabe sooner.

That night when she told Gabe about the invitation he seemed extremely happy to go.

"If Maggie will be with Don, it sounds like a lot of fun. I could use the connections for finding a job, that's for sure."

Each day that passed, bringing her closer to having to spill it all, her nerves became more intense. Restless nights and the inability to eat much, she'd drag herself around work, functioning on autopilot and caffeine.

It's going to be ok. He's a good man. You have to trust that, she kept telling herself.

৵

The event was at the Brick Hall, which was the fire department's association hall, and when they arrived, a river of people moved about. Some moved upstream, trying to make it to the bar, while others moved along with the current, going outside to breathe in the crisp air on the sidewalk.

Grabbing a beer for himself and white wine for Sarah, Gabriel handed his girl her drink and they both walked to the table they would share with friends. Michelle was excited to see Sarah and the women moved closer to Angie to talk girl-talk. Caleb and Gabe gave each other a knowing look and the two men shook hands hardily, like old friends.

Jimmy walked up behind Gabe and swatted his backside like in football. It startled Gabriel and he jumped when Jimmy popped him. This only made both Jimmy and Caleb laugh, then to make good with Gabriel, Jimmy high-fived him in a welcome of sorts to the evening.

"I am *stoked* you two could make it." Jimmy said. "I was talking to Caleb about how much I wanted to have you and Sarah come tonight because I think after tonight, you will truly understand this town. These are gonna be your people man."

The large hall, with its concrete floors and high ceilings, echoed with conversation and laughter. The soft sounds of country music wafted through the air and Gabriel felt very much at home there. With all the firefighters and their spouses milling about, Gabe could feel the camaraderie amongst these people and he knew they all loved what they did. He could see himself being a part of something like that, had he not gone the route of heavy equipment operator. Maybe he could talk to Jimmy about being a volunteer.

"What do you think?" Jimmy asked.

"Of this? Oh man, I think it's great. You all really do this every year, huh?"

"Yeah, and it's just getting started. Once dinner is served they are going to announce awards for the year. This last year being pretty hairy, there might be a lot of speeches. Afterwards some of the guys can party pretty hard. You'll see what I mean," Jimmy laughed.

"Well it seems like you all have a good time together. That's something special right there. Work together, play together. My kind of gang."

He looked across the table to Sarah, who was talking with the other ladies. She was staring at him with smoldering eyes and the sexiest grin it was killing him. *Wait for later,* he thought with a grin.

The guys were about to sit down when an older man in his mid-fifties walked up behind Jimmy and grabbed his chair, pulling it backwards to startle him. When Jim looked behind him the man and Jimmy both started laughing. Jimmy rose to greet him with a proper handshake.

"Hey, they just let anyone in here don't they?"

"Yeah, this is a classy joint. What are *you* doing here?" Jimmy razzed.

"Sarah and Gabriel, meet my Battalion Chief, Hank Bauer, and his lovely wife Anna. Gabriel here, is new to Lake County. He will be moving here soon to join this beautiful woman. Gabriel comes to us from Danville but originated from Oklahoma. How about that?"

"Oklahoma. You are a long way from home boy." Hank laughed.

"Yes Sir. I am. But I've found I really feel at home right here in Lake County. I work for an excavating company near Danville. I came here after your terrible fire and helped with the clean- up effort. You all went through quite a disaster here."

"Thought I'd sit here since you have a couple seats left and for whatever reason Anna seems to like your company. Or your wife's anyway."

"Hell yes. Pull up a chair," Jim said.

"Yeah, it was a helluva fire. Worst I'd ever seen in my thirty-five year career. If you're interested, we could always use more good young people and with your skills, it would be good to have you around. That is, if you all plan to stay here?"

He and Sarah looked at each other then and shared goofy grins. They both said yes they did at the same time. With that, the table laughed and Hank stood up.

"Babe, you want wine?" he asked Anna.

"Yes please. You want me to join you?" she asked.

"No, just sit and have your girl talk. I see the chief over there and should go say hello. I will be back."

As he walked away, Gabriel was reminded of his Uncle Mac. Neither of them were big guys, just average height and weight, but both had that undeniable something about them that was larger than life and demanded respect.

Jimmy leaned over to Gabe. "So Hank is a great guy. You really should get to know him. If you really think maybe you'd like to volunteer, we could work out a ride along for you."

"I'd like that. Sounds good. I was just thinking about how it would be great to be involved more in the community once I'm settled here," Gabriel said.

"If you do, you should try and ride along with me and the boys from A shift. We have three shifts and I'm on A shift with Batt. Chief Bauer. We have a really great group of guys on our shift, not that any of the others aren't great too. It's just that you get used to working with a group and you get pretty tight. We know how each other works and thinks. When you get to where you can read the other's thoughts, that's when you know you are spending a lot of time together. Anyway, I can set it up," Jimmy offered.

"That would be great. Thanks, man."

A large man with a huge belly walked up to the microphone on stage and announced that dinner would be served. Everyone was to take a seat. With that, everyone was returning to the tables and taking their seats as instructed.

Sarah squeezed Gabriel's hand when she sat down and the twinkle in her eyes warmed his heart.

With all eight seated at the round table now, the salads were brought over. The room was bustling with loud conversations, low music, and wait staff wearing black pants and white shirts buzzing around.

"I can see this is quite a big event," Gabriel said.

Hank looked up from his salad with a roll in hand, and acknowledged Gabriel's observation.

"I never miss it. My father was the chief here in Lower Lake when I was a kid. I ended up as an interim chief back in the nineties before the districts consolidation, and will retire out as a battalion chief in two years. Things have changed over the years, but I can definitely say it has been one helluva ride."

Hank looked over at his wife Anna, and she rubbed his shoulder. It was a simple look, a simple touch that somehow conveyed years of love and respect.

Sarah reached over to put a hand on Gabriel's knee under the table. She gave it a small squeeze and he turned to smile at his girl. She could read him like a book. Listening to Hank talk and watching the quiet ease of his relationship with his wife Anna, made Gabriel think just how much he wanted a life like that. Something to look back on with fond memories of camaraderie and community with a woman he loves. Looking at Sarah now, he knew that's just what he was going to have.

"So tell me, Gabriel, What is the next step for an Oklahoma boy? What do you plan to do after you move to Lake County?" Hank asked as he took a sip off his glass of beer.

"Well I was hoping to pick up a job running heavy equipment again. I've operated pretty much all heavy equipment since I was tall enough to do it and I'm pretty good at it. I was hoping you guys would have a good idea of where I could start looking first."

Caleb raised his eyebrows and while chewing the last of his salad began to talk over the music.

"Jimmy and I know lots of guys. With the clean up still in progress and all the new construction that will need to be done, we know quite a few guys looking for good operators, don't we Jim?"

"Yep. With your resume I'm sure you'll get hired," Jimmy said.

Sarah looked relieved. "Thanks guys. I knew you two would know what to do." She squeezed his knee under the table again and

Gabe felt something inside him shift, as though the universe was lining up just for them. This town. These people. This woman. He had a new life ahead of him and he couldn't wait to get started.

As Gabriel dove into his Tri-tip and Sarah cut into her chicken parmesan, Michelle started talking about how she was so happy to be with all the people who helped save the community.

"I didn't think I'd get this emotional about it," Michelle started. "It just means the world to me that we are here tonight with you guys, Jimmy. All of you are true heroes in my book. I can't believe what you do and that after such a horrible fire like The Valley Fire, that you can just keep doing it."

With a smile on her face and tears running down her cheeks, Michelle raised her wine glass in a toast.

"To the fire personnel and all emergency responders, I thank you all from the bottom of my heart for all that you do. And a special thanks to my wonderful brother-in-law, Jimmy and his wife Angie. We thank you so much for warning us to get out and for keeping our beautiful children safe."

"AMEN. Well said." Caleb agreed, as they all raised a glass and tapped them together.

With the dinner plates being collected and dessert coming around, Jimmy decided to jump up and grab one more beer. This left his chair momentarily open for Gabriel to scoot over and get a bit closer to Hank where he could ask some questions.

"So Hank, I was wondering about whether or not the fire service here would be in need for a heavy equipment operator. I'm pretty damn good on a dozer and I understand you all used a lot of them during The Valley Fire. What are your thoughts on that?"

"It's a damn good idea, but one you'll have to go through the proper channels. My best guess is to start inquiring at Cal Fire. I could give you a few numbers if you want, and you could let them know I sent you there."

"I'd appreciate that. I just like the sound of working with a group like this." Gabe said.

Hank finished off his beer and looked Gabe straight in the eye, sizing him up Gabe believed, "Well, don't romanticize it too much son. It's one ass puckerin' job runnin' a Cat up a hillside with fire on your ass. You gotta have balls the size of an elephant to do some of the shit I've seen guys do. Running straight into a fire, trying to head it off. If you still think that it's your bag, then by all means, look into a job there." A small smile curled the corners of his mustache. Hank looked as if he'd just seen what it was he was looking for in Gabriel, and gave an approving nod. "Something tells me you are up for the task."

"I think I'm up for it, but just to be sure, I'm going to sign up for some ride-along time with Jimmy and your crew. He said it would help me really see what you guys do."

"Well, if you'd have been here during The Valley Fire, you'd have seen more than you bargained for I'm sure. I know some guys that hung it up right afterwards. Others still can't talk about it. Then there's the young ones that found what kind of men they really were while fighting it. Made men out of them overnight. We have some damn fine women too and through the whole ordeal, the one thing I can say is a person's character comes out during times of stress like that."

"If you don't mind my asking Hank, what was your experience during the fire?"

"If you'd like to accompany me to the bar, I'll tell you."

Gabe whispered into Sarah's ear that he'd be right back and followed Hank to the bar.

"I don't suppose you know I own a ranch? Well I was driving off the hill from working it that day and headed back down to Lower Lake where my house is. I was going to shower and looking forward to an early evening. Well I got the shower, but didn't get the rest because a friend of mine called and asked if I knew what was going on with the fire on Cobb Mountain. That's when I turned the scanner on.

"My wife, Anna, was home and listening to it with me. Right away, I heard them ordering up the world for equipment. A huge list of everything under the sun and they needed it in a damn hurry. That's when I knew. I put my boots back on and kissed her quick. I told her, 'This is the one. The one we've all been worried would come.' I left and jumped into my chief's truck to haul ass back in the direction of Seigler Canyon Road.

"When I came outside of my house in Lower Lake, I didn't even see any smoke. By the time I reached the intersection of Hwy 29 and Seigler Canyon Road, I saw the huge column but it was lying over the mountain, being driven by winds. I drove up the mountain and to Hoberg's Airport first. The fire was through Big Canyon Road already. I wasn't on duty but started scouting it out anyway to report conditions.

"I called our chief up from my cell and he was already on a county task force as the leader. He instructed me to stay in the district to cover. Well, I drove back to my ranch and was covering as I was told. We were already low on equipment because so much was sent out on the fire. Then around four or five o'clock, there was a car accident on Spruce Grove South and Hwy 29. Everyone was trying to evacuate, cars were driving on the wrong side of the road headed away from the fire. The injuries were minor but the fire was burning toward them on both sides of the highway, so they just loaded the patient and got out of there.

"Because the fire jumped Highway 29, Hidden Valley was on fire, and all the power poles along that stretch of highway were all a blaze. It was an incredible sight!"

He drank some beer and looked out the window.

"I continued my coverage of the district, and around eleven o'clock that night, the fire was heading toward my ranch. We have a vineyard and walnuts, and I knew we might lose it all. There are several other residents up there as well so we needed to get structure protection in place for them. I didn't see my wife for three days.

"The fire was headed down the mountain and I could hear propane tanks blowing up like a warzone. But when it found its way into the base of Wild Cat Hollow, just below our vineyard, the winds died down and the fire just snaked around down there the whole night. That was our first break.

"I had a small local crew working with me, and by the next day a Cal Fire division leader sent me three dozers. That second night, those dozers cut line all night to protect several homes up there. That's what you'd be doing Gabe."

Gabriel was shaking his head. What kind of dedication does it take to know your own dream could disappear while you are focused on protecting strangers? How do you leave the people you love and drive towards danger, knowing you might never see them again? Like most kids, Gabe had always thought firemen brave. But the depth of personal sacrifice each of them made while trying to save their neighbors, had never been tangible to him. He looked at Sarah, eating her cake and laughing with her friends, and had to wonder if he could put her in a car alone to escape.

"You wanna hear the ending or am I rambling on too much?" Hank asked.

Gabe's attention snapped back. "Please continue. I'm on the edge of my seat here."

"We had to stay on our toes watching the winds, protecting our people to make sure it wouldn't circle back on us and get trapped. Looking back on it now, I'm glad about being able to save our neighbors and all the folks homes we were able to save, but there were a damn lot of folks that didn't have it so well. The weather conditions were different here in Lower Lake, and we know we were lucky. The fire storm that took Cobb Mountain, Middletown, and Hidden Valley, was a freak of nature so much so that I dare say the devil himself was running point.

"By day four, it rained. Less than half an inch but the humidity helped. That was our next break. I was driving my truck up the hill again to check the crews, and I looked behind me in my mirror to see the biggest, most vibrant rainbow I have ever seen. The whole thing. From one end to the other, making a perfect arch. I knew it was a sign that we'd done good and that the worst was over. It gave me so much hope, I stopped and took a picture of it with my phone to send to Anna. I will never forget that."

He turned then back to the bar and it was apparent he was done talking fires.

"Bartender. I do believe I brought in a large bottle of Buffalo Trace bourbon and I'd like a shot for myself and my friend here."

When they both were set up, Hank raised his shot glass to Gabe.

"Pain makes you stronger. Tears make you braver. Heartbreak makes you wiser, and bourbon makes you forget all that crap!"

Gabriel laughed and shot down the bourbon.

✍

Watching from across the room, Sarah watched Gabriel lean against the bar with the Battalion Chief. She felt so grateful that Gabe was making connections so he'd feel like this was his town too. It was important to her that he embrace living in the small town that she loved so much.

As the large man that seemed to be the Master of Ceremonies approached the microphone again, Gabe and Hank were returning to their table. The awards were about to start. When Gabriel took his seat, he leaned over to whisper in her ear.

"Sorry I took off like that. I think I'm making a lot of connections here tonight that will help me in getting a pretty good job. You look amazing, by the way," he said kissing her ear.

"Thank you. And if you keep making friends so easily, they are going to start calling you the Mayor," she teased and kissed him on his cheek.

❦

The room grew quiet as the Fire Chief, Willie Brighton, approached the podium.

"Good evening and welcome. If you are a guest and don't know me, I'm Chief Willie Brighton, of the Lake County Fire Protection District. It is my honor and privilege to award this evening's Best Fire Cadet, Rookie of the Year, and of course Fire Fighter of the Year.

"I hope you all enjoyed your food prepared for us tonight by the amazing Kennedy Klein, of The Harbor Restaurant. She has business cards waiting for anyone interested at the table by the door."

The Chief stopped for a minute to take a sip of water before he continued his speech. Gabriel thought he looked a little nervous. Maybe he just didn't like public speaking. But when he continued his talk, Gabe realized it was the content of his speech that was probably making him a bit nervous. It had been quite a year for this department and Chief Brighton was visibly emotional about it.

"On July twenty-sixth of this last year, the hell of the 2015 fire season really began. That is the day the first fire, The Dam Fire, started. Next was the Rocky Fire, The Jerusalem Fire, and then of course, the worst of them all, The Valley Fire. Over thirty-five percent of Lake County burned this year. Many of our neighbors, and even some of you in this room lost everything. For me personally, it feels like a surgeon that loses his patient on the operating table. For every home lost, that's like someone's life, and it's very personal to me, and I'm sure to all of you.

"But through it all, I've witnessed the best of humankind, reaching out to not only friends and neighbors, but to complete strangers in their time of need."

Sarah reached over to hold Gabriel's hand and just as she did, he noticed each couple at their table reach for their mate's hand for support.

"When folks were evacuated to the Walmart parking lot, the

store brought out food and water to the evacuees. They weren't the only ones. Again and again as people were evacuated, more local restaurants were bringing food to them. Citizens from all over made food and brought it to the fire department to feed our crews, and for some, it was the last dollar they had that they spent to prepare these meals. The local chapter Moose Lodge in Clearlake Oaks became and still is a camp for many folks that lost everything. They too have fed and sheltered these unfortunate souls in their time of need. Before Red Cross even showed up, our local people rallied together to provide clothing, bedding, and basic hygiene products for the evacuees. Animal food and trailers were offered up to help move livestock. It's overwhelming the generosity of our community. I have never been more proud to live in Lake County than I am now."

Chief Willie paused and took another sip of water. He stood a moment looking out over the sea of people that waited on him with patience and admiration. Each person in the audience was enthralled and the silence was palpable.

"I was at football practice with my son when The Valley Fire hit," Willie continued. "When I heard the call and all the equipment ordered up from Cal Fire, I knew I had to go. Like so many of you, I didn't return home to my family for days, and even when I did it was simply to shower, change, and leave again. On September 12, 2015, we couldn't have known the enormity The Valley Fire would become, or that it would take us until October 6th to call it truly out.

"Reports on conditions from the air and Cal Fire allowed their meteorologists to assess weather and to make predictions based on humidity, fuel modeling, and years of drought. This is so fire service can make plans on how to fight the fire. Unfortunately, the plans for how to fight the fire went past the next day's predictions. The Valley Fire became truly *unpredictable*.

"So what I would like to say to all of you tonight, is without your service, and without the resources that came in from outside the area, we'd have had more burned over crews, and more loss of life certainly. What you all do in fire service matters, and that is what we are here to celebrate tonight."

The applause was deafening. There was a standing ovation in the room with many people in tears. Once the room settled down, the chief's wife came up to help him hand out the awards. Every award had a story. And the audience stood to cheer every one of them.

The last award of the night was Firefighter of the Year and once again, the room got very quiet as Chief Willie Brighton, began to talk up the person and why they were to receive this special award.

"This person," Willie began, "was not on duty the day the Valley Fire broke out, and like many of you, he came to work anyway. He worked with me on the task force up on Cobb during the fire, and his engine was all over the place. He drove it into places most people with way more years of experience would have thought twice about going. No matter what I asked him to do, he did it without question, and took initiative to go into places that needed help before anyone else even spotted it. This person did all this while having to wonder whether or not his own family was safe because they had to evacuate. While working under great duress, this person showed extreme professionalism, had great instincts, and evacuated countless people, while helping to save as many homes as his crew could manage. Throughout the year, this person is not only a skilled engineer, but community leader, family man, and friend to all his colleges. It gives me great pleasure to award this year's Firefighter of the Year to Jimmy Hollings."

An explosion of applause erupted and Jimmy sat there at their table stunned. His wife, Angie had her hands over her mouth and tears were spilling down both her cheeks. Hank was patting Jimmy on the back and he slowly started to stand. Caleb stood up and shook Jimmy's hand at first, then pulled him in to bear hug his brother. He let go of Jimmy so that he could walk up to the podium and receive his award. The microphone was thrust into Jimmy's hand and he faced the audience.

"Any one of you could have received this along with me. I don't feel like I deserve anything more than the rest of you. We do what we do together as a team. The spirit to serve is what we are taught and it runs in our blood. Those of us that do it, don't do it for any other reason but to help our community. I love working with all of you and it's such an honor to receive this award tonight. I don't take it lightly. But without my wife and family's support, I know I wouldn't have gotten through this last year. It's been a tough one. Thanks to all of you for having my back and I will continue to have all of yours. This is truly an honor."

The Chief closed the awards portion of the evening with a few more words, then the music started up for dancing. Jimmy received many handshakes, hugs, and high fives, then he took Angie for a spin on the dance floor.

The rest of the evening was just as perfect, Gabe took Sarah for a few spins. He loved seeing her laugh and smile on the dance floor. When a slow song came on, he held her tight. Everything about this evening had been wonderful.

He leaned in and kissed her softly on the lips then laid his forehead against hers, taking a deep breath. Sarah reached up to cup his face in her hand. Gabriel then grabbed her hand and kissed her palm, then led her back to their table.

"Well you two lovebirds calling it a night?" Michelle asked when she and Caleb walked up to their table.

"I think maybe so," Sarah said.

"I'm so glad you guys came tonight. It was nice to have us all together again," Michelle said.

Sarah reached over and gave her friend's hand a squeeze. They congratulated Jimmy once more, then walked out with their arms around each other and stood on the sidewalk. Main Street was glowing from the amber lighting of the lamp posts, and it was quiet except for the music that flowed out of the doors from the hall.

They got into his truck and found their way back to Sarah's

tree lined driveway that led to her little house. The house where he hoped they'd live for many years to come, making wonderful memories together.

The promise of a romantic encounter at the end of the evening was kept. The two found each other in a slow and exploratory union, that kept them up most of the night, touching, caressing, and loving.

But later, as Sarah drifted off, Gabe couldn't sleep. He had rehearsed all week what he was going to say Sunday morning. He eventually dosed off, but as the sun rose, the sounds of birds chirping outside the window woke him and despite his lack of sleep, Gabriel felt like it was Christmas all over again. His heart was bubbling up like champagne was in his chest with the excitement of knowing something Sarah did not.

※

Sarah was turning over in bed as the light streamed in through the sheer curtains. Blinking the sleep from her eyes she saw Gabriel already awake and staring at her. He lay across the blankets in his t-shirt and boxer briefs, smiling at her and brushing her hair away from her face.

"What are you up to? You look far too happy this morning and the sun is barely up. What time is it?" Sarah asked suspiciously.

"It's seven, sleepy head. And I am happy," he said kissing her on her forehead.

A slow, wide, grin spread across her face then and she made an attempt to control her wild hair. "Do you have something on your mind, Gabe?"

"As a matter of fact, I do…I had a request. Something to ask you," he said sitting up.

Her face fell. What kind of question? Oh no, no, NO. He couldn't. He wouldn't! Not yet. She abruptly sat up then. Her eyes wide and she was pulling the blankets up around her chest to tightly wring them in her hands, twisting them like her stomach.

He was still smiling, her expression lost on him and possibly misinterpreted. Either way, he wasn't stopping.

"Sarah, soon I am moving here and I feel like my whole life is starting. I love you so much and I can't wait to wake up with you every morning. I want to know if you will be mine, *forever.*"

He pulled a box out from the blankets, hidden next to his legs, a sapphire blue velvet ring box. Yep, it was most definitely a ring box, small and square, undeniable. *Christ.* She had waited too long.

"Sarah, will you marry me?" he looked hopeful, eyes shining and staring into hers.

"I…I mean," she wanted to scream yes, but he'd probably run out as soon as she told him what she'd held back all these weeks.

"Babe?" he sat back studying her face now.

"Gabriel… the thing is, I want nothing more in the world than to be your wife."

He laughed out loud and opened the box to show her the most beautiful round cut, one carat diamond, surrounded by smaller diamonds that continued down the platinum band. She only looked at it a moment then looked up pleadingly at Gabriel, feeling guilt and shame wash over her. Damn. Why hadn't he waited until at least Valentine's Day or something?

He was pulling it out of the box and grabbing her hand to see if it fit when she shook her head and pulled her hand back away. Tears were spilling down her face and she turned and got off the bed, walking to stand in front of the window, wishing she could jump out of it and run away.

"Sarah?… What is it?"

She put up a hand behind her, asking for a minute.

Well it's come to this. You have to do it now. Jesus, I hope you didn't ruin everything. Just do it.

"Is it too soon, honey? I swear I didn't want to pressure you," he said sitting on the edge of the bed, ring back in the box.

She turned to look at him a minute then turned back to look

out the window. It would be easier if she didn't have to look at his beautiful, confused eyes when she spoke.

"There is something I need to tell you. Something I should have talked to you about a long while ago but just couldn't. Now I think I might have waited too long but…"

She heard him sit back and exhale. Where to start? She reached out and rubbed the curtain between her fingers.

"We were so happy. It was everything a girl dreams of. The high school romance that blooms into marriage, house, great jobs…and kids."

"Kids?"

Her lower lip began to tremble. Fat tears welled up in her eyes and spilled down both cheeks, but Gabriel didn't move to comfort her. He sat and let her finish.

"I became pregnant just before we started looking for properties for our bed and breakfast. I went to the doctor and it was confirmed. Everything looked great. I felt wonderful and excited. At my ten week appointment I got to hear the baby's heartbeat and it was like this little miracle from God was living inside me. But then…" Sarah trailed off and wiped her tears again before she continued.

"Then I woke up with cramping pains one night and found a pool of blood on my sheets. By the time we got to the hospital, it was too late," she sobbed, choking on her words. She heard Gabe rise from the bed and again she put up her hand for him to sit. She just had to get it all out. If he hugged her she didn't think she'd be strong enough to say it all.

"My body produces a lot of uterine fibroids that's what kept me from carrying the baby to term. The doctor said it was a miracle I even got pregnant in the first place, and it was highly unlikely to ever happen again."

She turned slowly now, more tears spilling down, and tried to meet Gabriel's gaze. She gave a shrug of her shoulders like, *there it is.*

"I'm so sorry, Sarah. That must have been… I'm just so sorry."

"Gabriel? Do you understand what I just said? Do you know what this means?" Sarah asked. "Gabe, I can never give you babies."

She stood staring at him waiting for him to say something but he couldn't. No words would form. He rubbed his face with both hands, eyebrows raised and obviously stunned. She couldn't sit. She excused herself for a minute to the bathroom, leaving him sitting there.

When she was alone she blew her nose and tried to straighten her spine. It was out. He would either leave her now or, if Michelle was right, they'd find a way to make it work.

Gabriel is an only child. He'll want to carry on his family name with a son of his own.

She had to just be strong and if this was it, then she wouldn't beg. She wasn't going to let another man destroy her again. That's what she told herself, but inside she was dying at the thought of losing Gabriel. He'd become everything to her and she just didn't know how to be alone anymore.

When she returned, he was still sitting there, looking like someone kicked him. As she spoke, she could hear the tight conviction in her voice. She had to stay strong.

"I understand, Gabriel, if you cannot continue this relationship now. I guess it was pretty selfish of me to even let things go this far between us without telling you. I hope you can forgive me. At times, I seem to be in denial of the truth. But anyway, you are free to go and I won't hold any grudges against you if you want out. No one could blame you," she said.

He seemed to wake up then and his eyes narrowed at her, anger in his voice. "Wait, just a minute," he nearly yelled. "You haven't even given me a minute to think about this without assuming I'd want out. God, Sarah, I love you. Doesn't that mean something? Maybe I don't want out. Maybe I just need a minute. Please don't go dismissing everything we mean to each other. I just asked you to marry me, for Christ sake!"

She stood in the doorway to meet his heated stare. She was holding on to her pride and digging in her heels, playing the stoic maiden. She didn't want or need his pity.

"Don't decide to stay with me Gabriel if you think somehow, someday we could get some kind of second opinion or other medical help. I've already tried. I've been assured from doctors that it's quite unlikely. Nearly impossible."

"Nearly?" he asked with raised eyebrows.

"YES. Nearly *impossible*. Look, don't you think I have already asked every question known to man? This is what drove my husband and me apart. I insisted that I could get pregnant again and I'd go on permanent bed rest, do anything the doctors said, just so I could have a baby. But he said he couldn't do it! Getting pregnant didn't mean I would be able to carry the baby and he wasn't willing to adopt. He said he would never raise another man's child. I was in agony. I cried all the time. I spent every night on the internet, searching for ideas and answers, risky procedures, and he couldn't take it anymore. We fought like crazy and before we knew it, we were talking divorce."

She couldn't take looking at his pained face anymore. She went to the kitchen and took coffee from the freezer then set it on the counter but couldn't bring herself to perform the next step. She sat down at the kitchen table, wondering what the hell to do next.

❧

She wasn't going to get away with just dismissing him and their relationship because she was scared. But what could he say? If he said he didn't want kids anyway, that would be a lie. He'd always envisioned having a couple of kids and ever since falling for Sarah, he'd secretly thought of them having a cute little girl that looked just like her and a son that, maybe, took after him. But that was not to be and he didn't know how he felt about that dream being wiped clean. In the back of his mind, he knew people adopted children everyday, he had just never thought of it for himself and wasn't ready to wrap his head around the idea. His girl was pulling away and he needed to get her back.

He stood up and followed Sarah into the kitchen. She didn't look up, her body so tense she might shatter so he stood at the sink, trying to find the words that would bring her back.

"Sarah listen, I won't lie to you. I've always wanted kids. But I want kids with *the right person*. The thought of leaving you simply because you can't have babies is not an option for me. You have my whole heart. I don't want someone else. Period. I think we just need to take this back a step and get through this thing together."

She turned to face him with fresh tears, "Well *this thing* is not going to have a different outcome. You are the one that needs to think about what this means. God knows I've had plenty of time, but it's news to you so… I don't know. Maybe you should leave, take this week and mull it over. What life will be like for you and me without kids, or me and kids that aren't biologically ours. You need to figure out if you can handle that."

"You would want to adopt?" he asked, maybe too surprisingly.

"Well I don't know! *Maybe I would,"* she shot back. "But obviously it's not for everyone and I just don't want your life filled with regret. I don't want to be your biggest mistake."

He couldn't stand it anymore. He pulled her into his arms, kissed the top of her head, her wet checks and forehead while she buried her face in his chest. The fight went out of her and he felt her collapse against him.

"We will get through this Sarah. Whatever happens, I am not letting you go. I'm in way too far over my head now. My life was set on a path with you the first time I laid eyes on you. That's just the way it is," he said.

She pulled away from him.

"I meant it, Gabe. I want you to take the week to decide. I need you to realize what you'd be giving up. I can't be the reason you are unhappy. I can't live like that, always thinking in the back of my head that you might regret your decision and it was all my fault. I couldn't bear that."

"Ok, fine. Have it your way. I will think about it. But, clearly, my mind is made up," he tried to joke.

"No, you haven't made up your mind. You only think you want to marry me. But you don't know yet how you feel about what our life will look like together because you haven't had the time to think about it. That is my fault. For that, I'm so sorry I didn't tell you sooner," she looked down shamefully.

He tried to get her to look at him. Those gorgeous eyes were now clouded over with a storm of guilt and sorrow. His heart was breaking and there was little he could do to help her.

Packing up his bag was painful. Neither of them spoke much. They mumbled things here and there, but both were in deep thought. His heart in his throat, his nerves shot, Gabriel felt the world had suddenly changed. Sarah had changed somehow. She was distant and guarded, more than ever. He worried the new and exciting feelings they had were somehow never going to be the same. He wondered if they'd be alright again. Relationships have to weather change and hard times. They'd both had more than their fair share in the past. He'd just hoped they were due good fortune by now.

He kissed her goodbye. Long, sweet, and desperate. Fear was a dangerous thing in a young relationship. Had they built a strong enough foundation in the short time of knowing each other? Would they be able to pull each other up through disappointment like this? Or was this fear and disappointment going to tear them apart? Gabriel was determined to hold strong to Sarah. He only hoped he could convince her he would.

"I hate this. Leaving things like this," he said. "I will see you next week though. It's going to feel like a million years away."

"Just wait and see how you feel," she said.

He pulled her tight and looked desperately into her eyes.

"Sarah, haven't you figured it out yet? I'd walk through fire for you. I will drive a million miles to be wherever you are. I want you to be my wife. I love you. Remember that."

She was crying but kissed him softly and put her hand on his chest to gently push him away. She nodded without speaking to show she understood, then backed up and crossed her arms over her chest.

He climbed up into the truck and shut the door. Starting up his engine, he rolled down the window and felt his chest tighten. He knew she needed him to be strong and confident though, so he gave her his best smile and winked at her with his baby blue eyes.

"I love you, Sarah McKinney. You are not getting rid of this guy. There isn't anyone like you in this world and I'm not letting you slip through my hands. Hope you can handle that." He smiled.

"I love you too, Gabriel Hart," she said with a small smile. "Drive careful and text me when you are home safe."

Pulling away from her was like a slow tearing of Velcro. It was loud in his mind, pulling and scraping his heart strings the whole way. She seemed sad and broken but he had faith that underneath, she was stronger than she knew.

❧

Michelle walked in without knocking. Sarah sat on the sofa, where she'd been since Gabriel left. Four hours now. When her friend arrived she was sitting in a pile of used tissues, the house was freezing, and she was half a bottle in to a Wildhurst Sauvignon Blanc.

"Well this is serious then. Where's my glass?" Michelle asked sarcastically. "And we are going to have to build a fire or something. Give me some blanket."

Sarah tried not to smile but couldn't help it. Michelle had that effect on her. She never let Sarah wallow too long...ever. She was the rock and even after losing her home, Michelle could always find the silver lining in every situation.

"You called, I'm here. Tell me everything. You told him the *whole story*, right? No more surprises then?"

"Nope. No more surprises. And I think I might have been a little cruel. Like, maybe I took out old feelings on Gabe," she crinkled her nose at Michelle.

"Oh hell, I'm sure you weren't half as bad as you think you were. That man would forgive you anything. But how'd he take it?"

"I don't know. Shocked, I guess. A little angry. But mostly, he was sweet," she said burying her face into a throw pillow.

Michelle laughed and poured herself a glass of wine. "Of course he was. I told you."

Sarah set the pillow back down and got serious again.

"NO… no we still don't know if he will want to marry me after all this. He hasn't had time to really decide how he feels about no kids, or adoption, or even how he feels about me after he thinks how I kept this all from him. UGH!"

"Wait. What did you say there? Marry you? Did you guys talk about getting married?"

"Oh, didn't I tell you? That's the best part of my humiliation. He actually proposed this morning before I got the chance to tell him. Yep. He had the ring and everything. GOD! I'm such a loser!"

"Holy shit."

"Yes, holy shit. I insisted he take the week to decide how he truly feels. I'm not going to tie myself up in a knot again, Michelle. I need him to be certain. And I need a partner that won't look at me like I've trapped him in some circus he didn't want. I love him so much. I do. But please tell me I did the right thing."

Michelle looked at Sarah with all sincerity and said, "Girlfriend, you have the strength of forged steel. I am so proud of you for standing up for what you need. You have really grown. I remember a time when you were the doormat, but look at you now. No matter what he chooses, you will be ok. And you will always have me."

Sarah hugged her friend and felt exhaustion run through her body.

"So where is this ring?" Michelle smiled

Sarah pointed to the kitchen counter.

Michelle was up and running to grab the velvet box. She flipped it open as Sarah sat glumly watching her gaze at the sparkling beauty.

"Oh, dear God. He really is a prince isn't he?" Michelle said staring into the box.

"Yes. But now I'm going to be tortured with having to look at that all week, not knowing if I will ever be Mrs. Gabriel Hart. He said he was leaving the ring here and we were going to work *this thing* out. He kept saying, *this thing.*"

Michelle set the box down and came back over to Sarah. She looked her square in the eye and didn't pull any punches.

"Now Sarah, don't go getting a chip on your shoulder. He was just given this information and I'm sure it *was* a shock to him. So even if he referred to your infertility as *this thing,* you are going to have to cut him some slack. He's a good guy. Don't project your old problems onto him. He's not the enemy here and you better not try to push him away just to protect yourself from getting hurt. You are already in love with him. Let him love you back. It's the biggest favor you can do for yourself."

✍

CHAPTER THIRTEEN

DECISIONS

THE WEIGHT OF Sarah's news pressed down onto Gabriel like a cumbrous, dark cloud. His chest ached as he lay in his bed, staring at the ceiling after his long drive back to the apartment. The sounds in his head were whirling and loud, making it nearly impossible to sleep. When he finally did, he was plagued by nightmares of drowning, reaching out to Sarah who was being swept away from him in a strong current.

His mind was so full the next day, he barked at the guys and found himself apologizing more than once. They'd started a tear down of an older business in Dublin where the building had so much rot and water damage, the new owner thought it was smarter to tear it down and rebuild in the same place. It was going to take Gabriel's crew a couple days to knock it out and do proper clean up. But his mind wasn't on his work. It was on Sarah.

He got through the day and found himself falling back into old habits of shutting down. He distanced himself from his crew and was pissed off at everything. That wasn't how he wanted to be though.

Once the guys knocked off for the day, Gabe headed to the office to do paperwork so he didn't have to go home to an empty, cold apartment. It was just like the old days. Work would see him through. Gabriel knew he needed to get a grip on what was happening in his life. He knew for certain he was in love with Sarah. He knew he never wanted to be without her. But he also knew he always planned on having a family. He'd hoped with her. Now that wasn't an option, or at least not the way he'd envisioned it.

Driving back to his apartment, he stopped off to pick up some Mexican take-out food and a six pack of beer. Sitting on his couch, he ate mindlessly, and flipped through television channels without really watching. He was looking at the screen, but seeing nothing. His mind was wholly on Sarah and their situation. He wished he was with her, sitting at her little dining table by the window, eating take-out Mexican food with her. Instead he was in his sterile apartment, isolated and alone.

He finished his food, set the plate on the counter and grabbed another beer from the fridge. He picked up his cell phone and stared at it. He wondered if she'd made it home yet. He knew she wanted him to think about it carefully, but he mostly just wanted to talk to her. He wondered if he was being too desperate in wanting to hear her voice. Would he push her away by his neediness if he called her? It was killing him that they were in this awkward place in their relationship and yet neither of them had done anything to create a fight or problem. It was all going so well. Now it felt like they were nearly breaking up and he had no freaking idea why.

What do you want, Gabe? He pondered the thought. Yes, family was important to him. He loved the idea of he and Sarah raising up kids that would run around and be loud, as he and his cousins did. Like Caleb's and Michelle's kids did, laughing and bringing joy to the house.

Reaching up to his chest, Gabriel pulled the medallion out from under his t-shirt that hung from his necklace Sarah had given him. The Trinity Knot symbolizing the three domains of earth, sea, and sky, also the past, present, and future. The one continuous line that looped around with no beginning and no end hung from his neck and he tried to pull strength from it. Sarah said she liked the symbolism of the Father, the Son and the Holy Spirit. Turning it over in his hand, feeling the etched lines and curves he thought of her, and he prayed.

Just then, his phone buzzed on the coffee table. Sarah had sent him a text message. Gabriel's heart leapt in his chest and he read her message.

"I was wondering how you were doing. I hope your day was good. I cannot stop thinking of how much pain I've caused you and how sorry I am. I really am just worried about you. I hope you are giving it some careful thought. No matter what you decide, I love you."

Gabe finished reading the text and decided it was a sign.

On the second ring she answered.

"Hey," she said.

"Hey you. I can't do this Sarah. I can't just sit here and think about everything without discussing it with you. This isn't *your* problem, Sarah. It's ours. And *we* need to figure it out together. Please, don't shut me out and pull away from me. I know you think on some level that you are doing me this great favor by giving me time to decide, but it's killing me." He said trying not to choke up.

"It's killing me too," she sobbed on the other end and it tore at his heart.

"Baby, I don't ever want a life without you. We've already lost so much, you and I. Let's not lose each other now too. I want to marry you. And yes, I want a family with you, whatever that ends up looking like. We can adopt if that's where it goes. But I know that even if that didn't pan out, I'd choose you. I will never want some phantom woman because she might give me children. I couldn't love anyone else the way I love you."

And just like that, he realized his answer. There was nothing more to discuss. He'd made up his mind and that was that. Gabriel was going to let go of this fantasy about a son that looked and acted like him and a daughter that was like Sarah. He would build a new dream and seize any happiness they could get. They would do it together.

When they hung up, Gabe was laying on his couch in the dark room, spare the television casting waves of light across the living room. He could see from his sliding door the neighborhood lights shining in the evening like fireflies of the south, but not quite as endearing. The tightness in his chest finally released. He felt like he'd run a marathon race and fatigue was taking over.

Eyelids heavy and sliding down, Gabriel started to feel himself floating in warm, tranquil waters. It was only for a moment and he took a deep breath and decided to take his beer can into the kitchen and get to bed before he accidentally slept there all night.

When he opened his eyes, Shelly was sitting at the end of the couch. She was wearing a flowing white dress and her hair hung down around her shoulders. Those deep brown eyes shining in the light of the television. Her knowing smile warmed his heart. How he had missed her.

"How'd you get here?" he asked.

"I have my ways. How are you Gabriel?"

"Oh, Shelly. It's been so long. I hope you understand. I didn't go looking but…"

"I know. Sarah is a wonderful girl. She's lucky to have you Gabe. *I was lucky to have you.* You deserve to be happy. Don't ever worry about that. It's all I ever wanted for you. You made the right choice tonight."

The light behind her grew brighter, illuminating her hair and shoulders. Gabe's heart beat faster. He wasn't ready for her to go, but he felt her leaving.

"Shelly, please don't leave yet. How do you know I made the right choice?" he asked.

"Because I know your heart. I know your future is waiting for you, so stay the course. Life isn't easy Gabe, but there's no need to worry about the past. I love you," she said as the light swallowed her up.

"SHELLY. Shelly. Shelly wait."

Gabriel sat up abruptly from the couch. Jimmy Fallon was on TV and the other end of the couch was empty. He could still *feel* her sitting at his feet. Oh, he missed her. But she'd given him her approval and that made all the difference. He didn't have to feel guilty anymore. He'd made the right choice.

∾

It was the longest week she could ever remember, waiting for Gabriel to return to Lake County, after telling him her secret. When he arrived, he brought a few boxes of his personal items to prove to her he was serious. He'd made his choice.

She'd waited for him to put the ring on her finger. She didn't feel right wearing it until he'd done it himself. They didn't make any firm decisions about adoption, but it was out there and it felt good. They both said they'd be open to it when the time was right. For now, they were going to revel in the splendor of loving each other and planning a wedding.

The next day they told her father, Don. He was just as pleased as Sarah had hoped he'd be.

"Oh Sarah, honey. This would put your mother over the top. She is smiling down at you for sure. I can't think of better news. Congratulations you two. And Gabe, I knew you had it in you, son. You are a smart man." Don said patting Gabriel on the back.

When the watercolors of sunset spread across the sky behind Mount Konocti, they sat on her father's porch talking wedding plans. A small, intimate ceremony was what they wanted, right in his backyard. It would be perfect.

After Gabriel finished the last job at the country club for Tommy, he'd be moving in with her, just a few months before their June wedding. The sheer joy of planning their wedding together took the sting out of him having to leave on Sunday. There was a light at the end of the tunnel now.

The days started to fly by after the plan was put into motion. Each week when Gabriel drove north, he brought a few more things to her little house in Lower Lake. He made every effort to prove to her that he was happy, and there was no reason for her to believe otherwise, but deep in the back of her mind, she couldn't help but wonder if at any moment, he'd change his mind.

Their friends were elated with the news. Michelle was not only busy planning the wedding with her, but repeatedly said, *I told you so,* about Gabriel being the one. They kept her father in the loop and he was so proud to be part of the planning process. It also occupied his mind, helping Sarah plan the details. They were only planning on close friends and family so about fifty invites. It was all coming together.

"I told Tommy and the gang at Dermont Excavating. Everyone is expecting an invitation. Can we do that?" Gabe asked.

"Of course. They are your people. They should be here."

He scooped her up into his arms. "*Our people,* now."

She smiled then. She didn't really know any of them but Tommy, but still she was glad he felt like that. By June, she'd meet them all. In the meanwhile, she just hoped his Oklahoma family would like her. She didn't want them to think she was some possessive, California girl that monopolized all his time. They'd not even discussed going back to see his family and now it didn't look like there would be any time to before the wedding. They both had so much to do.

Nights alone in her room she'd think of how soon, she'd not be alone at night anymore. He'd be there beside her. She stared at her engagement ring, shining in the moonlight, and think, *this is real. This is happening. I'm going to be Sarah Hart. Mrs. Gabriel Hart.*

Gabe made it to Lake County with his gas gauge dipping into the red zone so he pulled into the Shell Station on the corner of Hwy 53 and 29 in Lower Lake. Valentine's Day was on Sunday and he couldn't wait to spend the whole weekend with Sarah. He was putting diesel into his rig and watching the numbers turn on the pump when he heard a familiar voice from behind.

"Hey there, stranger."

Gabe turned with the nozzle still in his tank. It was Max, the bartender. He was wearing blue jeans and a t-shirt with a flannel, and work boots.

"Hey Max. What are you doing man? You look like you've been working today," Gabe said.

"Something like that. I'm uh…waiting for a friend. How have you been, Gabriel? How are you and Sarah doing?" he asked.

Gabriel couldn't mask his happiness and a smile spread across his face immediately.

"Things are actually going really well. I can't even believe it myself, but I'm going to be moving here very soon. Sarah and I are doing exceptionally well. How about you? You good?" Gabriel asked Max.

Max laughed a little and looked at the ground, shaking his head.

"I'm good, Gabriel. You don't ever need to worry about me. I just take things as they come," Max assured.

At that, Max looked up over Gabe's shoulder, and then turned to look behind himself, as if deciding which way to go. He looked back up at Gabriel and something in his eyes made Gabe wonder if he should be worried about Max. Either that or Max was hiding something that he didn't want to share.

"You ok, man?"

Max turned to look deep into Gabriel's eyes, "Yeah, man. I'm good."

Something made Gabe relax inside. Something he couldn't explain.

"Well, I've got to be going now. You take care of yourself, Gabriel," Max said. "I wish you and Sarah the best." He reached out his hand, and Gabe shook it.

"Thanks, Max. You take care too. I'm glad I ran into you," Gabe said.

"You bet. See ya," Max said and turned towards the station store. The pump clicked off and Gabe turned for a moment to place the hose back on the pump and screw on the tank cap. When he looked up, Max was already gone. In that short amount of time, he must have found his friend and left. Gabriel opened his truck door, looked around once again, and then jumped inside to leave. He hoped Max was ok.

On his truck seat sat a box of chocolates and some flowers for Sarah. He would give them to her right away when he arrived at her house. Valentine's Day wasn't something he had anticipated celebrating ever again. Now he was excited to spend the weekend surrounded by the gushy festivities, hearts and all.

She opened the door from the garage when he pulled up and her bright smile lit up when he stepped out holding the gifts. He was rewarded with soft kisses and an exceptionally long hug.

"I missed you," she said.

"Well I missed you more," he said.

They shared a late supper and got caught up on each other's week and she filled him in on the wedding planning. She and Michelle apparently had found *just the right wines* to serve at both the rehearsal and reception, and were talking the guys at the firehouse into cooking the meat for the event. She was very calm.

"How can you be so chill?" he asked her.

"Hmm? What do you mean?"

"I mean, aren't brides supposed to be stressed out?"

"This is what I do," she offered. "I am a planner. I think it's why I wanted to open my own B&B. I love the process of seeing an event through from beginning to end with every little detail. Strangely enough, it relaxes me. I just focus on making things beautiful."

"Wow. You are so going to have to teach me that. I mean, I'm really not like that at all. I mean it. I admire you for being able to just stay so grounded. Guess that's just one more reason to love you, Sarah McKinney, soon to be Hart."

The next morning, Sarah suggested they go to the Napa Valley and look for a dress before they went to the Valentine's Day fundraiser dance. She wanted him to come along with her. He didn't see why she needed a new dress for the occasion but was happy to accompany her.

"Should I buy some new clothes too? You are making me nervous that this thing might be more formal than I thought."

She started laughing at him. "Gabriel, I already bought an amazing dress for tonight and you are going to love it," she waggled her eyebrows at him. "But for today, I was talking about a *wedding* dress."

Her wedding dress. He gave her a quizzical look, not understanding.

"I know, I know what you are thinking. But I thought about it and I really don't want to shop alone and I don't want anyone else to go with me. I only want you to be with me. I don't care about old superstitions or traditions. This is just about you and me. What do you say? You want to help me choose a wedding dress?"

"Hell, yes I do. When you put it that way, I think we should make a day of it." Gabe dropped his voice to a sexy whisper, "But I will be trying to imagine this *amazing* dress you are wearing tonight, all day long. Bet it's sexy."

❦

Just like she planned, they went to the Napa Valley. The day was sweet with smells of wildflowers, moist earth, and hints of eucalyptus in the air. Stopping at a bakery in Calistoga, they loaded up on coffee and carbs before heading into St. Helena to a little dress shop called Lovely Lady.

Sarah felt like Julia Roberts in *Pretty Woman,* with Gabe as Richard Gere, watching her whirling out of the dressing room in dress after dress. Some were ivory, some white. Some were lacy and old fashioned, and some were satin. No matter what she tried on though, Gabriel said she was the most beautiful thing he'd ever seen. Sarah was so happy it radiated from her.

But then, she put on a dress that felt different. It was a simple, off the shoulder, ivory dress. It was fitted through the torso and fell loosely from her hips into a sleek, flowing skirt that flattered her figure with a timeless elegance. Gabriel was standing to stretch and glancing around the boutique so he didn't see her emerge from the dressing room. She quickly stepped onto the pedestal as the sales person fussed with the skirt. She was in the perfect position to see his face as he caught sight of her.

"Dear God," he whispered. She locked eyes with him and she knew, *this was the dress.*

"You like this one?" she asked playfully.

"Wow. Um… No. I don't like it. I absolutely *love* this dress on you."

He reached up and grabbed her hands while she remained on the platform staring down at him, never letting her eyes leave his. She felt regal in that dress.

"You don't think one of the other more fancy ones were better?" she asked.

"Sarah, you could wear a gunny sack and be beautiful, but this dress is you. It is… gosh I don't know. It's just that you look like an angel. My angel. Oh sweetheart. I am so glad you asked me to do this with you. We have to buy you this dress."

She was giddy now. She found her dress.

With the large box in hand, they left the Lovely Lady dress shop and happily set out for lunch in Rutherford at their favorite restaurant, The Rutherford Grill. They decided against going wine tasting and instead, spent 2 hours over lunch and drank wine there. The conversation drifted comfortably through the afternoon as they discussed when they would travel to Oklahoma to meet his family and decided it would make a wonderful honeymoon trip. They celebrated their plans with a decadent flourless chocolate cake with house made vanilla and lavender ice cream. She fed a spoonful to her handsome fiancé and could not believe how lucky she was.

Back at her house, they struggled to hold off falling right into bed together. Sarah insisted it would be sweeter later when time allowed for more intimacy. Instead, they got ready for the evening, sharing long looks and smiles as they dressed. She watched as he pulled on a dress shirt over his toned back and shoulders. He was beautiful.

"I had a wonderful time today, Sarah. I'm really glad you suggested we go together."

She touched his arm and looked up at him lovingly. "It's a pretty special way to start off our married life, don't you think? I loved the dress the second I put it on, but I loved the way you looked at me in it. That's what did it for me. So thank you."

If this was how things were for them *before* they were married, she could only imagine how magical it was going to be as his wife. They really were lucky.

Once Gabe was dressed, Sarah made him sit on the couch while she finished up. At the last minute she pulled the dress from its hiding place in her closet. It was completely different from the wedding dress. This one wasn't so much about timeless elegance as it was about feeling luscious and sexy.

The theatrics were worth it. When Sarah came out in the clingy, red velvet stunner with the plunging neckline and a small slit up one thigh, and the pearls he gave her, Gabe was speechless. This was going to be quite a night.

❧

The dance was in The Brick Hall, just like the Firemen's Awards, but this time the building was decked out for romance with white linen covered, round tables, and white lights everywhere. There was red tulle hanging over many of the lights coming from the ceiling for a festive ambiance.

The women were all dressed to the nines and the men all paled in comparison. Most guys wore blue jeans with dress shirts and cowboy boots. Some wore slacks like Gabriel and a few even showed up in their dress uniforms from either military or fire departments. It was quite an eclectic assortment of attires but the funny thing was, nobody really cared. They were all there to enjoy each other's company and support a great cause in fundraising for the local high school sports programs.

With cocktails in hand, and country music playing in the background, Gabriel and Sarah meandered towards their table where Caleb and Michelle had just arrived and were hanging their coats on the backs of their chairs.

"I just love your dress, Sarah. My goodness it's beautiful." Michelle proclaimed.

"Thanks Michelle. You look amazing too. Gosh I love that color on you," Sarah said of Michelle's soft coral dress.

"Hey, don't I look pretty too?" teased Caleb. "I had to diet for three weeks just to get my ass into these things. I'm wearing Sir Dockers tonight, in case anyone like Joan Rivers' daughter, Melissa asks. Last season, I believe."

They all laughed at Caleb's joke just as Jimmy and Angie walked up.

"The hell is so funny?" Jimmy razzed.

"Your brother is being the funny man again," Michelle said. "Thinks he's Red Carpet worthy tonight in his lovely Dockers."

"I believe I can give him a run for his money. If I'd have known some of these guys were going to wear their dress blues, I'd have worn mine. But I think my new Levi's and collared shirt are quite dapper. Don't you think so, Babe?" Jimmy asked his wife.

"Of course, sweetheart, but Gabriel went all out with the tie. You could take note of that for next time."

"Hey, don't drag me into this thing. I just did as I was told. Sarah said shirt and tie, I wore a shirt and tie," Gabriel admitted.

Another couple walked up then and Jimmy introduced them, "Gabriel, Sarah, this is my buddy Rick Patterson and his lovely wife Korina. Rick use to play football for Kelseyville back in the day, but we don't hold that against him…anymore."

Gabriel turned to shake Rick's hand. "Hey man, good to meet you."

The women were already in a lively conversation about their kids, their jobs, and finding the perfect dress for the dance. The guys just left them to it and went to the bar.

The men returned with the ladies' drinks and Sarah touched Gabe's shoulder as he handed off her wine and she went with the women to look at the auction items on the tables.

The guys were talking football, construction, and then Rick asked Gabe what he did.

"I'm a heavy equipment operator."

"Yeah, that's how he met Sarah. He came here for the Valley Fire clean up and Sarah was with Michelle at our place sifting through the rubble when this guy walks over from another site. Now we can't get rid of him," Caleb teased.

"Wow, that's quite a story. Nice something good came from that damned fire. I'm at Public Works and Korina is a Lake County Sheriff's dispatcher. We are glad to be getting everything behind us around here and moving on."

"I hear you," Gabe said.

They were announcing the beginning of dinner to be served. Salads were served first, followed by a prime rib entrée with steamed veggies and a baked potato with all the fixings. At their round table, the couples sat girl, boy style all around. Sarah sat on Gabriel's left and on his right was Korina Patterson.

Conversations had split into multiple exchanges. Jimmy and Caleb were talking with Michelle about something, while Rick and

Angie talked of something else. This left Sarah, Gabriel, and Korina to hold their own powwow. Korina asked him how he and Sarah met and when told, she thought it was romantic.

"That is a wonderful story, you two. My gosh, I can't believe how this fire has brought people together," Korina said.

"I understand you are a dispatcher. That must have been a tough job during the fire," Gabriel said.

Korina looked towards the windows. She seemed to be trying to rewire her brain for an appropriate comment. When she found her voice, it was distant.

"On September 12th, I was supposed to attend a friend's wedding. I never made it there. Instead I got to embark on a multi-day, back to back shifts of dispatching. On most days in the office we have two dispatchers. By the time the fire was in full force, we had up to five people in there and things were still going crazy."

She had Sarah's and Gabe's full attention now, as they sipped their drinks.

"When the initial calls started coming in about The Valley Fire, it was small and in a residential area of Cobb Mountain. It didn't sound unordinary. But then we kept hearing of spot fires and before we knew it, there were multiple fires all sparking off the one fire. They'd turned it over to Cal Fire by then and the calls really started to multiply as did the air traffic we had to deal with.

"In the weeks prior to The Valley Fire, there were two substantial fires called The Rocky Fire, and The Jerusalem Fire, which were both hairy in their own right. These both preemptively helped in a way because we dispatchers were pretty well dialed in on what we needed to do for such disasters. However, we could never have imagined the enormity of what The Valley Fire would become. Nobody could!

"They were calling up off duty people who were trying to leave town, or people on vacation to return and help. In all fields from Sheriff Deputies, to dispatchers, and any emergency personnel they could get, they were asked to assist. They had a Search and Rescue crew headed to training out of town and they too were asked to turn around and return as quickly as possible. The fire had morphed into not just some wild land fire, but an inferno that made it more important to evacuate and save lives now, and less important to save structures. And there were THOUSANDS OF SOULS that needed evacuating! It was all hands on deck.

"There was no time for personal feelings during this frenzy. We all had a job to do, but you know a lot of these people on the other end of the radios are like family to us at dispatch. We kept pushing it down, the frantic feelings and fear. We kept pushing it down deep because they needed us. But then we got calls with people screaming in the background, we got calls where we could hear the fire roaring and cracking…It got pretty damn real then.

"The fire had swept through Cobb Mountain area so fast and there were so many people that had to evacuate, the emergency personnel tried to jump ahead of the fire and start warning people down in Middletown to evacuate. Some of these people would get angry and say, 'well we don't see any fire here yet and it's quite a ways away from us so why do WE have to leave?' They had no idea what was coming and how unpredictable the fire was behaving. Most people cooperated but some simply didn't listen until the last possible minute and then the traffic to leave was atrocious! The Hidden Valley Lake area was at risk next so mandatory evacuations took place there next.

"Then something happened I can never forget. One of our officers was in there, trying to get people out. I heard him come over the radio air traffic saying, 'I'm trapped and there's no way for me to get out.' Well after we heard that at dispatch, for some reason, there was silence. No other air traffic, no phone calls ringing in, and complete utter silence in our office. I swear time stood still. It just stopped."

Gabe and Sarah looked at each other in disbelief. These stories, Gabe thought, were all so alarming.

"Of course, shortly after we heard him screaming for help to get out of there, and we experienced our deafening silence in the office, we then heard another one of our deputies get on the air and say he'd not only been able to save him, but his patrol car as well. They were both really lucky.

"Once the first initial day and wave of terror rolled over everyone, we got unbelievable phone calls from citizens offering up horse trailers to haul out their animals. There were other people offering up property to house these animals too. They were wonderful people of our community that just wanted to help.

"I worked that first day from 6:00am to 10:00pm that night, doing what I could before I felt safe enough to leave for awhile and go home to rest. It was sixteen hours working dispatch at high levels of stress, with people crying, screaming, and panicked, on the other end of the line. Countless people's lives that were forever changed and we had to somehow compartmentalize these sounds, feelings, and memories. I turned right around and was back at it the next morning at 6:00am. I did this for twelve days straight. Everyone was basically on call. Tensions were very high."

When Korina stopped and sipped more wine, tears were filling her eyes.

Then Gabriel spoke up.

"Korina, in my mind, people who we call when we dial 911 are true heroes. They are the first people we talk to in a crisis, and they are the ones that get help to come. You guys are the unsung heroes that usually are faceless to us, but the voice of an angel when people are crying out for help. Thanks Korina, for all you do."

Sarah was wiping away more tears than Korina by then. She agreed with everything Gabriel said.

"Listen, you guys, in the end we just have a job to do. It's the spirit to serve that keeps me going. I never forget that. No matter what kind of day I'm having or what is going on in my personal life, when I'm driving to work I have this mantra that I say over and over. *It's the spirit to serve, it's the spirit to serve.* I say it like a meditation almost. That's what keeps me going. Nothing more than that," she concluded as she raised her nearly empty glass of wine to both of them.

Sarah, Gabe, and Korina clinked glasses and sipped more of their beverages. Gabe decided in his mind then, that when he moved to this place, he was going to find some way to get involved to help the community more. He was really leaning towards being a volunteer firefighter.

Just then, dessert was served and Korina engaged in lighter conversation with Angie and Rick. Sarah excused herself to the bathroom to touch up her makeup, and Gabe walked to the bar for another drink for the two of them.

As he stood waiting for his order, he surveyed the room and felt a warmth come over him. These were people he felt he could be proud to be acquainted with. People of substance and values. It made him smile.

⚜

As the evening progressed, Gabriel took Sarah onto the dance floor, dancing together like they'd been doing it for years. Sarah was awarded one of the silent auction items she'd bid on. It was a kitchen gift basket and Gabriel happily paid for it as a woman came around to collect, and Sarah gave it to Michelle. It was a good night.

Saying goodbye to the three couples, they walked outside into the cold February evening. It seemed like the coldest they'd felt in a long while, watching their breath escape in steamy clouds from their mouths. Gabe put an arm around Sarah to keep her warm.

Michelle yelled from the truck window as Caleb was pulling out, "Hey Gabriel. You are going to have to share my friend Sarah, here pretty soon. You two have been so lovey-dovey, that I don't see her anymore. You guys come to dinner soon ok?"

Laughing at her, Gabe yelled back, "Tell you what, if you help me move, I'll buy you dinner." Sarah squeezed him tight around the waist and laughed at her friend's bossy tone. They really were so very lucky. The town was intertwined with so many giving, caring people, and some of the best of them were her friends. She knew as she looked at Gabriel, that her life was very blessed.

Once they got home, Gabriel had to stoke the fire back to life. Sarah was about to go take off her beautiful dress in favor of more comfortable sweat pants, when he stopped her.

"Whoa, wait one minute, Missy. You tormented me with wondering about this dress, then I watched you in it all night long fantasizing. You wouldn't want to cheat a guy out of the pleasure of taking it off of you, now would you?"

He walked up behind her, kissing her neck and pulling her hair to the side, she felt her skin come to life, tingling all over. He hunted for the zipper, then slowly unzipped her dress and turned her to face him, as he slowly pushed the dress down her body until it fell to the floor. The room was no longer cold to her, as she only desired for his touch and the heat coming off of his hands to keep her warm. Throwing her head back, he leaned down to kiss her throat and shoulder before scooping her up to lay her on the sofa, in front of the fire.

Their first Valentine's Day was loving, romantic, and very steamy in the end. She couldn't have dreamed up a better night.

CHAPTER FOURTEEN

WHEN PLANS CHANGE

THEY BROKE GROUND on the San Ramon Country Club project. Everything was going beautifully. The clearing of the property, and shoring up of the cliff with rip-rap was looking just as old man McElroy wanted it to. He was very pleased when he came to the sight. That made *Tommy very pleased,* so Gabriel was pleased.

Tom hired on a new operator named Sal Gonzalez, and he was to be the new Gabriel. It looked as if Gabe would be able to leave Dermont Excavating sooner than he thought and it was very exciting. Tommy just asked that he stick around enough to help get the project underway and help Sal along a bit. Gabriel was more than happy to do it.

But soon, they found there was more rock than they'd expected to find in the pond area, and it was beginning to slow them down as well. So as the contractors started building the Event Center, Gabe's crew was trying to move along with the valley part of the project now, but it was not on schedule. Gabe felt like he was getting an ulcer over it, and couldn't see leaving until it was back on track.

Each weekend, he and Sarah would plan more of their wedding. The excitement that they were planning their lives together mounted each time they talked. It was so thrilling to be so certain of a love like theirs. Their bond was growing stronger each day, and Sarah's calm approach to the whole thing helped him to relax.

Tommy finally just made Gabe set an end date. "It's not like I'm kicking you out dude, but stop feeling like you gotta hold my hand. Sal is gonna do great and with all this rock we are hitting, we might need to redesign and negotiate some changes. You can't be held up here forever. Just go man. I love ya, but go."

Hanging his head, kicking rocks with his boot, Gabriel decided he was probably right.

"Ok. Next week then. That's my last week."

He looked up at Tommy then, who was smiling a half smile. "Ok."

He told the news to Sarah. She was just as excited to start their life together as he was. He couldn't believe he only had one week left.

That weekend Sarah and Maggie went to buy table linens, place settings, and center pieces. Things were really coming together for their wedding.

On Monday morning, Gabe was more than ready to get his last week of work started. Today they were going to tackle some changes to the Country Club project pond area.

A small storm was predicted, but being March, it was to be expected, and they knew delays would happen. They weren't overly concerned. The meteorologists estimated an inch of rain over the east Bay Area overnight. That was nothing for Oklahoma, but here if the rain hit they would cut out for the day.

Daryl, the playboy transport driver, called in sick that day. Gabriel and Tommy assumed Daryl figured they'd be cutting out early anyway and was probably using it as a day to screw off. Either way, it meant they were down a driver and Gabriel was going to have to drive the Peterbilt transport over to the job site and haul the excavator. Slightly inconvenient, but Gabe actually kind of missed driving the big trucks so it wasn't that big of a deal.

Hoping into the Peterbilt 379, Gabe felt at home. The worn leather seat was comfortable and as he brought the engine to life, it roared like a tiger as he throttled it up. The sky was cloudy on the drive over from the yard but they all arrived and worked for a few hours without a single drop hitting the ground.

When the crew broke for lunch Gabriel said they should just call it a day and start loading the equipment because the first of the rain was beginning to fall and he didn't want to be stuck loading in a down pour if the sky opened up.

"Hey Sal."

"Yeah, man what's up?"

"Hey you've got skills dude. Tommy won't miss me a bit."

Sal had been running the Kubota backhoe until today, when he ran the excavator all morning before the rain hit. Gabe was impressed. Sal had proven to be an excellent operator that worked well with the crew and Gabe was grateful Tommy was going to have a fully manned crew ready to go when he left.

The backhoe was loaded up behind the Kenworth that Barry drove, and their labor crew drove out in the two utility trucks. Gabriel brought up the rear hauling his 320F L Cat Excavator. They were going to actually get a half day off and this time it didn't even stress him out.

Even with the rain's delay, they were running ok on time. Old man McElroy was happy and the Grand Opening for the event center promised to be a fun event. Maybe he and Sarah could come down for it. Driving onto Interstate 680, Gabriel was beaming, even with the heavy sky looming around him.

The freeway was darkening to a silvery river with a moderate amount of traffic. It appeared to be dusk even though it was only one o'clock in the afternoon. The heaviest traffic wouldn't hit for two more hours. He'd made a good call in leaving when they did. When Bruce Springsteen came on the radio, he sang out just like his dad and uncles did.

Suddenly a white Mercedes blew by him and weaved between him and the car in front of Gabe, cutting him off.

"What an asshole." Gabe said out loud to nobody.

They were in the far right lane when the car pulled back into the middle lane and blew by several more cars at a high rate of speed, disappearing into the haze of the rainy day.

"Idiot."

He had five miles to go to his exit and back to the yard where he hoped Diane had a hot pot of coffee on. It might have bothered some people that Tommy was so quick to replace him, but Gabe was just happy to not have to feel guilty for leaving Tommy hanging. It was only right that Dermont Excavating keep moving forward without him now. He had Lake County and Sarah to look forward to anyway.

Sheets of rain pummeled his windshield all at once and Gabriel had to put the wipers on high. The glowing of headlights reflected off the pavement, sending halos of fragmented light all around. He had to strain to see.

Then it was only red lights. Break lights. Lots and lots of taillights breaking everywhere.

A semi-tractor hauling equipment cannot stop on a dime. He put on his breaks while looking for where he could go to avoid running into, or over any cars. The trailer started to jackknife but Gabe pulled it out just before coming to a halt on the shoulder of Interstate 680 south.

His heart racing and palms sweating, Gabriel's eyes were wildly looking out his windshield through the streaming rain. The wipers thud, thud, thudded fast across the glass. He could see a jumbled mess of taillights and they were not going anywhere. Looking out, he realized he'd just missed a silver car that was just beside him. Had he not gotten off the road, he'd have driven right over the car. He then realized there was an accident just ahead.

He reached for his radio and called into the office.

"Diane. Diane this is Transport 1, can you hear me? Listen I'm a few miles from the yard and there's a big accident on 1680. I'm ok but I'm gonna go see if I can help."

"Ok, I'll call it in and I will let Tommy know. Be careful Gabe," Diane said.

Gabriel turned off the engine and opened his door. He was immediately soaked upon hitting his boots to the pavement. It looked like several cars had skidded to avoid the accident ahead but most of the cars near his rig were not involved, only stopped.

He tapped on the driver's window of the silver car just beside him. A woman, visibly shaken, rolled her window down.

"Are you alright?" Gabe asked.

The woman nodded her head yes and gave a weak smile. He looked around her and pointed to the clearing in front of his truck that she could easily pull over to.

"Pull over and wait there. It will be safer on the shoulder."

She nodded and started to roll her window up. Gabriel turned away from her window and was blinded by the headlights of an oncoming car. He jumped towards the shoulder and his rig, in the hopes of making it onto the skids of the Peterbilt and away from the impact, but there was little time. On the wet pavement where the gray from the road met the gray of the sky, a driver slammed on their brakes to avoid the silver gray of a car and didn't even see the man standing next to it. Gabriel was hit on his right side and thrown under the semi. His last thoughts were of Shelly, of Sarah, and how much he loved them both.

The wedding plans were going smoothly and basically there was nothing left to do until the week of the event itself. They still would need to buy the food and with Michelle and Caleb's help, and some of Jimmy's fire department friends smoking and cooking the meat, they had everything under control.

Sarah's father Don was very excited to be hosting their wedding and kept saying how her mother Jane would have loved it as well. The perfect backyard lawn under the canopy of walnut trees in the orchard, and her mother's cottage roses and beautiful climbers on the arched trellis, would be the perfect back drop to her ceremony where she would vow to love, honor, and cherish Gabriel the rest of their days.

While she was daydreaming of the wedding and how handsome Gabriel was going to look in his tux, standing at the altar, watching her walk up the aisle, her cell phone rang. She was in the store room at the winery, sorting the Wine Club of the Month bottles for pick up.

"Hello?"

"Sarah? This is Tommy Dermont. Listen, there's been an accident."

The air left her lungs and she sat down on a case of wine before she fell down. Her head was spinning and she couldn't hear correctly anymore. There was a slow motion about the room and a panic rose within her chest. There was only one reason for Tommy to call and say that. It was Gabriel, and it was bad.

"You there, Sarah?" he asked.

"Yes...What's happened to Gabriel?"

There was silence on the other end for what seemed like an eternity, but she wasn't sure she wanted to hear what he was about to say anyway. She hoped the silence would erase the truth and when Tommy finally spoke, it would be something as simple as Gabe lost his phone, or Gwen and I cannot make it to the wedding. But she knew better.

"It's Gabriel. Sarah, he's in the hospital. They had to fly him to UC Davis. There was an accident."

"What kind of accident?" she heard someone that sounded like her ask.

"There was an accident on the freeway on the way back to the yard and Gabe was hauling the excavator. He didn't get involved in the accident while driving. He stopped to help and was hit by a car."

Again the silence. She didn't know what to do. Her mind was racing but she couldn't form a definitive sentence. The only thing she wanted to know came out of her mouth.

"Is he alive?"

"Yes. But he's in a coma. It's medically induced because of the trauma. It's better that way. That's what they told me and only because I lied and said I was his brother. I'm on my way there now. If you want to head that way, I can meet you at the hospital."

It was nearly 4:00 in the afternoon and she was about to leave for the day anyway. Could she meet Tommy? Of course. How would she get there? Drive stupid. She was split into two parts. The conscious and subconscious Sarah were battling within her head with one advising the other.

"Um... yeah, I will be there. Where do I go?" she asked calm as you please on the outside but freaking out on the inside.

"Truly, I don't know. They were going to prep him for surgery when I called. I'd imagine just the Emergency Room area and ask from there. I'm sorry I don't know more," he said.

"Yeah, ok. I will just see you there."

"Sarah? Are you ok to drive? I mean, Gabriel wouldn't want you to drive over by yourself. You are everything to him. Be safe."

She took that into account then realized Tommy spoke as if Gabriel would have something to say about this. That he'd wake up and scold her for driving alone. That gave her the strength and hope she needed.

"Yes. I can do it. I will see you there."

"Sarah, wait. One of us should call his parents."

"Yes, definitely. Tommy, do you have their phone number? I just realized I don't have their number on me."

"I do, it is on his employee paperwork. I will do it."

"Thank you, I'm leaving work now."

Tommy agreed. "Sure. I will see you soon. Drive safe."

Hanging up, Sarah sat there on the box in the storage room of the winery. She could feel the beating of her heart hitting the wall of her chest and pounding in her temples. This was NOT happening again. A stupid, freakin' car accident would NOT take the man she loved once more. What kind of God would have her endure that kind of punishment? Surely she'd done something to piss off the Universe in her past life to deserve this kind of punishment.

She stood and found her legs to be sturdier than she'd imagined. She walked out of the storage room and found Michelle to tell her what was happening.

"Oh my God, Sarah. Do you want me to go over with you? I don't mind and I could even drive."

"No, I am fine. I can handle it. I just need to tell my dad. But I'm leaving so can you please tell the others. I will call you later."

She hugged her and went to grab her purse from the main office and flew out the over sized, double doors of the winery and to her red Honda parked a half block away on Main Street, Kelseyville. She just refused to believe Gabriel would be taken from her and that gave her the strength she needed to push through.

When she told her dad what was happening over the phone, he insisted she stop by his house to pick him up so he could drive them both over. Sarah declined.

"Dad, I'm already past Clearlake and headed out Hwy 20 so I will just call when I get there. I'm fine to drive, but can you please call Maggie for me, and Joe too? I will let you all know more as soon as I hear what his condition is. And Daddy?"

"Yes baby…anything."

"Please pray," she said starting to cry. "Please pray with all your heart."

"I've already started honey."

~

The white light of the headlights was the last thing Gabe remembered before finding himself walking down a country dirt road. The smell of moist soil filled his nose and the dewy mist from the recent rains played tricks with his vision. He was walking alone but strolling up the road towards him was a figure he couldn't quite make out. The beautiful oak, pine, and ash trees lined both sides of the one lane, dirt road and as the light filtered through the leaves, it danced across the water droplets that still hung onto the branches.

As the person drew nearer, Gabriel recognized the man with the big smile and kind eyes. It was Max, the bartender-contractor. For whatever reason, Max seemed like he was expecting to see Gabe. The two met right in the middle of the road and shook hands.

"It's good to see you, Max. I wondered what became of you. You must have been really busy lately huh?" Gabriel laughed.

"Yes, very busy. I hear you too have been quite the busy guy. Planning a wedding, driving back and forth every week from the city to see Sarah, and now this huge task before you, it all sounds like quite a lot."

The two turned together and walked in the same direction Gabriel had been headed, Max walking slowly with him step for step. Gabriel looked up through the trees and couldn't believe how beautiful a day it was. Even through the mist, the colors of the trees and plants were so vivid green and he thought he'd never seen a sky so blue.

"Yeah, that job with the country club is finally going to come to an end and I will be free to move. I can't wait."

"I wasn't exactly talking about the job with Dermont Excavating, as the huge task before you. I was talking about fighting for your life."

Gabe stopped walking. He shook his head in confusion but Max just kept looking at him with those kind eyes. What did he miss? What was Max talking about?

"I don't understand. Why am I fighting for my life?"

"It was really nice of you to check on that woman on the freeway, Gabriel. I just wish you would have waited in your truck," Max said.

Suddenly the whole incident flashed before Gabriel again and he remembered. He remembered bits and pieces but he realized with horror, what Max was suggesting. Gabriel remembered waking up under the semi to voices yelling and asking if he could hear them. He remembered lying in the rain soaked road as they strapped him on a board. He vaguely remembered the feeling of being lifted and the loud sound of the rotors. Then he just remembered walking down the road and meeting Max.

"What the hell is going on Max? I'm alive. I'm here right now aren't I? But…" Gabriel then realized he didn't know where *here was*.

"Listen, the choice is yours. It's never easy, but you have to choose. You are one of the lucky ones, not everyone is given a choice. Either way, I know you will do the right thing," Max said.

Max nodded his head towards the mist, down the road ahead of them. Gabriel turned to see what he was looking at. Again, in the foggy air a figure was walking towards them. This time, the person was much smaller and Gabriel strained to see who it was.

"You are a good guy, Gabriel. I hope you are strong enough to make the right choice," Max said.

"What choice?" When Gabriel turned to look back at Max, he was gone. Completely confused, Gabriel turned to look back down the road and he saw Shelly walking towards him. She was more radiant then ever and smiling at him just as Max did, all knowing and relaxed. Her hair was flowing and hung long around her shoulders. Gabriel's heart ached at the sight of her.

"My God, Shelly, what's happening?" he pleaded.

"You are being given a choice, Gabriel. For whatever reason, you have the choice to stay or …or not," she said.

"Am I dead Shel? How is this even possible?"

He reached out to grab her hands. She took both of his in hers and Gabriel felt the warmth of her touch. The familiar connection they had with each other wasn't gone, but his heart ached just the same. The thought of leaving Sarah behind and putting her through such pain nearly broke him in two.

"You are not dead, Gabriel. You are just stuck. You have a choice. You can continue to walk in the same direction and the love and beauty you feel here only grows stronger. If you turn around..." she turned him by the shoulders to look behind him in the opposite direction, "you will go back to the life you were living. It will be difficult, trying and sometimes very messy, but it will be your life."

What Gabriel saw in the opposite direction down the road was a view into a hospital room of himself. He lay waiting on a bed with tubes coming out of him everywhere and beeping monitors hooked up to him beeping. He was banged up pretty good but he was alive.

"Shelly, if I go back—will I just be a burden to Sarah, and my family? I don't know what to do." He said spinning around to look back down the beautiful road.

"Only you have the answer, Gabriel. Just know, whatever you choose, I love you."

Then she vanished and left Gabriel standing in the middle of the dirt road.

"SHELLY!" He yelled.

When it was clear he was on his own to decide, Gabriel dropped down in the middle of that road, collapsed with grief and turmoil, uncertain of which to choose. Then he did what his mother always told him to do when he was unsure, scared, or lost. He prayed.

❧

In a foggy dream, Sarah made it to the UC Davis parking lot without really recalling how she'd made it there. She decided it was better to not even think about how she'd made the two hour drive in her mental state and instead, focused on finding the Emergency Room.

Looking around, she wasn't sure where to start. The place was large and had two counters, three corridors that led away from the waiting area, and she wasn't sure if she even came to the right place. She decided to just start with the closest counter and begin asking questions.

"Excuse me ma'am? I am looking for where they bring patients that have had to be flown in. My fiancé was airlifted to the hospital and I'm not sure where to look."

"Can I have his name please?" the woman behind the glass window asked.

"Gabriel Hart. He was flown in somewhere around two o'clock today from the Bay Area. Please, I don't know where to go," she pleaded, her voice shaking.

The woman behind the counter picked up a phone as she was looking at her computer monitor. Her hands clicking across the keyboard, as she looked down through her glasses at the screen. Sarah felt as if she might vomit. Up until she arrived and had to actually face what was coming, she didn't even think it was real. Now that she stood in front of the woman who would lead her to Gabriel, it was all very much real and terrifying.

"Yes, it's Natasha. I'm calling about the patient, Gabriel Hart, that arrived at 1430 via air ambulance. His fiancé is inquiring."

There was a long pause and Sarah thought she might start screaming. She wanted to be with him, find him and crawl into the bed with him...INSTEAD OF HIM. She wanted him to look into her eyes and tell her it was all ok. She wanted him to just take her home and away from the damn hospital. She hated hospitals. *And now her Gabriel was in a damn hospital.* She could feel herself starting to lose it when the woman hung up the phone and looked up at her.

"He's in surgery. Go up to the third floor and follow the signs to Surgery and Emergency Services. Check in with the desk clerk, she will make sure the doctors know you are in the Family Waiting Room. His brother is already there waiting."

Pressing the up button on the wall, the dreaded waiting began.

Sarah knew far too well of the waiting. The waiting for news from the doctors, the waiting to have her husband's body transported back to Lake County, the waiting for his service to be over, so she could wait alone forever wondering if he ever truly loved her. She never did get an answer to that painful question. Only Gabriel made her life make sense again. Only Gabriel made her feel like she was alive again. If she lost him too, Sarah didn't know if she would have the strength to go on.

As the doors opened on the third floor, Sarah came face to face with Tommy Dermont. Tommy pulled Sarah into an awkward, if not obligatory hug to try and comfort her. It didn't work.

"Sarah, I'm so glad you made it. We can go to the Family Waiting room over here," he motioned as he steered her with an arm around her back and they walked in the direction of a long corridor.

The anxiety built again inside of her, like a bubbling fire that branched out through her torso and limbs. Her mind was beginning to have racing thoughts again and the urge to scream sat just below her throat, lingering in her chest wall. Sarah's eyes became wild and she pulled away from Tommy, unable to continue this trance-like walk to the *God damned Family Waiting Room.*

"No." she said louder than she intended to speak.

Tommy looked at her alarmed and clearly didn't know what to do. He looked around the nursing area with an uncomfortable, apologetic look. The two nurses at the desk snapped their heads up to see what was happening in their otherwise quiet space.

"I'm sorry," she continued, running her hand through her hair, "but I'm not ready to go into that room until I get some answers. I have to know the extent of his injuries. I need to know what to hope for. I need to know if Gabriel is going to die or not. Somebody has to know SOMETHING."

A woman came out from behind the desk and approached both Sarah and Tommy with a sympathetic look on her face. She was short in stature, large in girth, mid 50's, and had her reddish colored hair pulled back into a bun. She extended a hand to Sarah to shake and put her other hand over Sarah's, holding Sarah's one hand in both of hers.

"I'm Valerie, the lead nurse for staffing in our Surgery and Emergency Services Department. Let's step into our conference room for a moment and maybe I can help."

Sarah knew the woman just didn't want her to make a scene right there in front of all the other patients and families waiting. Truth was, Sarah didn't want to make a scene either and she felt immediately embarrassed but somewhat relieved the woman would be able to give her and Tommy some answers. Tommy also looked relieved that this Valerie stepped in. The three walked over to the room she offered.

With Tommy and Sarah securely inside, Valerie softly closed the door behind them. It was an all white room, with cream colored, over-stuffed chairs, white tile floors, and a few end tables in white painted oak. The only art work on the walls, were pictures of hands, reaching out and light shining behind them, as if God were reaching towards the people in the room. Sarah wondered if he were really there with her or just mocking her. It was becoming difficult for her to not become angry with Him at this point.

"Please, take a seat," Valerie motioned to the chairs on the side wall. She took a chair closest to Sarah, and Tommy sat on Sarah's other side, waiting just as anxiously for what Valerie would tell them.

"I understand your frustration in needing answers so I will try my best to fill you in with what we know now. Gabriel was flown here after sustaining serious injuries. The good news is that the medic crew said he was semi-conscious for a few minutes on the scene but that he had a lot of pain so they gave him medicine for the pain and that's why he lost consciousness. He has a fractured shoulder, some broken ribs, and a punctured lung. The most serious thing that they will be monitoring is swelling on the brain. He took quite a blow hitting the pavement.

They will want to make sure he doesn't develop hypoxia. His spine is fully intact without fracture and he was moving his limbs on his own so there doesn't appear to be any paralysis. He went into surgery for his lung and they are going to make sure there isn't any other internal bleeding. He is young. He is strong. We just have to hold tight. If you are praying folks, that's all we can do for him right now."

The woman patted Sarah's knee and gave a half smile, half pleading look to them both, obviously hoping she'd gotten through to them. Tommy spoke while Sarah was still processing.

"So he didn't ever code or anything? He never had to be resuscitated?" Tommy pressed.

"Not to my knowledge, sir. No."

"Well that's a relief. How long should he be in surgery then? To repair the lung?" Tommy asked.

"I'm really not sure on that. It all depends on what they find when they get in there. He took a hard blow and they need to be certain there isn't any other bleeding. I really don't want to speculate. We can give you updates though as we hear from the surgery room."

"Thank you, Valerie. We appreciate you talking with us. Should we stay here or wait down the hall for more information?" Tommy said while looking at Sarah, in case she had something to say.

She couldn't say a word. Sarah was still absorbing and somewhat frozen. She was looking at the floor now, wringing her hands in her lap. She felt herself going numb in shock.

"Ma'am, do you have any questions for me? Do you understand all I have told you?" Valerie asked Sarah.

She looked up at Valerie with a blank stare and just nodded her head in acknowledgement. Yes, she heard. She comprehended the conversation. Sarah just didn't understand why she was going through this all again. What she wanted Valerie couldn't give. Sarah wanted a guarantee. A guarantee that her Gabriel would be just fine and walk out of here with her to go home together forever.

"Ok, well you two can stay here a few minutes after I leave and when you feel ready, make your way down the hall to the Family Waiting Room so we can keep you updated on Gabriel's progress."

She stood and walked to the door. Before leaving she gave them both one last sympathetic look, nodded, and then walked out, closing the door behind her.

"He's going to be ok, Sarah. I just know it now. He is too strong to not come through this. I know it. You just have to believe it, too," Tommy said reaching to hold her hands that she was vigorously wringing in her lap.

Looking up at him with tears spilling over the rims of her eyes, Sarah nodded without words. She wanted to agree. She wanted to feel certain. She wasn't.

Tommy reached over and hugged Sarah, whether she wanted him to or not. He obviously needed reassuring himself and she felt badly she couldn't give him any. God had let her down so much before and she was afraid to allow faith to pull her through now. She'd lost her mother, lost her baby, lost her husband, and almost lost her father. She was reluctant to ask Him to allow her to keep Gabriel. What comfort could she be to Tommy if she had little faith herself.

Before she knew it, they were both crying and soon Tommy stood, trying to collect himself and put on the brave face for Sarah. She knew it, so she did the same. They needed to walk down to the Family Waiting Room for updates on Gabriel anyway and blubbering wasn't going to get them anywhere.

By the time they both settled into the new room, Sarah realized it was closing in on eight pm and she needed coffee. She also needed to take a walk. She offered to bring Tommy back some coffee. He started to say he'd accompany her but she waved him off. He luckily took the hint she needed time alone to process and mill over what might be coming. Agreeing to a coffee… black, he let her go without any arguing. Sarah put a thankful hand upon his shoulder before heading away to the elevator.

Alone on the ride down, Sarah realized it wasn't the cafeteria she was headed to. First, she needed to go to the hospital's chapel. It was on the second floor and when she arrived she was alone there. Nobody else to mourn, pray, or beg to God, took up any space in the little five row chapel. Stumbling to the front row, kneeling before the stained glass window and Christ hanging just in front of it, Sarah began to sob. Her shoulders shook up and down in a silent convulsion of pain.

"PLEASE." She begged. "I don't know what you want of me. Please God, heal Gabriel and bring him back to who he once was. Don't take him from me, please. I'm begging you, God. I'll do anything. I'd rather you take me, God. Take me instead. Just don't leave me here without Gabriel. Please don't put me through this pain again. I just can't bare it. I don't want to live without him."

She cried until she was spent and the suffering she felt dried up her conscious emotions to the point she felt like an empty shell. All she could do now was hope God heard her and wait. Wait once more.

It took a while, but eventually she felt ready to leave the little chapel. She stopped in a bathroom to wash the dried tears from her face and purposefully avoided looking in a mirror. She knew it would be terrible and didn't need one more thing to worry about. At the cafeteria she bought two large coffees and took them back to the Family Waiting Room where Tommy eagerly took his cup from her. There still was no news. She went to the window to stare out at the darkness. Just as she was checking out emotionally the elevator doors opened up and a woman stepped out looking a bit lost. It was Maggie. They locked eyes and Sarah stood frozen in place while Maggie nearly ran to her and threw her arms around her little sister, giving her the strength she needed so desperately.

As they stood in the hallway, a serious looking man in scrubs came into the room. Tommy stood and Maggie grabbed Sarah around the waist and Sarah felt instantly grateful for it. She was feeling much weaker than she'd ever admit and having Maggie with her allowed her that honesty inside, even if she wouldn't tell a soul. The whole world was upon her shoulders right now and she needed every bit of support she could get. She wanted her mother. She needed her strength. And just as the man was about to speak, Sarah silently asked her mother to be with her to help her bear the news she was about to receive.

"Are you Sarah, Gabriel Hart's fiancée?"

"Yes," she managed.

"I have news from the operating room."

She simply nodded. There wasn't much else she could muster. Speaking was becoming more and more difficult. Whatever the man had to tell her she was not given the privilege of being ready or not. He'd tell her regardless. She began to shake and felt her knees give out from underneath her and she stumbled into her sister. Maggie and Tommy both lunged to grab her and help her to stand. Before Sarah knew what was happening, the man in scrubs was motioning for another nurse to bring a wheelchair. She was seated in it and without news about Gabriel, Sarah was taken down the hall to an exam room with Maggie and Tommy right behind her.

She just wanted Gabriel. It was the last thing she thought of as she fainted and slumped into the side of that cold wheelchair without even hearing the condition of the man she loved, who was fighting for his life in a room right down the hall.

⁜

The soft sound of constant beeping filled Gabriel's ears with a familiar rhythm as he woke from the dream. At first he couldn't open his eyes. Maybe he was still dreaming. One eye, then the other opened slowly with the weight of steel gates.

As his vision began to focus he realized he was in the hospital. He was intubated and unable to speak, with a tube down his throat. He felt himself start to panic and beeping on the monitor got faster. A nurse appeared at his side and quickly tried to calm him.

"Relax. Please don't try to talk. I will have this thing removed in a moment. Just let me call the doctor. Don't move just yet."

He laid his head back against the pillow again and tried to look around. Tubes from everywhere. He hadn't dreamed it at all. It was real. But he could move. He could think clearly...or maybe clearly. He tried to wiggle his toes. They worked, that was good. He tried to move his arms but it was so painful he felt a stabbing throughout his shoulder and ribcage that shot straight threw him. Not good. Then Gabriel looked down to see his entire torso was bandaged and he couldn't bare to look anymore. Instead, he lay there and just tried to wiggle his fingertips. They all moved too.

A tall man with silver hair walked in wearing green scrubs. Gabe had about a million questions he needed answered but couldn't talk with the damn tube down his throat. He was starting to feel like coughing but suppressed the sensation the best he could.

"Hello. I'm Doctor Warner. You were in an accident, Gabriel, but I think you will recover just fine. I'm going to remove the tube we have in you that was to help you breathe during surgery. You will feel a slightly uncomfortable tug but then it should just leave you with a slightly sore throat."

The nurse and doctor had the tube removed in a few minutes and Gabriel began to cough. It hurt so much in his chest that he tried to stop the spasm immediately. Taking a deep breath was far too painful as well. His eyes were large, with a questioning look of, *what the HELL is wrong with me*, addressed to his doctor.

"You have some broken ribs and we had to repair a punctured lung. There is a tube for air to escape the chest wall we need to leave in another day but I am pleased with the way the procedure went. Yes, you will be fairly sore for a few weeks but after that, each day should be better than the one before. We didn't find any other internal bleeding. You are a lucky man, Mr. Hart. Other than that, you have a pretty severe concussion that we will be monitoring and it might leave you feeling dizzy, nauseated, or a bit disoriented."

He said these things to Gabriel as he was shining a light across his eyes. The nurse was preparing something in a syringe to put into his IV. Gabriel watched them still unable to form any words, but he saw how the doctor was recording some things on a clipboard. The tall man looked at a tape coming out of a machine next to the bed, and then suddenly, a blood pressure cuff began to automatically inflate around his arm. He jumped, a bit startled, not knowing it was even on his arm.

"No worries, Mr. Hart," the nurse said. "It will automatically take a reading of your blood pressure every half hour then we will adjust it to every hour. You are just waking up so we need to check all your vitals... It's a little high, but that's to be expected for now. Once your pain is managed it will come back down."

She injected something into the IV and nodded to the doctor, then left the room with the door open.

"Nurse Gates just gave you some morphine. It will help with the pain. You should be able to talk, but try whispering first. Can I answer any questions?"

"Am I going to be Ok?" Gabriel managed in a gravely whisper.

"As far as I can see, yes. You will remain here in our post-op ICU area today but if all goes well, we can move you to the main floor tomorrow or maybe the next day. It all depends on how you fair throughout the first 24 hours. You were brought in yesterday afternoon and were in surgery until nearly midnight. It's almost seven a.m., now. You just need to rest for now, Gabriel. Anything else?"

He wanted to rub his eyes but one arm had the IV in it and felt so heavy, the other was wrapped and bandaged up. He looked at both of them then his chest area.

The doctor wrinkled his brow and acknowledged Gabriel's predicament. "I know. It looks pretty bad now and you must be uncomfortable, but you broke your shoulder on impact with the pavement. It was set in place but you won't be able to use it for a few weeks. Over all Gabriel, this will be at least a four week, maybe up to eight week recovery process if there are no complications. I'm afraid you will need help when you go home to convalesce."

Then Gabriel's heart jumped and he wanted to fly up out of his bed, but the pain shot again right threw him and he lay against the pillows once more. The doctor put a hand on his forehead.

"Easy there. What is it?"

"SARAH. I need to tell Sarah," he said wincing at the pain.

The doctor laughed. "You don't have to worry about that. She and your brother, Tommy, and a woman named Maggie have been here all night. We just had to get you through recovery before we could allow any visitors. They've been informed of your condition and are eagerly waiting to see you. I will let the nurse's station know it's ok for a few *short visits*. *Short* being the operative word, Gabriel. You need your rest. Understood?"

Gabriel nodded and a small smile crept onto his face. He closed his eyes and exhaled a sigh of relief.

God gave him yet *another chance* when it seemed he'd lost everything. He'd made the right choice. He had a life with Sarah waiting for him. He still didn't know if seeing Shelly was part of the concussion, part of an anesthesia dream, or if he'd seen a glimpse of Heaven. He didn't know if Max was part of that dream or if he was a spirit, guiding him along. Either way, Gabriel was grateful. He'd suffer through the pain of this recovery with gratitude, knowing he had a life he always dreamed of just waiting there for him to embrace.

The morphine took over and healing warmth washed through his body. Gabriel trusted that it was all going to be alright, and he fell fast asleep, smile on his face.

∾

In the dark places of her mind, Sarah had gone where she hoped to never go again, and that was where she almost lost her faith entirely. She'd promised God, that if he brought Gabriel back to her that she'd stop being angry with him for the loss of her mother, the loss of her child, and the loss of her husband. She would just be grateful for who she still had in her life and for bringing her Gabriel and giving her that second chance of a happy life. Now it seemed God followed through on her request and so much more. They were going to be able to go home together in a few days and shoulder sling or not, they'd be married in June as planned.

When the doctors allowed her to go in to see Gabriel, she tried to brace herself for the worst scene. After all, he was hit by a car. It would take all her control to not crawl into the bed beside him. But when she walked into the room, he had scratches across one side of his face, and his jaw was a bit swollen on the same side, but otherwise, he looked like Gabriel. The tubes and monitors, bandages across his torso and catheter bag were the worst part of seeing him. Then he opened his eyes and those electric blue beauties melted her heart. She started to tear up but a smile was plastered all across her face. He smiled back at her and she knew he'd be alright.

"Gabriel. Oh Gabriel, I am so glad to see you." She said standing at his bedside and moving strands of hair away from his eyes.

"Don't cry baby. I'm going to be alright," he said in a horse voice.

"I just didn't know…we weren't sure… Oh, I just wasn't going to believe it was true until I saw you for myself. I love you. God I was so scared." She said and kissed him gently on the cheek.

"I know. I'm so sorry you had to go through all this. But I promise you we are going to be fine and as soon as I get out of here, we are going to finish our wedding plans."

She laughed, and then she remembered to tell him about his parents.

"Gabriel, we called your family in Oklahoma. Your mom and dad took the first flight out today and should be here this afternoon. I reassured them that the doctors said you would be ok, but your mother insisted on coming and I can't say as I blame her. You are her baby boy and she nearly lost you once, so don't be mad we called, please."

He laughed a little then winced in pain. He shook his head to let her know he wasn't angry.

No worries. My poor mom will be shaken up until she sees me for herself, just like you. Anyway, you two will meet in the flesh now, only I just wish it were under better circumstances," he said.

There was a soft tapping on the door and standing in the doorway were both Tommy and Maggie, smiling and looking sheepish. They didn't want to intrude but couldn't wait any longer to see Gabe.

Sarah motioned them in and stepped aside. Tommy peered down at his friend and shook his head with a smile on his face and Maggie just stood there grinning too.

"You really know how to get all the attention don't you, Bro?" Tommy said. "I'm really glad you are going to be ok."

"Me too." Maggie said. "We've kinda grown accustomed to you being part of the family and you gave us all quite a scare."

"Hey, sorry you guys. Maybe if I hadn't taken off my reflective vest before driving back, the guy would have seen me. But I'm going to be alright. I'm hurting now, but that just means I'm alive and quite frankly, I'm glad I feel it. Much better than the alternative. Just don't make me laugh. It hurts like hell."

The nurse came back and broke up the party. She said Gabriel needed his sleep.

Sarah was reluctant to leave and the gang could see it so they all said their good-byes until later and the nurse gave her five more minutes alone with him.

"I don't know what I would have done if…" she began.

Gabriel squeezed her hand she offered him and shook his head.

"Don't. Don't do that. We are going to be fine. I'm not leaving you. I would fight like hell, you know that, right? I want this life together just as much as you do so let's not play the *what if game,* Ok? We have too much to look forward to."

She nodded and realized he was right. He couldn't reach to kiss her or lift his arms easily, so Sarah leaned over to kiss him as softly as possible on his lips. They were dry and cracked a bit but warm. She quietly said a prayer of gratitude that she was able to do that and it made her smile.

When she left, the nurse asked her to sign for his personal effects and handed her his wallet, a watch, and the Celtic knot necklace she'd given him for Christmas that was to protect him. Squeezing the pendant in her hand, she smiled and walked away.

Chapter Fifteen

Looking Forward

A FEW WEEKS LATER, Sarah went with Gabriel to his apartment to close it up and make the final move. Hi physical therapy was going well and he was getting stronger every day. He still had limited use of one arm, but the doctors were confident that would continue to heal and he would be good as new.

They were boxing his clothes when Gabriel came across something that gave him pause. He sat a minute and just stared in the drawer, then looked sheepishly at Sarah.

"I'm not quite sure what to do with these."

He almost looked apologetic at her, with large saddened eyes. But there they were. All his pictures of Shelly.

"May I?" she asked.

Gabriel handed Shelly's picture to Sarah. His hand moved slowly, almost apprehensively towards her.

"She was really pretty. I can see how you would be drawn to her," Sarah said with a small smile.

"She was. You are very pretty, Sarah. Beautiful. I really don't know what I'm supposed to do with these now though. I just…"

"You keep them, Gabriel. You box them up and keep them. Someday, you will want to look back on your life and Shelly was a part of that. I have no issues with you holding onto something that was a part of you. It won't get in the way of our future. She was important to you," she said as she handed the picture back to him. "You keep them."

After kissing him on the cheek and squeezing his arm, she gave him some time alone. She headed to the kitchen and left him standing there holding his past in his hands. She smiled to herself, fully understanding how that small gesture could give him peace because she too, had a past. They were each other's future now, and their past shouldn't give them cause to be sad. There was too much to look forward to.

After the donation truck left, they dropped off the keys with the apartment manager and made the drive back to Lake County before it was dark. The May evening was warm with the smells of tarweed and grass. The sun was setting as they turned onto the driveway, and the oaks were looming above them with their gray-green leaves swaying in the breeze. They were home.

They sat in the truck just looking at one another for a moment and smiling. This was it. They were never going to be apart again. This was going to be the first night of their *happily-ever-after*.

⁂

The next day they decided to knock out as much unpacking as possible. On Monday, Sarah would have to work and Gabriel had an interview lined up with Cal Fire as a dozer operator, thanks to some calls made, by Battalion Chief Hank Bauer. He'd already interviewed on the phone and this call back to meet in person was pretty hopeful.

Sarah started unpacking the kitchen boxes while Gabe worked in the bedroom. He decided to start taking Sarah's dresser drawers out of her dresser and put them on her bed to make it lighter for moving. They were going to put her dresser along another wall to make room for Gabriel's to come in.

Once he'd removed her drawers, he eyeballed the dresser itself.

It seemed pretty small so he went to the side and with his good arm, pulled it up and out, away from the wall. He did the same with the other side and figured he could make slow progress like this across the room. When he started to move the other side again, he saw a piece of paper behind the dresser.

Gabriel reached down and picked up the binder paper that was folded in threes. He opened it up to find a hand written letter. At first he wasn't sure he should read it but his eyes wouldn't let him stop. Though his mind knew it *should not* permit him to continue reading because a personal letter, not addressed to him, should be forbidden to read, and he knew he was breaching privacy, Gabriel continued to read the entire letter.

Dear Sarah,

I know you probably don't want to hear anything I have to say at this point and I don't blame you, but I feel what I have to say is important and hope you will continue reading this letter.

For starters, what happened between us wasn't your fault. I really should have been there for you and I wasn't. I was far too wrapped up in my own pain and didn't want to see yours or even deal with my own. It was just easier to bury it and for that I am sorry. Even though I'm sure you won't believe me, but the loss of our child was just as painful to me as it was to you. The thing is, you were always stronger than me. You wanting to adopt...that's just not me. Then you trying to find new ways to have another baby just scared me even more and I knew I couldn't go through that again, so I pushed you away. I wasn't brave enough to even try. Again, I am so very sorry.

The affair was not like you think. I didn't seek it out. She is nothing compared to you. Maybe there was just too much pain between us and I was looking for the first thing that made me feel good again. It's no excuse, but there it is. I told her it was over. You need to know that. Not that I expect you to forgive me or for us to patch it all up. It's just something I thought you would want to know

I have a job out of town but when I get back, I hope we can at least talk. After all, we have a lot of history together. Years of loving you are not going to just fade away. Even if we decide to split for good, I want you to know that you have been the love of my life. I feel like I have taken every dream you have ever had and torn them to pieces, and for that I will never forgive myself. All I can say is, I hope you know that although I have shown it poorly, I have loved you, still love you, and will always love you, and I am sorry for all the hurt I have caused you.

Forever,

Max

"What's that?" Sarah asked.

Gabriel visibly jumped and his wild eyes flew up to meet hers. She gave him a quizzical look and then started to walk over to him. Instinctively, Gabe drew the letter up towards his chest to shield her from seeing. He didn't even know what to think. His mind was spinning from what he'd just read and he knew he had to show her.

"Um…Sarah? I found something behind your dresser, and I don't think you have ever seen it."

Gabriel handed her the letter and as she sat on the bed reading it, he stood up before her and watched as her eyes flew across the page, tears welling up, and one hand went trembling up to her throat as she read.

When she finished she looked up at Gabriel with confusion.

"Where did you find this?" she whispered.

"It was just here," he pointed behind the dresser. "It must have fallen back there and you never found it. He must have written it before he left and it slipped behind the dresser."

He kneeled in front of her, taking her hands in his. Kissing her fingers, Gabriel tried to comfort Sarah and he smiled up at her. Silent tears fell on her cheeks.

"I told you Sarah, that there was no way any man could not love you. And Max loved you. He…"

Gabriel stopped mid sentence and looked up at Sarah. He suddenly felt like pieces of a puzzle he didn't know he was supposed to solve were coming into place. He slowly stood and walked over to the window and looked outside.

"What is it Gabriel?"

"Max…He's…He was your husband."

"Yes."

"Um…Can I see a picture of him? I mean…I'm just curious now and need to put a face to the name. That's all."

"Just there," Sarah pointed to the hope chest below the window.

Gabriel opened up the chest and pulled out a wedding album. Inside, standing next to Sarah was Max, the bartender with the kind eyes and deep dimples. It was him. But how could that be? Gabriel's head was spinning and his mind was feeling like it was too full. Then he remembered the dream, after the accident. Max was the first person he saw before talking with Shelly. It was Max that had led him to Sarah all along.

It was Gabriel's turn to need to sit down. He gently put the album back into the chest and closed the lid to sit down on it and try to make sense of it all. He was staring at the floor, not really seeing it, but remembering the things Max had said. Suddenly, Sarah was standing next to him.

"Thank you," she said.

"Huh?"

"I said thank you. For finding this and showing it to me, thank you. I guess I needed to know and now I do. Max was a good man. We had our problems, but he did love me. I really needed to know that so I could forgive him and move on. Now that part of him I carry with me can make me happy instead of sad."

She wiped tears away from her eyes and put on a true smile. Gabriel gathered her up in his arms and held her. She rested her head against his chest and he stood swaying her gently back and forth. This was the strangest, yet most wonderful thing he'd ever experienced.

❦

It was finally June. At her parent's house the decorations were being brought in. A full white tent outside with a prefab dance floor made of engineered wood was set up along side of the lawn area. At the end of the lawn, the white arbor had her mother's antique roses climbing from both sides in pale shades of pink and white. Chairs with white ribbons were on either side of the white runner, facing the arbor, which would serve as the altar where Sarah and Gabriel would say their vows. Michelle and Caleb brought in loads of large potted plants and flowers to put all around the backyard deck, and Jimmy and his guys set up some white pop up awnings along the BBQ area and picnic tables for the food. Sarah smiled and thought it looked more than beautiful. It was perfect.

Their lives were turning out just as they planned it. Sarah was to continue working at the winery and Gabriel was cleared for work, starting with Cal Fire right after their honeymoon. When they saved up enough money, they talked about maybe giving Sarah's dream of running a B&B a shot. It was fun to talk about anyway.

As they planned, their wedding would only have around 50 guests coming, and it was to be a simple, country wedding at the home where Sarah's mother last cooked, gardened, lived, and loved. Her father was thrilled and both Joe and Maggie came home early, along with her husband and kids, to help with the preparations.

Once again, Don had a full house and it filled his heart with pride and happiness. Anyone could see it.

The rehearsal dinner was at a Chinese restaurant called Happy Garden, in Clearlake Oaks. Both families came together and along with Gabriel's parents, his Uncle Mac and Aunt Fiona flew out for the occasion.

When the banquet room they'd reserved was in full on party mode with loud voices and second rounds of drinks being ordered, Don pulled both Gabriel and Sarah aside.

"Sarah honey, I wanted you to have something from your mother and me."

Gabriel and Sarah gave each other a look.

"But Daddy, I don't understand."

Her father pulled out a small box from his jacket pocket. It was a ring box in black velvet that she recognized immediately. Her hands flew to her mouth and tears started to form in her eyes upon seeing it.

"My mother, your grandmother Ilsa McKinney, was given this ring by my father, Joseph McKinney. He gave it to her as a promise he'd come back and marry her after the war. You know this story, Sarah," he said opening it and handing it to Sarah.

Sarah started to laugh through her tears.

"Yes. I do. Then Grandma McKinney gave it to you when you fell in love with Mom and you gave it to her as a promise ring. Mom wore this every day. Even after you were married, she wore it on her right hand."

The ring was a round ruby surrounded by diamond chips in a platinum setting. It was old and quite elegant. They all stood staring at the ring. So many memories came to Sarah looking at this ring.

"I want you to not only wear this at your wedding, but I think after all you have been through, your mother would agree that you should keep it. I think Janie would like that. Besides, you two will keep your promises to each other, just as your grandparents did, and my Janie and I did. Love is a difficult road. The journey rises and falls countless times, but the fire between two who truly love can withstand it all. And for two who have been burned by life's tragedies in love, you have both risen from the ashes and found love once again. Cheers." Don said holding up his glass of wine.

Shaking as he put it on her finger, Sarah couldn't help but wish her mother were there. But now, she would look at the ring every day and see her, as well as Grandma McKinney.

Gabriel grabbed both his and Sarah's glasses from the table, handing hers to her once the ring was on her hand, and the three toasted, misty eyed and laughing.

She looked around the room, then at Gabriel. One year ago, Sarah had thought her world had ended. She never imagined she could be in the place she was today. She never imagined she'd be able to trust, or love again. She had felt damaged and empty inside, until the day this wonderful man walked into her life. Because of him, she felt stronger, happier, and more confident than she'd ever felt. He brought her back to herself, while loving her like no one ever had.

Together, they would face life's challenges. They knew how to lean on each other for strength. And she knew, they'd embrace every bit of joy that came their way.

The End

ACKNOWLEDGEMENTS

Writing this book became extremely personal for a lot of people. I held countless interviews with many people who experienced this monster fire first hand. There were so many who touched my heart, but some helped with the book itself in giving details, even though it was enormously painful to relive. Although it's still a work of fiction, there are many true elements in the story.

I would like to thank Fire Chief Willie Sapeta, for sitting with me for hours giving details on not only the Valley Fire, but all the terrible fires that lead up to The Valley Fire in 2015. His commitment to our community is profoundly sincere.

My wonderful friend who was a veteran Lake County Sheriff's Dispatcher, (and wishes not to be named), gave insight into the world which many forget orchestrates all the response teams. She leant vital information to this project and I am eternally grateful for her many years of service.

The center of my world, my husband Charlie, who listened to and answered my many questions about the fire, and gave me an interview from his perspective as well, I cannot thank him enough. As a wife of a battalion chief, I can honestly say that when he responds to calls, there is a part of me that goes out there with him and I'm never quite whole again until he returns.

My daughters, both beautiful, grown women, have always

inspired me to reach for more. I thank you both for your love and support.

My dear friend April, who read the first, (very rough), draft of this novel to give me her honest opinion... thanks for believing in me. Having lost her home on Cobb Mountain to the fire, I know it was immensely difficult for her to read some of the scenes. Thank you for your input and raw truth.

Tim and Jamey, you are rock stars! Thank you for always inspiring so many of us with your fortitude. It is a blessing to call you both friends.

Josh and Jess, without you guys and Chernoh Excavating, Gabriel Hart would have been a different kind of contractor. I will always be grateful for your dedication to our community.

I'd like to acknowledge The Best Western of Clearlake, The Main Street Bar & Grill, Wildhurst Winery, The Saw Shop, Park Place, and Lower Lake Coffee, Gregory Graham Winery, and Happy Garden Restaurant.

And lastly I want to thank the people of Lake County. There are many of you out there who have supported me from the beginning and I really couldn't have done this without you. This is my love letter to all who persevere, who never quit believing.

LAKE COUNTY STRONG!

ABOUT THE AUTHOR

Patti Diener has called Lake County, California, home since she was three years old. She's a wife and mother, but writing was her first love, having written since she was in the fifth grade. This is her debut novel. Look for how this book came to be at pattidienerwrites.com and leave a comment about *After The Fire*.

Already well into her next novel, you can be sure there is more to come. The next book is also about a small town with a big heart, and romance is in the air. Look for sample chapters in 2020 on her website.

Made in the USA
Lexington, KY
07 December 2019